CHRISTOPHER CARTWRIGHT

THE LAST AIRSHIP

This one's for my wife,
Maricris,
who is the best thing that's ever happened to me.

PROLOGUE

Munich, Germany, 24 September 1939

It was exactly twenty three days since Germany had invaded Poland, setting into motion the largest war the world had ever seen.

Peter Greenstein looked up at the giant in the clearing. Like a dark cloud in the night sky, she created an ominous silhouette above the opening in the already obscured forest of the moonless night. He had waited almost two weeks for the arrival of the dark moon. It had very nearly been too long, and might have easily cost all of them their lives.

She was a magnificent ship, exquisite to her core.

He had her built exclusively for use by the wealthiest people of her time. The Magdalena stood thirty feet high and one hundred eighty-five feet in length, only slightly shorter in length than a transatlantic Zeppelin. Her lines were more sleek and her propellers proportionately larger, making her the fastest airship ever built.

He was proud of her.

She was the greatest achievement of his fifty two years of

life.

Unlike the Zeppelin, which was designed and built for the masses, the Magdalena was built for the few. From the outside, she looked like a race car, built for speed. Inside, her opulence flowed from every point, like a stately cruise liner. The luxury of her coach house had tried in every way to meet the expectations of those privileged few who would ever travel inside her, in absolute comfort.

Peter's heart sank when he thought about the reason she flew tonight.

When he commissioned her four years ago, he never dreamed that she would be used for such a purpose. Tears welled up in his eyes as he considered how few lives she would save.

Why should I save only the rich? He knew the answer. *Because I can't save them all and I'm going to need their wealth to start a new life.*

Tonight, her luxurious coach house would carry just two families, and an old friend of his, a professor from the University of Berlin, who would be travelling by himself. Peter would pilot her along with his chief engineer, Franck Ehrlich. There would be no other crew tonight, no exquisite culinary delights would be served, the guests would have to help themselves to their drinks, and no entertainment would be provided.

All told, it amounted to just eleven people on board, and the guilt of his failure flowed through him. Peter promised himself that he would try to make another trip back, that as a single man without a family he had an obligation to do so much more for these people.

But, after all, he was just one man, how could he possibly save millions?

The people aboard her tonight were some of the richest in all Europe. Old money. The sort of wealth that takes more than a generation to build.

He watched as the Rosenbergs arrived.

They were the first, and it gave him hope as each one of them quietly made their way up through the forest and into the gondola.

Peter recalled the story of how their great ancestor, Timothy Rosenberg, opened the first Rosenberg Bank in Germany in 1775, after receiving the advice of a bright young banker by the name of Mayer Amschel Rothschild.

Rosenberg specialized in difficult finances; lending when and where others would not. Higher risks with higher possible gains were a gamble that paid off well for him. Once established, the bank expanded. Although now a legitimate bank with more than forty shopfronts, rumors of its underlying ties to criminal organizations had never ceased. The Rosenberg Vault was a privately owned bank with the reputation of trading in suspicious circles. Although Rosenberg had never been convicted of running a criminal enterprise, his funding of certain syndicates, terrorist organizations and violent wars was well and widely known.

All four passengers appeared sullen as they took their seats.

It was hard to imagine that such a powerful family could be cowed by a regime that was in its infancy. Only Sarah, at age six, the youngest amongst them, had the strength to offer a polite smile.

"Thank you, sir."

"You're most welcome aboard, Sarah. All of your family is," he said as he smiled kindly at the child.

Her older brother, Werner, walked dutifully behind her without saying a word. His arms struggled under the weight of the wooden trunk he carried, the burden of which he shared with his father, Hank. Hank was sweating, despite the snow outside. He looked pale. The stress looked as though it might cause him to suffer a heart attack at any moment.

Peter could only imagine what such a family would choose to take with them on this journey, which had such limited space available.

Mary was the last of the Rosenbergs to board the ship.

She wore an expression of superior disdain for the others on board. He wondered how much of it was the result of a lifetime spent at the top of the pecking order, or if she wore that look today in order to conceal her own terror at the night ahead. Wearing a thick fur coat, the only item of jewelry in plain view was a large blue diamond amulet, worn above the curve of her breasts.

Somewhere in the back of his mind, he recalled the name of that famous stone.

Then, there were the Goldschmidts.

Margaret Goldschmidt was married and had two sons. In 1927, her uncle, Ernest Oppenheimer, a German immigrant to Britain who had earlier founded the mining giant, Anglo American, along with American financier, J.P. Morgan, took over De Beers. Peter remembered the controversy over the diamond conglomerate. It was a ruthless syndicate, one in which the value of its diamonds were set at artificially high prices. Oppenheimer built and consolidated the company's global monopoly over the diamond industry. De Beers became a cartel of companies that dominated the diamond market, its mining operations, retail shops, diamond trading, and industrial diamond manufacturing sectors. De Beers was currently active in every category of industrial diamond mining: open-pit, underground, large-scale alluvial and coastal mining, and there were whispers that they were even experimenting in deep sea mining for the future.

Peter also remembered that Margaret had married Karl Goldschmidt, whose family was in the gold bullion trade. He had no idea which family made the other richer, but together, their family had grown in both wealth and power. It was because of that wealth that they had survived this long. Peter had no idea of the extent of their fortune, except to say that it couldn't be spent in any one person's lifetime.

The simple fact that Margaret Goldschmidt was here tonight was proof of her vast fortune.

"Is this thing ready to go?"

He could tell that Margaret hadn't even considered whether or not there would be others joining her. Her family had taken a massive risk by getting out of Munich tonight, and it appeared that all she could think of was why they weren't already off the ground.

"Soon. We're still waiting on one man."

"Really?" She did nothing to hide the fear on her face and then said, "Aren't we an obvious target sitting here like this?"

Peter dismissed the urge to inform her that he himself had returned to Germany tonight, and that he had waited nearly two hours for his guests to arrive so that he could save their rich, entitled lives.

"I must beg your patience for just a little while longer, and then we'll be airborne."

Karl, her husband, then shook his hand as he walked through the door to the gondola. "We appreciate your help, Mr. Greenstein, really we do. Our friends and neighbors, the Hasek family, was taken yesterday. They had planned to leave tonight also. We're all a bit shaken up," he said, as an explanation for why his wife was behaving so badly.

Reaching his hand up in apology, Peter said, "Completely understandable. We're all very distressed by these events. Please assure her, we won't be here any longer than we have to be."

He watched as their two boys took their seats. At the ages of four and five, they had no way of knowing the severity of the risks taken by all who were aboard tonight. Their father had instructed them that they were playing a game of hide and seek, a game in which people were searching for them, and that it was essential that they remain as quiet as possible. They were both sitting, their posture rigid, and working hard to not make any noise; occasionally failing and having a little giggle, they were immediately hushed by their mother.

Then, there was Professor Fritz Ribbentrop, a late reservation.

Just this morning, the professor had contacted him, at the Magdalena's mooring site in Switzerland. Peter had been reluctant to accept any additional passengers, but he had been to university with the professor, who had been adamant that he needed to escape tonight.

Ribbentrop hadn't mentioned what had happened, but Peter was certain that it was important. Fritz was known to be an exceptional scientist, and a valued worker; he was a loyal fascist who came from a clean Aryan bloodline.

He wrenched his mind seeking an explanation for the strange phenomenon.

Why would Fritz, of all people, need to escape the Gestapo?

Were it any other man, one less honorable, he might have worried that he was walking into a trap, but Fritz was not that kind of man. Even if he believed it to be in the best interests of the Nazi party, the professor would have felt that using such a ruse would have been dishonest.

Peter looked at his sorry human cargo.

With the exception of Fritz, who had still not arrived, he didn't see himself as the equal of any one of them. Although he himself was an heir to a great fortune, his path through life had been decidedly different than his passengers. He was an outcast amongst his own family. Even after the events of the past week, a week in which his father had died and left him the title of Baron Greenstein, he still did not feel as though he was one of them.

Unlike the rest of his family, he had turned his wealth towards science, studying at the great Berlin University of Aeronautical Engineering. The Magdalena was his brainchild. Capable of travelling at twice the speed of a normal Zeppelin, she was a marvel of both modern engineering and opulence. He would have liked to build her for the masses, but the masses were unable to afford such luxuries as travel by dirigible. Consequently, for the sake of science, he turned to those whom he despised, to fund its development.

He studied the two families and wondered what they'd say if they knew they were waiting for the arrival of the most honorable fascist who Hitler had ever considered his close friend.

Rumbling far away, he could hear the muffled yet distinct sound of a four stroke engine. The BMW R75 motorcycle. Designed specifically as a military vehicle, Germany had so far only released the first line of production—for use by high ranking Nazi SS officers.

Doctor Fritz Ribbentrop was the last passenger to arrive.

The man wore his short hair brushed back from his forehead. Years past being blonde, it now bordered on completely white. A pair of riding goggles covered his attractive dark blue eyes. His face was clean shaven for the most part, with the exception of a small and almost entirely white moustache.

It was easy to guess that as a younger man, he had most likely been highly sought after by women.

He wore a simple green coat and matching trousers, the coat fully buttoned up against the cold. He had the luxury of leather gloves, with which he skillfully gripped the handlebars as he made his way up the narrow, snow-filled path through the black night and the scattered pine trees.

Riding his motorcycle was the only joy in life still left to him. It was the only joy that the mighty German military machine would allow him to keep. And, he was one of the privileged few, whose scientific ability allowed him the luxury fuel allowances which were denied to all other civilians.

He knew he should have abandoned the motorcycle further back along the trail, but it had taken him longer than he anticipated to leave the university today, and without it, he would never have made it here in time to board. He, of all people, knew the danger that he brought the Magdalena tonight. The sound of his motorcycle attracted attention and made them an easy target. He justified the risk to himself with his belief that his purpose was far more important than the rescue of a couple of rich, Jewish families.

He could see the airship in the distance.

It appeared quite vulnerable. Even in the dark, the Magdalena's enormous canopy marked a great area against the night sky.

He was relieved to see that the four propellers at rear of the gondola were already turning and the two side, stabilizing blades, were rotating at an idle. The airship would be ready to launch at a moment's notice.

He rode his R75 right up to the ship's mooring line and then released his grip on the handlebars unceremoniously as he dismounted. The bike fell to its side, but the motor could still be heard running smoothly, evidence of the strength of its simplicity.

Fritz panted heavily as he made his way through the thick, snow-covered, metal stairs carrying one small suitcase. He climbed up to the open door of the gondola.

"You're late," said his old friend, Peter Greenstein, curtly. The man was crouched down at the door. Peter looked outside one last time and immediately closed the door behind Fritz.

Fritz didn't bother apologizing for his late arrival. He wasn't sorry at all. If he could have been here sooner, he would have been.

He studied the interior of the gondola as he approached the others.

It was spacious, more like the interior of a grand yacht than an aircraft, he decided. It felt like a yacht too—even moored several inches off the ground, the slow, rolling motion of the gondola reminded him of the gentle feel of riding an ocean swell.

He heard the large, powerful engines increase in pitch. The swaying motion stopped, as the mooring cables were cut and the Magdalena was finally free to begin her journey.

His right arm instinctively reached for the nearest chair for balance. Smoothly, the giant craft began its vertical rise into the air, like a helium balloon released from a child's grasp. He also sensed a slight forward motion, similar to the feeling one experience when an escalator ascends.

There was only one vacant seat, and he carefully made his way toward it.

The windows sloped outward, so that he could look straight down and watch the scenery roll by beneath his feet, not that there was much to see below on this dark night.

"This must be yours, it's the last one," said a young boy, whose voice was far from breaking. "Thank you."

He noted that the boy's father quickly admonished him for speaking to a stranger.

He took his seat, glad to relinquish the weight on his unsteady feet.

Thank God, it's going to be safe.

Two seconds later, he heard the barking sound of a German machine gun being fired.

Walter Wolfgang perused the report in front of him.

It was bad. The Fuhrer was going to be most displeased. People in Germany disappeared, or were frequently made to disappear, these days. But today, of all days, to lose such an important person, was to invite severe criticism. It was the man that he, specifically, was assigned to keep his eyes on.

The Fuhrer himself had given him this assignment. He, of all the loyal members of the Third Reich, had the exact qualifications and position to carry out this important task.

And now, he had failed.

How could I have let this happen?

A clean shaven man in an SS uniform entered the room, carrying a manila folder imprinted with the words "Top Secret" across the front.

"Heil Hitler," the officer said, as he saluted.

"Heil Hitler," Walter dutifully replied, returning the salute.

The officer had come directly from #8 Prinz Albrecht Street in Berlin—Gestapo headquarters. Walter shivered, just thinking about it. Everyone feared the Gestapo, even himself, Germany's most loyal servant.

As a civilian, he held no military rank and had no authority.

In actuality, he was secretly working for the Fuhrer on a most important assignment. The Gestapo, he realized, could and did send fear through everyone. Should he object to their interference, by the time news of his complaint reached the Fuhrer, the Gestapo's punishment would have already been meted out.

He understood precisely why the SS officer was standing before him today.

"So, he left work early today?" The officer spoke each word slowly and carefully, as though he were actually interrogating Walter.

Does he not realize that I want to catch Ribbentrop as much as he does?

"Yes, he did."

"Has he ever left work early, previously?"

"No, never." Walter fidgeted with his briefcase as he spoke.

"And . . . you just let him leave?"

"We are civilians. Both he and I are working diligently for the Third Reich, but he is my superior, and if he says that he has to go, then I cannot stop him."

"Where did he say he had to go?" The officer persisted, without raising his voice—he never had to. If a person was being questioned by an SS officer, they listened carefully.

"He told me that he was meeting with another professor today. The meeting was to take place at his house."

"But, you say that you went to his house and no one was there?"

"That's correct." Walter replied.

The skin along the SS officer's strong jawline tightened in frustration. "And, I have men at his house, even as we speak, determining whether or not Ribbentrop has taken anything with him."

Walter sat patiently in his tan leather chair, feeling like a child attending one of his own lectures; a child who had failed to demonstrate satisfactory understanding of a concept and was now to be instructed as to what was expected of him.

Someone knocked at the door.

It was probably another SS officer. No one else in their right mind would interrupt an ongoing interrogation by an SS officer otherwise.

"Yes, who is it?"

"Rutherford, Sir. Heil Hitler." The young man, little more than a boy, in his starched SS uniform saluted.

"Heil Hitler." The first SS officer didn't invite the younger officer to take a seat. "Now, Rutherford, what do you have for me?"

"He's been spotted riding his BMW south." Rutherford struggled to disguise the pleasure of his own success.

"He's trying to escape Berlin on his motorcycle?" His incredulity was visible. "He must know that he can't escape Germany that easily. He must have found help. Where is he now?"

"He's on the A9 motorway. Do you want us to bring him in for questioning?" Rutherford asked.

"No, I want you to follow him. Arrest him once he has met with his contact."

These people have no idea! Walter was horrified that SS were going to risk Ribbentrop's escape so that they might have a chance at catching his accomplices.

The SS officer then looked at Walter, and said, "You'd better pray that we catch this prick."

"You have no concept of what's at stake," Walter replied.

Peter gripped one of the levers with his right hand. It controlled the angle of the two forward propellers. He pulled backwards on it, and then turned to the pair of levers beside it, which increased their forward thrust. The idling sound rose to a higher pitch, but nothing happened.

Franck then released their mooring lines.

The Magdalena was now floating unrestrained.

A moment later, the airship started to move forward, ever so slightly.

Peter's hands gripped the large wooden steering wheel adeptly, it was not too dissimilar to those which might be found on a sailing ship. Like its naval counterpart, the wheel controlled an oversized rudder at the rear of the airship, allowing directional control.

A careful movement of his left hand on a somewhat smaller wheel allowed the rear four propellers to pitch the nose up, while preventing it from yawing from side-to-side. On the wall to his right, where his co-pilot Franck sat, were a number of pressure switches, valves and toggles that controlled the pressure of both helium and air, as well as the distribution of ballast.

Peter felt good to finally nose up with the pitch control wheel so that the Magdalena could reach for the sky.

It was painfully slow.

All dirigibles were.

There was nothing you could do about that. Tonight, Peter felt the slowness. He felt as though he was running from a monster, but, as if in a nightmare, his legs were stuck in the mud and he couldn't get away fast enough.

Finally, he felt the Magdalena climb and start gaining forward speed and momentum.

With both hands fixed firmly on the steering wheel, he kept the enormous, lumbering aircraft under control. With its six engines, six propellers and filled with helium gas, whose buoyancy constantly changed depending on the temperature and atmospheric pressure, piloting the Magdalena was like a combination of flying an airplane and making a scuba dive at the same time.

"We're just about to clear those pine trees, Franck. Once we're over them, we should be ready to switch to flight configuration.

"Copy, that."

Peter's heart stopped as he heard the rapid staccato of machine gun fire.

"What the fuck is that?"

"Machine gun fire, but are they shooting at us, or at a ground target?"

His hand pulled the two levers on his left back further, this increased the speed of the rear four propellers from1450 to 1700 RPM, which was just above the maximum recommended RPMs for the advanced Daimler-Benz engines.

It seemed pointless.

The extra strain on the engines barely increased their speed at all.

Ahead of them, he could hear the sound of more gunfire.

Suddenly, the area directly in front of the pilot's cabin lit up with sparks.

"Holy shit! We're hit."

"What's our pressure?" Peter was still in control, despite the disaster. He was very glad that he had opted to use the more expensive inert gas, helium, rather than the cheaper and much more highly volatile gas, hydrogen, which had proved so fatal in the Hindenburg Disaster of 1937.

Franck looked over at the gas pressure gauges.

There were fourteen separate helium compartments within the Magdalena. Each one had its own pressure gauge and release valves to prevent explosions during air pressure changes, and separate helium cylinders to increase buoyancy if required.

"Still 5.2 millibars in all fourteen compartments."

"Okay, copy that. Let's check the rest of our systems to see if anything else has been damaged."

"Everything looks all right." Franck then started to tap the compass. "Damn. It must have knocked off our forward gyroscope."

"Okay, we'll have to work something out by dead reckoning." Years of piloting had taught him to work on a problem rather than to panic over something you couldn't change.

Because of the metal used within the gondola, an interior compass was made fundamentally useless. To circumvent this problem, the Magdalena had a mounted gyroscope at the nose of the ship.

The sound of the machine gun fire was becoming quieter with distance.

Just a little further and we'll be out of their range.

"Okay, we've reached 25 mph. Let's switch the ship to flight configuration and see if we can increase our speed some more."

"Copy that," Franck said, as he pulled the levers before him, to a horizontal level. Now, the Magdalena was using its fins, not its engines, to control the ship's motion.

Like a ship in water, the Magdalena's steering wheel felt as though it was having more of an effect on their direction now that their speed had increased.

The ship now flew more like a yacht with a rudder. As such, Peter had to contend with other factors, such as air currents and thermals. It had taken years of experience, but he had learned to make minor adjustments early for expected changes.

"Good, our speed is picking up. It's now at 30 mph." Peter then noticed that his left hand was struggling to keep the pitch of the nose straight and level. "Can you check the helium again, she seems to be sinking?"

Franck ran his hands over each of the gauges and then he stopped at number fourteen. It was the one that was placed in the nose of the ship.

"It's already down to 3.5millibars. We're quickly leaking gas from compartment number fourteen," Franck said.

"Okay, we're going to have to re-route some of the helium from the other tanks."

"Copy that." Franck started to make the adjustments on the valves to move helium from the remaining thirteen compartments to the front. "Sir?"

"Yes?"

"How long can we keep her in the air by doing this?"

"I don't know. Four, perhaps five hours?" Peter said. Then, tapping on the pressure gauge to make certain the swivel stick hadn't become stuck, he said, "It will be close, but we might just make it. We're going to lose some gas as we fly over the mountains. I'll get up into the canopy shortly and see if I can repair the helium bladder by myself."

After a couple of minutes the Magdalena seemed to return to her normal flying capabilities, and, with the exception of a faulty compass, they were on their normal route for the night. They might still make it.

Their planned route was going to take them east, over Lake Constance at the base of the Alps. Then, by maintaining a more northerly route, they would avoid the Alps and enter Switzerland over Mount Uetliberg. At the entrance to Zurich, in northeast Switzerland, Mount Uetliberg rose to an elevation of 2850 feet above sea level.

A zeppelin had a maximum ceiling height of 650 feet. The Magdalena was not a zeppelin, and Peter had specifically engineered her for travel through Europe which has a number of high mountains. As the airship rises, the helium expands, and contracts when it descends. In order to maintain a constant pressure within, a ballonet is installed, which is simply a bag of air, which is inflated or deflated in order to maintain a constant pressure inside the envelope despite changing air pressures. This, in turn, allows the helium to expand and contract. When the ballonet is completely empty, the airship is said to be at its "pressure height."

The initial design of the ballonet size determines an individual airship's maximum change of altitude capability. The Magdalena had a maximum change in altitude of 4000 feet, but it could, in theory, continue to rise indefinitely if the expanding helium was constantly released. The problem was that by doing so, you would waste a lot of helium.

Peter set his course at a dead reckoning.

"Okay, Franck. I'd better get back there and make sure our guests are all right. Keep the nose between those two stars there," he said, pointing in front of him.

"Copy that." Franck said, as he gripped the steering wheel and then added, "Don't take too long. I might need you up here."

"You'll be fine."

Peter opened the door of the forward pilot gondola and stepped out onto the open air gangway to the primary gondola. The cool air was refreshing. He looked at the trees, which looked more like grass, scattered over the hills far below. There were no lights on. Concerns over British air raids still prohibited the use of lights during night time hours. Behind him, he could just make out the center of Berlin.

He loved it up there.

Many of the people he studied with were interested in building faster and more powerful planes. They said that after the Hindenburg disaster, airships would become antiquated. It was a shame, he thought, since this was the way he wanted to see the world.

He wondered if he'd built the last airship.

Like all engineers, Peter inspected the frame of his precious canopy first, before checking on his human cargo. From the outside it appeared intact, although he dared not shine a flashlight on any of it in case he exposed the Magdalena to attack. He was certain that some of the bullets had placed little holes inside her canopy, and the subsequent loss of helium would be insurmountable. He opened the hatch above his head and climbed inside the canopy.

He shined his flashlight through each helium bladder, one by one, listening for the telltale hissing of a gas leak.

Peter barely prevented himself from crying out when he first saw it.

If there was a small hole in the helium bladder in compartment number fourteen, at the bow of the Magdalena, he could fix it, but there was no way he could possibly repair the three foot tear he saw before him.

Without wasting more time, he climbed back down to the air gangway and then opened the door to the primary gondola and his guests.

Everyone inside the gondola was so quiet that, at first, he didn't even realize what had happened. Then he saw her. It was young Sarah. Her skin was so white, that he wondered whether she might be dead. Then, he noticed that the professor had torn part of his shirt and used it as a tourniquet to wrap around her arm.

She was still breathing.

"Is she going to be all right?"

"Yes. She's been shot in her arm, and has lost a lot of blood, but I believe she will make it—so long as we get her to a doctor before morning."

"Peter, what happened?" Margaret, Sarah's mother, asked as she accosted him.

"We were fired upon." To Peter, it seemed like such an obvious answer to a question that barely required one.

"But of course we all realize that. What I want to know is, are we okay? I mean, will we make it?"

"One of the bullets tore a hole in compartment number fourteen, and we're venting large amounts helium. Also, our magnetic gyroscope has been shot to pieces, so we're flying somewhat blind, but yes, I believe we will indeed make it."

Peter looked at Margaret.

The edge of her lip curled as though she had just bitten something pungent, "This is your fault for waiting so long before taking off!"

There was nothing he could say in response. It was true, if

he'd left earlier, Sarah wouldn't have been shot. "I'm very sorry. Now, I must continue making inspections of my ship."

He then walked to the back of the gondola and stepped out of the door and into the open air gangway to check on the motors in the rear gondola. Ordinarily, he would have a team of at least five mechanics and an engineer on board, to constantly assess the engines. Tonight, they would simply have to make it on their own.

Before Peter shut the door, Fritz followed him through it and said, "Thank you for waiting for me. Let me assure you, it was important."

Peter imagined that every passenger aboard thought that their life was important. He knew damn well that they would have made a clean getaway if he hadn't waited for Ribbentrop. "Let's just hope we make it, Fritz. If we don't, their deaths will be on your head."

"Of course, they will," Fritz replied with a shrug of his shoulders, seemingly comfortable accepting such responsibility.

Again, Peter wondered how it was possible that such a senior member of Hitler's regime to feel the need to escape tonight, and hoped that he hadn't misjudged his old friend. Peter didn't consider it for long. He still had a job to do, if any of them were going to make it out of Germany safely.

All four engines in the rear gondola seemed to be in fine working order.

He listened to the pitch of their hum. Like any good engineer, his ears told him all that he needed to know. *They're fine. At least that's something.* He then walked back, through the primary guest gondola. Everyone was quiet this time, and he didn't wait around to hear them voice their complaints again.

No, he thought. *He's not like any one of them.*

He then opened the door to the pilot gondola, and asked, "How are we looking, Franck?"

"Good. Nothing's changed. The slope is increasing, and I've raised the angle of our nose by one degree to maintain our rate of ascent."

"Really? It seems a bit early to do that." He checked his watch. They had been in the air for just under an hour. "Are you certain?"

Peter could already see the mountain up ahead.

They had apparently made a mistake with their dead reckoning, but, like all fools, Peter decided to continue, lost. He took hold of the large wooden steering wheel again and said, "Okay, I have command. Let's start our ascent."

He pulled the lever which changed the angle of the four rear propellers and then tilted the elevators, built into the side of the canopy, so that the angle of the ship increased to eight degrees. It was a little sharper than was normal, but he didn't want to waste any helium. It might be uncomfortable for some of the passengers who would be unaccustomed to it.

They started to climb.

He watched as his altimeter increased.

Every thousand feet they ascended took them closer to the Magdalena's ceiling. Soon, they were flying at 3500 feet.

In the distance, the mountain continued to rise ahead of them.

"Where are we, Franck?"

"Your guess is as good as mine, sir. Could it be St Gallons?"

"No, too high for St Gallons."

Peter calmly got out the book of maps, which contained aerial photographs of the landscapes and mountains. None of them seemed to match the area over which they flew. When he got to the last of the maps, frustrated, he handed the book across to Franck, and said, "Here, see if you can find anything you recognize."

They were approaching the Magdalena's maximum ceiling height of 4000 feet, and their altimeter reading kept rising. The mountain ahead of them showed no signs of leveling off.

There was no point in trying to turn the airship around, they just had to keep on going.

Then they attained their final possible height, and the mountain looked as though it was going to go on forever.

"Okay, Franck. I need you to vent some of that helium. It's the only way; we'll just have to refill the compartments once we start to descend again."

"But we're almost out of helium already."

"I know that. God damn it, but we don't have any other choice, do we?"

"No, sir."

Peter listened as the distinct sound of gas being released by the blow off valves, which were designed to avoid rupturing the hull, were each opened.

And still they climbed.

At 10,000 feet, Peter noticed his dizziness.

It was one of the first signs of hypoxia and he couldn't ignore it. There simply wasn't enough oxygen up there to breathe, at that altitude.

He looked at Franck, who was concentrating on taking slow, deep breaths, in order to help his oxygen starved brain continue to function.

"How are you doing there, Franck?"

"I'm all right, but if this mountain is much taller, we're all going to die of hypoxia long before the Magdalena runs out of helium." He didn't sound frightened, he was simply stating the facts.

"Well, that's one thing going for us, isn't it?"

Neither of them had the strength or breath to laugh.

"What's that, straight ahead?" Franck asked.

Peter strained his older eyes to try to just see clearly.

"My God, I think that's the top of our mountain!"

"Thank God!"

Far up ahead he could see the lights of a town.

"Thank goodness, we made it." Peter pointed at the lights. "Look at that!"

The lights confirmed that they were finally out of Germany.

"We're out of Germany, but where?"

"I have no idea."

Peter's dizziness subsided as they made their descent, but his headache seemed to hang on.

The slope was riddled with rocky ledges, snow, and enormous pine trees. Peter was worried about where they might safely land the Magdalena when they ran out of helium, and drew blank on a solution.

"We're out of helium," Franck reminded him, as his worst fear was realized.

"Okay, we can do this. We'll have to adjust for it by increasing our angle of attack and the RPMs of our fine Daimler-Benz."

Peter did just that, but the Magdalena seemed to keep falling.

He watched, as the altimeter dropped at the rate of 200 feet per minute.

"Okay, Franck, we're going to need to lose some of our weight, or we're going hit the ground pretty hard."

"Copy that. I've already dumped our water ballast and our air. What else do we have?"

"Franck, I want you to go back to the passenger's gondola and see what else we can dump from there. You'd better let them know we're going down, too. Throw out their precious cargo, if you have to."

"Okay, I'll try."

"And Franck, don't take too long. We're going to need to find somewhere to put her down soon, and I'm going to need your help."

Professor Fritz Ribbentrop watched as the engineer opened the door from the open air gangway. There was nothing casual about his movements.

"Quick, we've run out of helium and we're losing altitude fast. I need everyone to help me throw out anything that isn't bolted down."

He noticed that the men seemed to comprehend what he was asking much faster than did either of the women or young children, who simply stared blankly back at him, as though he'd just issued a completely mad order for them to jump out of the airship.

"Should we dump the alcohol?" asked one of the older gentlemen, who was holding his wife's hand, and whose face seemed to maintain a perpetual scowl.

"Yes, that would help very much."

Himself, the two other men who appeared to be in their

fifties, and the engineer, all quickly got to work throwing the expensive wines and other spirits off the ship. It almost made him laugh to think that he was destroying more valuable liquor than he would ever have had sufficient funds to consume under normal circumstances.

The side tables were the next to go overboard.

"You're going to need to help me with this. It's too heavy," he said to the man next to him, as he tipped the refrigerator.

"Okay, but how are we going to get it through the door?"

He took large book that was on the shelf used it to strike the large glass window in front of him. As it shattered, and the glass pieces fell to the ground far below, he said, "We can push it straight out here."

It took a little bit of rocking, but they soon had the thing tipped over the side.

The bookshelf went next.

Soon, the formerly luxurious gondola was reduced to eleven chairs, its occupants, and their personal effects.

The engineer, who had come from the pilot house looked at the large, ornate altimeter that was situated in the middle of the gondola, just as an old grandfather clock would be placed aboard a luxury steamship. The arm still rotated clockwise, indicating that they were losing altitude.

Their rate of descent had slowed, but not stopped.

"Okay, everyone's baggage must go," the man announced, as he tried to grab Fritz's suitcase.

"I'm afraid this one isn't going anywhere," Fritz said. His stern voice giving no doubt about his seriousness.

"Don't be daft, old man, we're going to crash. Your luggage isn't worth it," the man said as he began to tug at the suitcase.

"I told you, this one isn't going anywhere." It was the comfort and authority with which Fritz spoke, as he pulled his Luger pistol out and aimed it at the other man, which made him appear so frightening.

"Are you nuts?" The engineer asked.

"Yes." Fritz looked at the engineer through his horrified eyes, "You have no idea what terrible thing I've done." He continued to point his pistol at the engineer, motioning to him to throw another passenger's luggage out the window. "You'd better throw out their luggage, and do it quickly or else we might indeed crash."

The man shook his head in dismay, but said nothing.

He then began to pull at a large wooden trunk, belonging to one of the other passengers.

"If he gets to keep his stuff, why can't we?" The trunk owner asked, looking at his wife for reassurance.

"Because, he has the gun," The engineer said, smiling impatiently. "Now let me throw this thing overboard."

He tried to lift it by himself, but couldn't.

Frustrated, he removed a small knife from his belt that he normally used to cut tangled mooring lines, and stuck it into the locking mechanism.

The trunk sprang open, revealing more than a hundred gold bars, each bearing the emblem of its wealthy owners: a G and O joined by an infinity symbol.

"No, you can't throw this away! It's everything we have—our entire life savings. How else will we start anew?" The woman, he noted, had broken her sensibilities at the possibility of seeing her fortune nearly lost to the ground below.

Her husband then placed his foot on the base of the trunk and said, "I'm afraid this isn't going to be thrown out."

"Oh yeah?" The engineer asked. He now had the look of a crazy man, staring blankly, like someone who'd been pushed past breaking point and snapped. He reached down and picked up one of the gold ingots. "Watch this!" he said, tossing the brick bar out the window.

For a couple of seconds, it seemed as though all activity inside the gondola ceased.

Fritz watched, his pistol still pointed at the others, the rich passengers, he decided, had finally lost their aristocratic cool composure, and the only man who was working to keep the ship airborne looked as though he'd finally given up caring about the fate of any one of them.

It was going to become violent in here.

At that moment, Peter's voice could be heard over the intercom pipe, "Franck, get back up here, we're going down and I need your help."

Peter looked at Franck as he came through the door. His face was flushed and his nostrils flared dangerously. He must have had trouble removing the passenger's luggage, he guessed.

He then took another look at his altimeter, which indicated that their rate of descent had decreased to 100 feet per minute.

"It's no use. We're going down. Can you see anything below?"

The landscape looked harsh and lethal to the airship. The rocky outcrops on the mountain would slice her wide open at the speed at which they were descending and they needed to maintain that speed to retain some lift. With the exception of the rocks, this entire side of the mountain was covered in densely packed pine forest.

"Over there, how about that open place?" Franck was the

first to spot it.

"Where?"

Franck pointed to a spot. It was a large field or clearing, covered in white snow.

"I see it. That'll do nicely."

Three minutes later, the Magdalena hit the snow-covered ground hard. Bouncing and shuddering, she slid for a long while along the icy ground, finally coming to rest. The altimeter indicated that they were at an altitude of 7000 feet. They were incredibly high up the mountain to have been lucky enough to find such a clearing.

"Christ almighty!" Peter panted, excited and out of breath. "That was close, but we made it!"

He then looked over at his co-pilot. A loud sound—a crack like that of distant thunder—could be heard . . . and *felt*. The airship lurched.

"What in the hell was that?"

Franck opened his mouth to respond, but Peter never heard his reply. They were both dead before they even knew what happened.

In the once luxurious passenger lounge, Professor Fritz Ribbentrop calmly looked out the window.

He, of all the passengers on board, realized exactly where they were.

It was a reasonable mistake for the pilot to land here. If he hadn't grown up climbing these mountains as a boy, Fritz might have made the same mistake, in their shoes. He didn't blame them for it.

With the composure of a man who had accepted his fate,

Fritz then made sure that his single suitcase was still securely locked and carefully handcuffed to his wrist.

Maybe it is for the best that it never reached its destination?

A weight had been lifted from his chest, as though the stress of the past few weeks had finally been lifted from him.

It was the last thought he ever had as he clutched the single suitcase tightly to his chest.

CHAPTER 1

Sydney Harbor, Present Day

Sam Reilly took the helm of his custom built fiberglass 68 foot ketch, *Second Chance.*

At six foot exactly, he was only slightly taller than the average man, but his arms and shoulders were wide from years of physical labor, and his legs were strong as tree stumps, giving him a solid, yet wiry appearance.

Physically, he was the product of hard labor, which the sea demanded of him.

He had pensive, dark blue eyes, and the sort of cheeky smile that says, *I can have it all.* If life had taught him anything, it was that he of all people, could. His gaze showed determination, and the calluses on his hands displayed the tenacity required to make things happen. He was amiable by nature, but he suffered from a general distrust of his fellow man. Sam felt at his most calm when he was on his own.

Today was one of those days.

The weather was warm and there was a moderate northerly wind of 15-20 knots. To every weekend sailor on the harbor, it looked like a great day for a sail. For a person like himself, who'd built his life on the sea, he intuitively sensed the disaster ahead.

He knew it with the certainty of a chess player, who had seen his own demise in forty or more moves ahead; there was going to be trouble at sea. Sam knew it by the calm air, the pale blue sky, the unusually large swell that didn't quite match the local weather conditions, and, like anyone with enough experience in a given field, he just knew it instinctively. His subconscious mind had picked up all the telltale signs and had given him the outcome; there was going to be one hell of a storm.

Sam had just completed his first year at the international sea salvage company, Deep Sea Expeditions. He'd promised himself that he'd never enter the business after what had happened to his brother, Danny. But some things are just meant to be, and try as he might to avoid it, he eventually realized that he must return to the world that he grew up in—the one in which he truly belonged—the sea.

It was the first time he'd taken leave since he started working for Deep Sea Expeditions. Two weeks was all the time he had, unless something came up. Auspiciously, he'd noted that Cyclone Petersham, which was about to slam into the northern Queensland coast of Australia and the tropics, was moving south. If his predictions were correct, which they almost certainly would be, the storm would collide with the terrible low, now forming off the coast of South Australia.

The collision of these two systems would produce a narrow trough between a tropical high and a southern low, a condition known as a squeeze. The weather would become horribly dangerous, and the seas would become incredibly violent and unpredictable.

The same sort of weather that killed 9 people in the 1998 Sydney to Hobart Race, and crippled another 39 yachts.

These were precisely the conditions for which *Second Chance* had been built to withstand; not to fight. Sam had learned long ago that you never fought with the powers of the sea, unless you wished to be crushed by them. Instead, your aim should be to follow the sea's commands by making simple adjustments.

As he looked up at the clear blue skies, Sam knew how close these conditions were to those which he and his brother had faced during that terrible day more than ten years ago. He had been lucky. That's all it was. It had never been a question of skill under the circumstances, just dumb luck. His brother, Danny, had sadly not been so lucky.

Sam had spent a long time frightened by the sea; he had even told his mother that he would not enter the family business, but as time passed, he knew that there was only one way to beat the nightmares from his past. He could never avoid it. He had to return to where he belonged. Where, deep down, he knew it was the only place he felt truly comfortable.

The ocean didn't care who your father was, or how rich you were. Out on the ocean, you were only as safe as the sea allowed you to be. Out there, you were just another one of the sea's trillion lifeforms, no more or less important than any other.

As Manly harbor came into view, Sam made his final tack before leaving Sydney Harbor and then he turned due south, toward a cold hell.

Sam sailed alone.

There was no way he could explain to anyone why he chose to sail solo. His father, the only person to whom he didn't have to explain it, understood exactly why he made this choice, as would only a fellow solo yachtsman. His mother never would understand, and he himself didn't quite understand it either. It was something he was driven to do. He had to do it, just like the salmon returning to the same creek of its birth to spawn; he was searching for a resolution to a problem which he'd spent the better half of his life trying to fix.

It would take *Second Chance* two days to reach Bass Strait. Then, when the storm was at its worst, he would take her through the strait, south around Tasmania, before returning. All told, he would be gone for no more than a week.

Will I find the answer in this one or at the bottom of the sea? He didn't take the question lightly.

He loved these trips as much as he feared them.

The challenge of solo sailing was rewarded by the sole ownership of the achievement. A yacht, with its sails trimmed to perfection, its course correctly synchronized with the swell and the current, was the easiest thing in the world to manage as a solo sailor. *Second Chance* was 68 feet in length and carried more than a thousand feet of sail. A head sail, stay sail, main sail, and mizzen, could be controlled by a six-year-old child, if managed correctly.

In truth, if he had done his job as skipper, he would have little else to do but enjoy the journey.

The sea, he knew, was as kind as it was unforgiving.

Over the course of the next twenty-four hours, little changed. The swell had risen to fifteen feet, but it was a following sea and comfortable enough to sail with. The wind then increased to 35 knots. It was enough to worry a weekend sailor, but only just enough to start to see the full potential for which *Second Chance* had been engineered.

Not enough to create any misgivings in his mind.

Sam wasn't one of those sailors who felt that he needed to round the Cape of Good Hope in a dingy using traditional methods of navigation and hand steering the entire way, simply in order to prove his seamanship. For him, it was all about being there, in the middle of one of nature's most violent spectacles, sharing in its power without being overcome by it.

Sam had no misgivings about using all the wonders provided by modern science. *Second Chance* certainly wasn't a production yacht. She was built for one purpose only, chasing storms.

She was the product of years of development by the finest shipwrights, naval architects, engineers, and actual sailors. Built with the kind of money that could hardly be spent in a single lifetime; the sort of family wealth into which Sam had been born.

Her hull was fiberglass with carbon fiber chine and a full keel, making her exceptionally light, strong, and stable. Equipped with state-of-the-art autopilot, GPS navigation, IAS, radar and satellite phone and internet, some might argue that Sam wasn't a real sailor.

Fortunately, as his eyes carefully perused the advanced instruments at his navigation table, he really didn't give a shit what people thought he was doing out here; as far as he was concerned, this journey was for him alone.

It was 8p.m., and although the sun had set more than an hour ago, the bright full moon gave a seductively clear view of the ocean around him.

This was his real home.

The swell, already reasonably large, was flowing in a consistent direction, and had none of the usual roughness to it. Tonight, he would sleep soundly.

He climbed down the stairs and into the main cabin. Still wide awake, he flicked open his laptop. It was connected to the main information and satellite system which had cost him a fortune to have installed onboard *Second Chance.*

On the top of his computer screen, there was a picture of a mailbox and to the right of it appeared the number 3.

He clicked on the icon.

At times, he was unsure whether or not he loved or hated having access to such communications while at sea. He found three letters in his inbox and about a dozen more in his spam filter. Two messages were from Deep Sea Expeditions. He hit skip—they were probably after him, and with this storm coming in, they were going to need everyone they could get, and they were probably trying to rescind his leave. He was on holiday, so it was not his problem. This storm was for him.

The last email was from Kevin Reed.

Sam had studied at MIT with Kevin, but had never had any particular relationship with him. Kevin had been studying Geometric Variances, while Sam had been studying Oceanography, before moving on to get his Master's in Microbiology. He couldn't for the life of him come up with a reason why the man would be emailing him now. He was pretty certain he hadn't signed up for any alumni. Besides, he wasn't old enough for a reunion anyway.

The very thought of it made him laugh.

He opened the message and started reading.

Dear Sam,

My wife and I have been in Europe on a six month climbing holiday. You will never believe what we found! This was the only one, although we continued to search the area for two weeks before we were willing to let it go.

I was wondering if you could tell me where it could have come from, and whether or not you think we might find more like it?

Attached was a Jpeg file showing a small gold ingot bearing at its center, the impression of a letter G and a letter O, separated by an artistically designed infinity symbol.

Any advice you could impart would be much appreciated.

Kind regards, Kevin and Sally.

At the bottom of the letter, were the words: *do you want to come on a treasure hunt?*

Sam laughed at that.

Why is it that when people know that you work for an underwater salvage company in the role of Special Operations, they automatically assume you're interested in treasure hunting?

He studied the picture for a couple of minutes.

Gold had never held any special interest for him. After all, what was he going to do with it? What piqued his interest was the story behind how the gold came to be.

He then forwarded the image to Blake Symonds, a merchant banker in Venice. A friend of his father's, the man specialized in gold bullion and fine European antiquities. If anyone knew about where the ingot had come from, it would be him. With the photo attached, Sam asked the simple question, do *you know whose emblem this is?* He then drew a red arrow pointing to the G&O impression.

That done, Sam climbed into his bunk and went to sleep, while *Second Chance* sailed on south toward Hell.

Tom Bower was sitting in the dark hull of the Maria Helena, staring at his laptop. Despite the powerful air conditioning, his face glistened with beads of sweat as he examined the catastrophic low that was rapidly approaching the northeast coast of Australia.

He had hazel brown eyes and a permanent smile, which best expressed his happy-go-lucky attitude towards life. His dark, curly hair and olive complexion suggested a Mediterranean ancestry, even though he was a third generation American. At six foot four, he was considered much too tall to be a pilot, and even less suitable to the world of cave diving. At both of which, he was an expert. At the age of twenty eight, Tom had already achieved more than most people would achieve in a lifetime.

His general demeanor was relaxed, and he believed that he would always manage to get through whatever happened to him. His smile was kind, and his friends often found his insouciance, despite any given disaster, as one of his most endearing yet infuriating traits.

In front of him, were a multitude of meteorology reports.

Even after having discussed the weather with the three brightest meteorologists in the world, the best information he could gather was not much better than what had been available when he was a child.

There was a cyclone heading towards the northeast coastline of Australia, and depending on where it hit, there would almost certainly be a lot of damage to people, buildings and the environment.

All the science that was designed to protect them could sink right to the ocean floor, for all its usefulness today.

Tom had spent four years in Florida as a young boy while his father was posted there with the Navy.

He knew all about hurricanes, and he always hated them.

As a boy, he promised himself that he was going to move as far from water as possible. When he finished secondary school, he joined the Marines as a helicopter pilot, happy to have distanced himself from the sea and the risk of hurricanes.

Not long after his initial training, he served in Afghanistan, where he mainly performed Hot Drops with Navy SEALS and Medevacs. It was dangerous work, but at least there was no enormous body of water below him.

Two years ago, his chopper had been shot down. Of the twenty men aboard her, he was the only one to survive. It was pure luck, nothing more. There wasn't anything he could have done to change that outcome. He should have been killed with the rest of them. When he attended their funerals, he felt no desire to change places with any one of the good men who had sacrificed their lives so that America could protect its way of living for future generations.

He felt no survivor guilt, but all the same, when he looked at their loved ones, their wives, children, parents, brothers and sisters, there was simply a deep well of pain inside him, which could never be repaired even with the military might of the U.S. Marines.

Tom tried to continue on with his military career, but it was pointless.

Much to the concern of his father, Tom eventually applied for an honorable discharge from the U.S. Marines. It had taken months for his discharge to be finalized. As a highly awarded helicopter pilot, with three separate tours of duty to the Sand Pit under his belt, he could only assume that despite his father being adamant that he would not intervene, he was indeed responsible for the delay. When it eventually came through, Tom signed the paperwork, handed in the last of his uniforms, and walked home from the base.

When he arrived home, Sam Reilly was there waiting for him, with a job offer he couldn't resist.

Although they had been childhood neighbors, they came from very different walks of life; both struggling with their unusual vicissitudes with equal enthusiasm and tenacity. Tom's own father was an Admiral in the Navy, and although he earned a salary well into six figures, and was even on a first name basis with a number of Senators and Congressmen, was considered relatively poor in comparison to the others living in the affluent community of La Jolla, California.

Sam, on the other hand, had more money than he would ever get to spend in his lifetime. The two men shared a similar love for cave diving since childhood. Once they reached adulthood, much to the disappointment of his friend's father, Sam decided to join Tom, and the two became cadet helicopter pilots never had any aspirations to reach Flag rank in forty years' of service to the Marine Corps.

The two of them completed their pilot training and Sam had even served the start of one tour of duty in Afghanistan with him. But then, for no reason that anyone could comprehend, Sam had returned stateside and completed his studies at MIT. There had been some unsavory sentiment throughout the military that once Sam had tasted the awful realities of war, he had used his father's influence to bring him home again.

To this day, Tom had never discovered the real reason behind his mate's sudden and early departure from the Marines, but he doubted very much that Sam had been incompetent and Tom was incapable of believing his friend to be a coward. Sam had returned to MIT to complete his Master's in Oceanography, and the two men usually met several times a year to go cave diving together. It wasn't much, but it was all the off-time that the Marines would give him, and all that Sam's studies would allow.

He was surprised to see Sam at the door on the very day that he had received his honorable discharge. It might have been sheer luck that their two lives were about to collide once again, but, although he believed in luck, Tom also knew that Sam was often the precursor to its development.

It wasn't a coincidence.

Sam must have known what was going to happen.

Tom still remembered their conversation fondly, despite his current position, and the irony of all that he'd been offered.

It occurred just over a year ago now.

"I was formally discharged from the Corps today," Tom

said.

"So, I was told." Sam looked cheerful and then said, "I'll bet your dad was stoked."

"Mom's already called to give me the heads up that it will take him a while to cool down after this one. Anyway, that's about all with me. I have no reason to feel sorry for myself. The truth is, I gave the Corps six years of my life, and three tours of duty in some of the most hostile conflicts in recent history. I'm glad to be out. I never had any aspirations to be an Admiral in forty years' time like my old man. Now, since I doubt that you're here to cheer me up, what do you want, Sam?"

"My dad has convinced me to return to the family business."

"I thought you hated what your father does?"

"No, I'm indifferent to the whims of an overly rich hyper-intelligent man child." Sam smiled again as he described his father. "Despite what he wants, I won't ever become Global Shipping's next Chief Executive Officer."

"So, you'll become what, a tugboat Captain?" Tom said, incredulously knowing that his friend wouldn't find that interesting either.

"No, he wants me to take over one of his smaller auxiliary companies, Deep Sea Salvage."

"Salvaging big ships and tugboat driving?"

"Not exactly, but I suppose we might be responsible for something like that. He's offered me the position of Director of Special Operations, which is a fancy way of saying that I pick the work that I want to do, which is primarily ocean research, deep sea salvage operations, and water quality studies."

"What did you just say to the offer?" Tom asked.

"I said, it depends whether or not I can convince you to leave the Marines and join me." Realization slowly dawned in Tom's eyes, as Sam continued, "My old man told me not to worry about it. You were thinking of quitting anyway."

"I got a phone call at 8 a.m. today, telling me that the paperwork had finally gone through! When did you speak to your dad, Sam?"

"We talked at about 7:30."

"That bastard! He's the only person who has ever gotten the best of my father, and he controls the world's largest Navy."

"Yeah, not to discuss whose is bigger, but my dad controls the world's richest one. So, what do you say, do you want to have an adventure or do you want to find out what other bureaucracy your father intends for you join?"

"You know I hate the ocean!" Tom knew that this wasn't an entirely true statement. Since he'd nearly been killed by a hurricane during his boyhood, he'd subsequently had a number of nightmares regarding the sea and so, when he met and befriended Sam, he'd spent years being dragged out into the ocean on adventures with him. Hurricanes still scared the shit out of him, but he had learned to love the ocean as much he'd come to deeply respect its awesome power.

"No, you don't hate it. You're just a little frightened of it, that's all. That will actually help where we're going. Besides, we mainly look after diving operations, deep sea retrievals and leave the ocean disasters to the other guys. I can put you in charge of Special Projects. Besides, we need a helicopter pilot. What do you say?"

"It sounds like a lot more fun than moping about here," and just like that, Tom had been hooked into a life at sea; a life in which he discovered a place and happiness he'd never before known.

Tom laughed as he recalled the conversation, and remembered how both Reilly men had the unique power to convince others to join them, regardless of their original intentions.

Tom's thoughts returned to the present.

Despite the heavy soundproofing in the operations room, the 40,000 hp twin diesel engines could be heard humming away in the background as they propelled the Maria Helena at full speed towards the troubled Hayward Bulk, somewhere off the coast of North Queensland, Australia.

Tropical cyclones, he knew, were the southern hemisphere's equivalent of his dreaded hurricane.

The Hayward Bulk was a 500,000 ton supertanker.

It was on the Japan to South Africa run when its engine impeller broke and the supertanker's built-in safety system cut the power to the engines to protect it. The Mary Rose, which provided offshore support to the vessel, had refused to come to its aid because cyclone Petersham was on its way.

The Hayward Bulk was one of more than thirty supertankers owned by Global Shipping. Deep Sea Expeditions was its smaller arm. It's CEO and owner, shipping mogul and old man, James Reilly, had contacted the skipper of the Maria Helena and informed him that they were being diverted from their current duties in Townsville in order to deliver a team of engineers and some heavy equipment to the lame ship.

If they reached her in time, Tom would be required to fly them over to the troubled vessel.

For twelve months his good luck had kept him away from any such disaster at sea. As he stared at the meteorological reports on his laptop, Tom realized that Cyclone Petersham was going to be one of the worst to ever reach this part of the world.

Fate, he realized, was inexorable.

The swell had risen above forty feet, and for the first time since leaving Sydney, Sam started to wonder if he'd gone too far this time. Where the waves had previously been spotted with whitecaps, they were now walls of water, forty feet high and covered in white, angry, frothy sea. The wind had risen to 80 knots, gusting up to 120.

To make matters worse, the extreme low off the coast of South Australia was just about to collide with the southern tip of Cyclone Petersham's low. This would form the most deadly of barometric systems, known as a squeeze. Seen on a synoptic chart, the two lows could be identified by a number of gradient pressure lines, with an area of relative normal pressure in the middle about to be squeezed between them. There was no rational way to predict how the sea would respond to such a collision of natural forces.

Sam relished this type of meteorological event at sea.

Below deck, barely audible above the sounds of the storm, he heard his satellite phone ringing. Only three people in the world had this number—his father, James Reilly, his meteorologist, Mark Stanton, and his best friend, Tom Bower. Even his mother didn't have it.

Whatever had happened, it would be important.

He stepped down the ladder and picked up the phone.

"Sam here." Despite the cold air, he could feel the sweat on his hand with which he held the phone against his ear.

It had to be his father.

He'd already spoken to Mark earlier today, and the man had made it abundantly clear that there was no possible way to tell, with any reasonable certainty, what the hell was going to happen when the weather systems collided. So, that left only his father, who never called unless there was a problem. Sam decided to hope that it was Mark on the phone, telling him the storm was going to be worse than he'd originally predicted.

"Sam, its Blake Simonds." There was a pause after that. *What the heck is Blake doing ringing me?* "I got your picture," the man continued, as though he'd anticipated Sam's lack of response as an indicator of non-recognition.

He'd almost completely forgotten about the gold ingot.

"Oh, yeah, do you know where it's from?" Sam asked.

"Yeah, it's from the Oppenheimer and Goldschmidt family." He could tell by the tone of Blake's voice that the man assumed that everyone knew about the family.

"Never heard of them."

"They were an extremely wealthy Jewish family who disappeared during the Holocaust."

"Don't you mean that they were murdered?" Sam corrected him.

"No, their deaths couldn't have been kept secret, not even during the Holocaust."

"Any idea where they are now?" Sam asked.

"No." Sam heard Blake sigh on the other end of the line. "But that's just it. No one's heard from them since."

"Any relatives?"

"No, the last anyone saw of them was when they tried to escape Munich on the Magdalena." Blake sounded excited, as though he was close to discovering something of great importance.

"What's the Magdalena?"

"She was a luxury airship, like the Titanic's equivalent of a Zeppelin airship. It was said that her owner, a Mr. Peter Greenstein, made a number of trips aboard her, attempting to rescue rich Jewish families in the early days of the war."

"Just the rich ones?" Sam, having grown up with a father who considered himself in financial trouble when his name didn't appear in the Top 10 Rich List in Forbes Magazine, found that irritating and typical.

"It's what I heard." Blake said.

"That figures." Sam had seen firsthand what was offered to the rich. "What happened to him and the rest of the people on the Magdalena?"

"Well, that's just it. They were never seen or heard from again after the night that the Oppenheimer and Goldschmidt family disappeared."

Now, the story behind the treasure hunt began to pique his interest.

"Thanks for that."

"Not a problem. You haven't found the gold, have you?"

"No, just doing some research for a friend. Say, how did you get this number?"

"My father told me the story about the lost Magdalena when I was a boy, so when I saw the image, I just had to know the answer. I rang your father and told him that it was urgent that I speak with you. He gave me this number. Said you wouldn't mind. By the way, he told me to give you his regards and that he hopes your new job is working out for you."

It had been a year since he'd reluctantly taken the job, but he and his dad didn't talk too often.

"Not a problem. Thanks for that."

"Hey, if you find anything more on the final resting place of the Magdalena, I'd love to know about it. Can you keep me in the loop?"

"Sure."

He hit the end button on his sat phone and then scrolled down through his address book until he reached Tom Bower's number.

He hit the call button.

Sam heard the first and the second ring. He never heard the third one. Instead, there was a loud bang as an unusually large wave hit *Second Chance's* portside, very nearly causing her to broach and flooding her. Dropping the sat phone, he heard the sudden rush of water engulfing the center cockpit.

He looked at hatchway high above him, and saw a wave of sea water breaking overhead.

It was too late.

His hands instinctively gripped two of the many cabin holds, before the torrent of water swept through the open hatchway and all light disappeared from his world.

CHAPTER 2

Cyclone Petersham had reached its peak on the morning of August 25th, just as the Maria Helena reached the failing ship.

Tom, along with the ship's skipper and a number of the other scientists aboard, were in the operations room, sitting at its large rectangular table. At the head of the table sat the Maria Helena's skipper, along one side of the table sat Tom and several of the scientists, who currently lived on the ship, and along the other side sat four engineers, whom Tom had flown in from Cairns earlier that morning. At the foot of the table, stood an empty chair, in which Sam Reilly would ordinarily be seated as Special Operations Director of Deep Sea Salvages.

Unlike the knights of the round table, the Maria Helena, although civilian, still maintained a clear chain of command. The skipper held the ultimate responsibility for the safety of the ship and everyone on board, and ordinarily, were Sam on board, he would be charged with the primary responsibility for their mission.

"As you're all aware, the Hayward Bulk has now been without its propulsion system for almost forty eight hours," Matthew, the skipper, stated with calm, clear, efficiency. "And, given her location during this upcoming cyclone, and both the immediate and long term risk to life and the environment if she is reefed, we have offered our services to get these engineers and equipment on board the stricken vessel."

No one spoke.

Everyone in the room knew that the fact that Global Shipping, their subsidiary's owner, was responsible for the potential disaster, was why they had been diverted to this mission.

Matthew spoke again. "We have received reports that the Hayward Bulk has dragged both her anchors and is headed for the coast of Cairns. The greatest problem however, is that she will never make land since the Great Barrier Reef lies between the two."

They were too late.

"What's she carrying?" It was the first time Tom had spoken since the start of the meeting.

"It's classified."

"Bullshit! Global Shipping is a civilian cargo fleet. All ship contents must be logged in and identified."

"Look, let's just say that the cargo the Hayward Bulk is carrying would be lethal to every bit of sea life, and human life, for that matter, for hundreds of miles." This time, the speaker was one of the engineers who had recently boarded the Maria Helena.

"I can't believe they've done this! What the hell are they carrying?" Tom didn't bother to hide his complaint.

"Tom, that doesn't matter right now. Can you land on the Hayward Bulk in this weather?" Matthew, the skipper of the Maria Helena, brought him back to the problem at hand.

"I can't even take off in this weather, let alone land in it." Tom was incredulous that he was even being asked such a ridiculous question.

"There are twenty three of our guys working on board her right now. If we can't get this new impeller to them, their deaths will be nothing when compared to the three hundred thousand deaths that will occur when they collide with the reef."

"What is she carrying?" Tom persisted.

"I told you, I can't tell you that."

"Piss off! You expect me to risk my life for my duty, but you won't tell me what it is I'm trying to save. No way!"

"Okay, can we speak about this privately?" Matthew implored.

"No, we're a team here. By the sound of things, old man Reilly's already put all of our lives at significant risk. I think we all deserve to know why." Tom raised his voice only slightly, but to everyone in the room who knew him well, it was akin to a declaration of war, coming from an otherwise entirely placid man.

"It's carrying uranium. It's not supposed to be anywhere near the reef, but it is." The speaker's badge identified him as Malcolm Ford. He wore a black Armani suit, which made him look like a businessman rather than an engineer. He was most likely a company representative—there to make sure that Global Shipping didn't bear the blame for this venture.

He'd been sitting quietly amidst the other engineers. Behind his fine glasses was the face of a man who confidently held complete authority over the situation. The man had taken his place among the other engineers who had also remained silent until that point, but this man seemed different. He was not simply an intelligent engineer. He was there for another purpose, although what that purpose might be, Tom couldn't imagine. The man hadn't apologized at all, but simply confirmed what Tom had suspected.

Who is this guy?

"But there's no way she could do that without special approval! The ship would need to be specifically certified for it. There's only one way that it could get that kind of approval . . ."

Tom stopped short, remembering the close relationship James Reilly had with the Obama administration.

What has that self-absorbed prick got us into this time? Sam was really going to be pissed off at his old man when he found out what had happened. Not that Sam had seen eye to eye with the old man since his mother split with him in the aftermath of Danny's accident.

"We don't have time for bickering." Matthew's voice was stern, but not antagonistic. "Can you fly or not?"

"If you can ride out the worst of this cyclone until she meets the eye of the storm, I might be able to take off and make the transfer."

"Okay, it's not an ideal solution, but at least it's a chance. How much of a window do we have?"

"If I time the takeoff perfectly, it will only be a matter of minutes between takeoff and landing on the stricken ship. We're not likely to get another chance to try to take off again if this plan doesn't succeed. So, what are the chances this will work?"

"I know the chances are slim, but they're absolutely zero if you don't get that part to the crew of the floundering Hayward Bulk."

"I get it . . ." Tom said, acknowledging that he would do it. It was never a question of whether or not he would risk his life to serve the greater good, but a matter of knowing why he was risking his life at all. "I'll go warm up the chopper."

Tom looked out the rear hatchway of the Maria Helena's doghouse.

The enormous Westland WS-61 Sea King helicopter could only just be seen through the spume of violent windswept water, resting precariously atop the small helipad located on the aft deck of the sky blue Maria Helena. Its skids had been secured to the deck as a normal precaution to prevent it from shifting as the ship naturally rocked on the swells of the open ocean. Today, their strain could be clearly seen, as the ship dramatically lurched in the violent swells. In this weather, Tom imagined that any sudden release from its restraints would result in it being flung off into the sea, just like a bull rider in a rodeo.

The storm was raging at its worst as they neared the eye of the cyclone. It was a scientific fact that the narrower the base of a cyclone was, the faster were the wind speeds it generated.

The restraints used to secure the helicopter were rated to hold more than forty tons, considerably more than the helicopter's fifteen ton weight. Even so, Tom would have much preferred to wait until the weather eased before preparing it for take-off. The problem was that they would have such a small window of opportunity to successfully make the transfer to the Hayward Bulk that the helicopter would need to be completely ready to take off the second they entered the eye of the cyclone.

Tom watched as the deck rose and fell several times before he mentally pictured a pause long enough to race from the Maria Helena's protected doghouse to the helicopter's cockpit door.

Seeing his best chance, he sprang into motion.

Reaching the Sea King just as the entire rear deck of the Maria Helena dropped thirty feet down a trough, his hand gripped the winch man's bar on the right hand side, as his legs fell out from under him.

Tom didn't wait for the ship to fully right itself before opening the cockpit door.

Stepping up into the large cockpit, he started his meticulous checklist, preparing for take-off.

With his left hand, he switched the Master Battery/Electrical Switch to the ON position. Instantly, the lights behind the cockpit instruments glowed a soft red. Next to it, his hand flicked the Master Avionics Switch to ON. The backlight of the avionics turned a reassuring soft red.

Looking to the right side of his control panel, he confirmed that the fuel level was reading FULL, as he always maintained it after any mission. The Fuel Valve Master was then switched to ON; the Nav Lights were switched ON, *not that anyone else in their right mind would be in the air right now.*

He gave the 'all okay' signal with his thumb and fore finger, signaling the engineers to join him. The spare impeller they were to deliver had already been brought on board.

Tom turned his head to face the back of the Sea King and watched as the four men climbed inside. Each man was sweating and unwilling to meet his eyes. Unlike the Navy SEALs he'd met in his former life with the U.S. Marines, these men were private engineers and unaccustomed to this level of risk.

Then, the fifth man opened the front passenger door.

"How soon before we can go?" It was the business man from the earlier meeting. Unlike the other engineers in the helicopter, this man exhibited none of the telltale signs of a person in distress. He might just as easily been jumping into a taxicab on the way to an important meeting.

"Soon," Tom said. He then looked around at the scared faces of his passengers, and said, "Are you gentlemen feeling lucky?"

"They tell me that you're the best helicopter pilot in either hemisphere," the man seated next to him said. The grey hair at his temples indicated his age, and he carried his strong, athletic build, one befitting a much younger man, with an air of confidence. "So, do we need luck here?"

"We're about to fly inside the eye of a cyclone," Tom said, as he tried to fake an untroubled smile. "I'd say we could use a little bit of luck. I'll make you a deal. I'll get you on the Hayward Bulk and you just make sure that you get her to operate under her own power in time to save all our lives."

"It's a deal."

Tom turned his head to the window, watching as the storm raged in front of him. The high winds were literally lifting the water out of the ocean.

How much worse could it get?

Tom then watched as the radar system produced a clear image of the opening ahead. The Maria Helena was about to enter the eye of the cyclone.

Tom's left hand adjusted the throttle until the main rotary blade RPMs reached 100%.

His right hand tapped the reset button, zeroing altimeter.

"Maria Helena this is Sea King, Yankee Victor Charlee Zero Niner."

"Go ahead Sea King."

"We're ready to jump ship the second we're through the razor's edge."

"Copy that, and good luck."

The Maria Helena's bow rode the enormous wave.

Once entering the eye, the storm was gone.

As though God had turned off a washing machine. In place of the turbulent sea, there was a placid lake. On board the ship, the pitch of the powerful diesel dropped, as its twin propellers ceased the hard work of trying to maintain forward momentum in the swell. There was an eerie absence of wind, and a seaman could easily be forgiven for thinking the storm was over and that he'd been lucky to have survived it.

Tom's mind returned to the present, as he saw the stricken Hayward Bulk in the distance.

"Here we go, gentlemen."

The ground crew then manually disconnected the tethers.

His left hand pulled on the collective.

Instantly, the collective pitch of the rotor blades increased, creating lift. The sound of the Sea King's powerful Rolls Royce engine could be heard, as Tom increased the throttle to maintain RPMs, and then they were airborne.

At eighty feet, Tom could see just how small the eye of the cyclone really was. He wished the Maria Helena could have closed the gap between the two ships.

Approximately one nautical mile ahead of him was the damaged super tanker, bobbing around in the relatively calm water, with no more control over its destiny than a floating plastic bottle.

Tom immediately adjusted the pitch for fastest straight and level flying.

Behind the damaged vessel, Tom could see a vast crest, a barrage of water. It was at the far end of the eye of the cyclone, quickly approaching. He realized that it was highly unlikely that they would make it in time.

No one aboard the helicopter spoke, yet everyone had the same thought—they were all going to die.

For each hundred feet they flew towards the Hayward Bulk, the outermost wall of the eye seemed to advance two hundred feet closer.

Tom felt like a child who feared with certainty that he would be the last one standing at the end of a game of musical chairs, he would be crashing his helicopter at the same time the storm would reach the Hayward Bulk.

Five hundred feet from the Hayward Bulk, he watched the small ripples crease at the back of the vessel's hull, then turn white—the storm had returned.

They were too late.

With the wind speed at over one hundred knots, it was going to be very hard to put the Sea King down on the helipad.

Tom started making the descent.

Unlike a normal descent by helicopter, this was more like a controlled fall than a standard approach.

Below him, the storm blew the enormous antennae off of the radar tower on top of the ship.

He was coming in fast.

When his rotors finally hit the other side of the eye of the storm, he could do little to maintain control. It was more a case of his forward momentum and gravity keeping him moving towards the helipad.

His arms and feet fought with the pedals, joystick, and collective to keep the helicopter from crashing into the sea, at a speed much faster than his mind could ever grasp purposefully. He was now relying solely on his subconscious ability, developed over many years of flying.

No longer concerned about crashing, but simply about staying out of the sea, Tom threw caution to the violent wind.

In doing so, he overshot the helipad.

Two hundred feet past the helipad, further along the hull of the Hayward Bulk, he slowed his rate of descent, hovered for an instant, and then elegantly dropped onto the deck of the crippled vessel.

The skids could be heard breaking apart as the Sea King set down hard.

Tom immediately reversed the pitch of the rotor blades, so that instead of creating lift, they forced the helicopter down hard against the deck, stopping it from being blown off into the sea.

They were alive.

For now.

"Okay, everyone out!" Tom turned his head and saw the pale faces of his terrified passengers.

No one moved.

"The wind is going to blow her overboard pretty soon, so I suggest you all get out of here if you want to live."

It was enough to get them moving again.

Tom watched as the four passengers struggled with the 150Kg impeller.

"Good luck."

"Where are you going?" said one of the engineers, who looked even more startled than before, if that was even possible.

Tom smiled.

"Just cleaning up the deck." He then raised the collective to full, locked it in position, rotated the angle to the portside, and stepped gingerly out of the helicopter.

The Sea King then disappeared into the ocean.

"Well gentlemen, there goes the only chance we had of taking off again," Tom said calmly. "I've done my part. Let's hope to hell that you're able to do yours."

"Come on, let's get this stuff down below," said the oldest engineer with an air of fatalism.

CHAPTER 3

Sam watched as the wall of water rapidly approached.

There was little that he could do about it. *Second Chance* would survive or she wouldn't. His only option was to hold on.

He turned away, his back facing the oncoming barrage of water and closed his eyes. Taking one last deep breath, he grasped the inside grab bar with all the strength in both hands, and hoped that today wasn't going to be his last.

The turbid wave of water hit him with the force of a Mac truck. The initial impact nearly rendering him unconscious. The strong flow swept his feet out from under him, and his hands, locked onto the grab bar, fought to prevent him from being flushed down the galley passage way.

The water was just starting to recede as a second wave struck the port side.

Sam had just enough time to take one more deep breath before the entire area was swamped with water again.

He thought his ship may broach and then roll, but *Second Chance* held true to her name.

Slowly, the water receded. Sam heard the familiar drone of the powerful automatic pumps deep in the bilge kick into life.

Picking himself up, he scanned the cabin.

It was going to take a lot of work to clean her, and some of the electronic equipment would need to be replaced, but all told, he had escaped lightly, he decided.

Another large wave struck, and he heard the mechanical workings of the autopilot struggling to maintain her course.

Then, he heard the sound that is every sailor's worst nightmare.

It was the sound of a cable snapping under pressure, followed by the sudden jolt of the yacht as its rudder stopped struggling to maintain her direction. The tiny storm jib, the only sail which remained, and formed a triangle no longer than a couple feet, could now be heard flapping in the wind.

Sam didn't wait to feel the pounding of the giant swell on his port side. Without the rudder, there was no way to control how *Second Chance* would face the oncoming swell.

In these seas, failure to run with the swell could only result in catastrophic damage to his yacht and his certain death by drowning.

He climbed up the stairs and stepped out through the tiny hatchway.

The storm surrounded him now. If he failed to gain control of the rudder within minutes he, and *Second Chance,* would be well on their way to the bottom of Bass Strait.

The autopilot was flashing and making an irritating noise as its computer tried to determine how to make adjustments. It was completely ineffective as long as the cable running from the steering block to the rudder was broken.

Sam hit the wait button on the autopilot in utter frustration.

He didn't need to hear that sound anymore. Then, without waiting to harness up and run a travel line, he quickly made his way to the transom. There, above the enormous rudder, were the remains of his old weather vane and next to them, the emergency tiller.

A simple, direct link to the rudder, the tiller was of little mechanical aid to steering, but it was something; the emergency tiller gave Sam at least the possibility of steering *Second Chance* by hand.

Sitting aft Sam had little protection from the giant waves, running from behind him. If another wave flooded his deck again, harnessed or not, the force would send him overboard to his inevitable death.

As if to emphasize his exposure, a medium sized wave broke and splashed over him; its icy chill immediately jarring his mind into making a change in his course of action.

The one saving grace was the fact that up ahead, his tiny storm jib, little more than a couple of feet of canvas, provided just enough speed to maintain a strong enough flow of water over the rudder to keep a course. Sam angled *Second Chance* diagonally along the large, breaking swell, a motion more like surfing with the wave than fighting against it.

He was in for a long night if he were to survive at all.

His survival so far had been more about luck than skill, he acknowledged, but by the morning the storm had settled.

The next day, he limped to the outskirts of Hobart, where he was able to anchor in the lee of the mountain and make repairs. Running a second steering cable on *Second Chance* was easier than it sounded, because Sam had insisted on a redundant set of cables running side by side.

In the end, that repair took under an hour, but he then spent the next two days draining the bilge to protect the inner hull from salt water corrosion.

On the third day, Sam set the autopilot on a northerly

heading, trimmed the sails, and commenced his long journey home to Sydney, where more serious repairs to his flooded yacht could be made.

Two hours later, well on his way north, and with the weather relatively calm, Sam took one last look at the horizon, checked his instruments, and climbed into the bunk he normally used when he was offshore.

Sam's eyes closed, and comforted by the direction of the compass at the end of the bunk, he slept.

Tom watched as his beloved Sea King helicopter disappeared into the sea.

The wind was too strong and the landing space too poor to ever manage to keep her on the deck of the Hayward Bulk. Flying her back to the Maria Helena wasn't even an option. She crashed into the sea a mere twenty seconds later, floating for a couple of minutes, and then swamped by a large wave.

Its sinking was enough to bring Tom back to the problem at hand.

The four scientists, who had been aboard the Sea King, along with a number of other crewmen from the Hayward Bulk, made their way down into the bowels of the ship, with the gigantic impeller.

Tom followed them to the entrance of the hull.

A stupid smile crossed his lips as he considered the ridiculousness of the situation, and his inability to now have any effect on its outcome.

The impeller, designed to bring in cold sea water to actively cool the engine, had split. Consequently, the engine wasn't being cooled, and left unrepaired, would ultimately cause the engine to seize, turning a $20,000 repair job into a $1,000,000 need for a new engine. To avoid this, Global Shipping's chief engineer had ordered a built-in safety system for each of his engines, to automatically shut down the engine should the impeller cease to draw in water.

The result of such a simple system was that everyone on board the Hayward Bulk, and potentially another three hundred thousand people, living in and around Cairns, were going to die, despite the engine being fully operational.

The irony of the system's theoretical safe guard almost made Tom laugh as he watched the four engineers struggle to maneuver the massive impeller deep into the hull, where it could be fitted to the enormous super tanker's engine.

Tom was just about to follow them, when he noticed that the man in the Armani suit, who appeared unsettlingly confident about the situation, was following the rest of the engineers to the door, but just before entering it, he looked around and then continued to walk toward the front of the ship.

What's he up to? Tom wondered.

Following him, Tom didn't even attempt to hide. The wind was gusting so strongly, and there was so much sea spray in the air, Tom feared that he might likely be blown overboard before the man even realized that he was being followed.

The closer the man came to approaching the bow, the more Tom worried about what he was up to. There were no working engines at the Hayward Bulk's bow, so why was he headed there? Tom fully intended to find out.

The man was carrying a work bag, but for what purpose, Tom didn't know.

Ahead, the man opened one of the hatchways into the hull, looked from right to left, and then disappeared below.

Tom ran ahead, trying to catch up.

He opened the hatchway and listened. The soft background lights, that allowed the crew to see the inner workings of the ship's bowels, allowed him to see only a short distance ahead. Down below, he could hear the sound of someone moving fast, skipping a number of steps as they descended; not that Tom could hear very much over the sounds of the storm.

The man may have had a valid reason for being there. It seemed reasonable to assume that if he were an engineer with a purpose, he would be running down the stairs.

Tom followed the stairs to the bottom.

The bilge could be heard, the ship having already taken on large quantities of the water which had flooded the deck, and was now swishing around the bottom.

Once he reached the bottom and looked around, Tom couldn't see where the man had gone. It appeared to be a dead end, which served little purpose other than to provide buoyancy. Tom turned around to see if he could find another direction in which the man might have gone.

Shining his flashlight around the large room it appeared to serve little purpose. At the furthermost point of the bow, two comparatively small engines could be seen, which must have been used for the bow thruster.

At the portside engine, something caught his eye.

Tom saw the faint glow of a single red dot which was flickering on and off. Ordinarily, Tom wouldn't have given it a second thought, but in the absence of any other light, the single red light seemed out of place.

Climbing down to the engine, he placed his hand on the red light. It glowed on his hand as though its source was emanating from elsewhere.

His eyes followed the beam to its origin, and then stopped.

On the side of the hull, and about ten feet above him, were two single sticks of dynamite wired to a timer with a red LED light. As explosives go, it wasn't much, but it was certainly enough to blow a big hole in the hull, one big enough to sink the Hayward Bulk—if cyclone Petersham didn't sink it first.

Tom's mind grasped the outcome.

Above him, he heard the sound of a single steel bar sliding over the top of the hatchway.

He was trapped.

CHAPTER 4

The man in the Armani suit was feeling good.

Everything had fallen into place perfectly. At first, after his partner had destroyed the impeller, he'd been worried that they were going to be able to repair it before he could reach the stricken ship. Then, he heard about the cyclone, and the solution presented itself.

Malcolm Ford, a senior engineer for Global Shipping, was in Sydney at the time. It would be easy for him to offer assistance to the damaged ship. It would also provide him with more credibility, as the crew of the Maria Helena would most likely have never met the man.

The gamble had paid off, but he was worried that the pilot seemed to sense that something wasn't quite right. The man appeared too aware, much brighter than usual. After research, he discovered that the pilot was Sam Reilly's right hand man in Global Shipping's special projects division—Deep Sea Expeditions.

As it was, that problem had been taken care of.

Now, he had less than an hour in which to retrieve it. He was going to have to work fast, but he was confident that he would have it in time.

The man ran back towards the main pilot house—the

superstructure located at the rear of the ship, which housed the crew quarters, Navigation Bridge, and control tower.

To his relief, he didn't run into anyone on his way there, and he quickly opened the door and stepped inside. The sound of the storm was instantly cut in half as he closed the door behind him.

He'd seen the schematics of the ship more than a week ago, and knew exactly where he was going–down more than a dozen sets of stairs, until he reached the bowels of the ship.

In the ordinarily locked room, he picked up the swipe card that his friend had left for him and unlocked the door.

The room was small when compared to the vast size of the rest of the Hayward Bulk. It was dark, with no portholes to let in outside light. He turned the lights on, but they did nothing to make the place feel more homely.

At the far end of the room stood a single bed, and next to it was a laptop computer.

He turned the computer on and waited until the security login page booted up. Then, quickly typing in the alpha-numeric code, he watched as the startup screen changed to his homepage.

In the top left-hand corner, he clicked on a file labeled, "Time to go."

Opening the file, his heart began to race as he realized that he was close to achieving his goal. He clicked the "proceed" button, and the tool bar showed the time remaining before the process was complete.

Leaving the laptop open to continue running its program, and confident that its owner would be too focused on current events to return to it, the man casually departed.

The smile never left his face until he was free.

He had done it.

He'd betrayed a man, and stolen something even more valuable than money.

Tom, unable to move the hatch above him, quickly returned to the place where he'd spotted the bomb. There was no identifiable timer, so he had no way to determine how much time he had left.

Tom realized that it didn't matter.

He was going to have to find a way of disposing of it. If he failed, the Hayward Bulk was going to be destroyed, and everything they'd done to save the lives of everyone within a thousand miles of the place was going to be for nothing.

To the right of the bomb, he found a spool of heavy chain. It weighed a lot and he was barely able to carry it to the steps above the bomb. Once there, he unrolled it as fast as he could and lowered one end. He then wrapped the other end around a bollard until it locked upon itself.

He then carefully descended the large chain links until he reached the bomb.

It was only comprised of two sticks of dynamite with a simple internal timer. Someone from his unit probably could have disarmed it without thinking twice. Unfortunately, he knew nothing about bombs.

He grasped it in his right hand and pulled gently.

It separated from the wall easily enough, and since he was still alive, Tom thought that he was doing well so far.

Although he didn't know much about the bomb itself, he'd seen enough explosives during his time in the Corps to know that people didn't usually rig these with long timers.

He carried it to the top of the stairs and affixed it to the hatchway door.

If it detonates before I get out of here, it's going to create my escape route . . .

Tom returned to the bottom of the stairs and started banging against the steel dividing wall, which made up part of the ship's watertight safety compartments. It was foolish to think that such a sound might be heard above the sound of the cyclone, but it didn't stop him from trying.

He found a fire extinguisher and used it to ram the side of the steel plate.

After banging away for ten minutes, Tom took a break, followed by another ten minutes of banging. At the end of his fifth attempt, the resonance of his banging was much louder than it had been at the start.

At first, he didn't realize its origin; his ears still ringing and his head throbbing.

When he looked up, he realized that above him a ten foot hole could be seen where the hatchway had been.

He'd found his exit.

If only there was enough time left to save the Hayward Bulk.

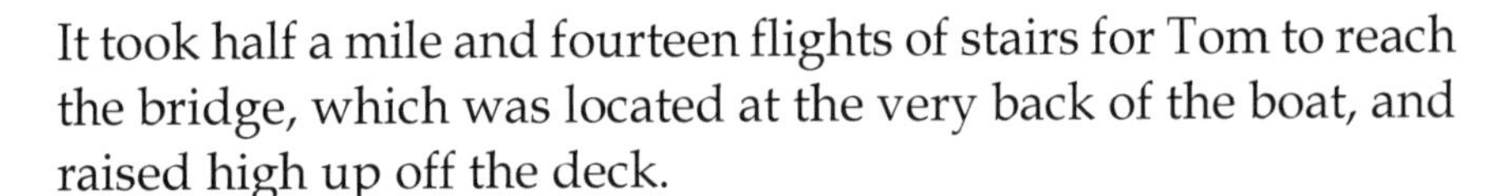

It took half a mile and fourteen flights of stairs for Tom to reach the bridge, which was located at the very back of the boat, and raised high up off the deck.

"Captain Ambrose?" Tom greeted the man, whose white beard and captain's hat would easily identify him as the very image of any sea captain anywhere in the world.

"Yes," he acknowledged, his eyes looking Tom up and down, "and you must be Mr. Bower, the pilot off the Maria Helena?"

"That's me, and we have a serious problem."

"We sure do, son. It appears that despite your valiant efforts, we're going to hit that reef and tear the hull of my ship open as if it was a sardine can."

"We'll get to that in a second." Tom paused, he had no idea how close they were to the reef. "One of the engineers who I transported on to this ship, a Mr. Malcolm Ford, is not who he says he is. I caught him planting a bomb at the front of the ship, and now I have no idea where he is."

"Christ, my day just gets better and better." The captain looked confused. "But why would anyone want to destroy my ship?"

"Most likely because of your payload and the catastrophic repercussions of its possible spill in these waters. It will be the worst terrorist attacks in history!"

"Are you kidding me?" The captain laughed. "Our payload is going to go straight to the bottom. The only harm it will do is to any fish who are unfortunate enough to be swimming underneath us when we sink. Nothing else will come of it."

"But, I was told you were carrying a load of uranium?"

"What, through the Torres Straits? Are you nuts? Jim Reilly would never allow it—not that he'd complain about the environmental risk, but if he were caught carrying uranium, the EPA would fine him so much that even he would never afford to sail a ship in these waters again."

"Then what are you carrying?" Tom asked.

"Coal."

"Just coal? Anything else? Why would James Reilly request all this support and risk all of our lives if you're only carrying coal? What else would someone be after?"

The captain opened a special shipping manifest and noted

an entry dated two weeks ago. "Jim Reilly was aboard just before we left Japan. He accessed his private vault."

"He has a private vault?"

"Sure does. It's rumored that he has a private suite on all of his supertankers, but this is the only one with a private vault."

"Really?" Tom couldn't imagine why James Reilly would need that. "What does he keep in it?"

"I have no idea, I've never known. I do know that it's not drugs—I know that much for sure. We've had many drug-sniffing dogs come on board at some of the ports we dock at, and I've never seen a single one of them stop and alert at his vault."

"How often does he access his vault?"

"Not very often, perhaps a couple of times a year." The Captain's eyes widened. "Whatever it is, we can safely assume that it's quiet valuable."

"Why do you say that?"

"It generally comes to us via a number of a private security vans. You know, the kind they use to transport gold and money around for banks. Only, Jimmy's different, he likes to use a number of them. Each one is armored to the hilt. They all crisscross their routes, so that any would-be pursuers are at a loss as to which van holds his valuables. In the end, there are usually three vehicles that enter the hull. When this happens, the old man is always on site. He says that he doesn't trust anyone, and he has used that specific team for years. He then locks it away and he may or may not retrieve it for months or even years later."

"And you've never found out what it was?"

"No, never. What Jimmy doesn't want you to know, you simply don't ask."

"So then, once he locks whatever it is in his safe, who keeps it secure?"

"No one. Like I said, 'It's secured in his private vault.'"

"What's to stop someone from boarding the ship and breaking into it?"

"The vault can only be accessed from the outside, along the waterline when the ship is empty. Then, when the ship is loaded, the entrance is well below the waterline, making it next to impossible to access when the ship is moving."

"What about a submarine or divers?" Tom asked.

"Impossible."

"Why?"

"The Hayward Bulk is a 500,000 ton super tanker. Do you have any idea what sort of pressure is created near the hull of this ship when it's moving?"

Tom nodded his head. He had a fair idea where the Captain was going with this.

"Anything that comes close to the ship would be pulled into her wake and destroyed in a matter of seconds."

"I get it."

He really didn't, though. Tom had known James Reilly for years and other than being well past suffering with megalomania, the man had always seemed quite pragmatic.

Why would he transfer something so valuable this way? He could easily afford to transport it by plane, or some other secure method. If it was illegal, what could possibly be so rewarding that he would risk everything he already has?

Tom already had an answer to his own question—*more money.*

"What if the ship were to sink?"

"We have state-of-the-art lifeboat aboard. We'll evacuate well before the Hayward Bulk reaches the reef, and you'll find that we'll be quite safe."

"No, I'm sorry," Tom paused. "What I mean is . . . from what you've described, whatever it is that James Reilly is transporting, it is worth more than your ship, and we all know that even the best crew and ship can't stay afloat indefinitely without risk. So, what happens to his prized possessions?"

"They would still be quite safe."

"Even if the ship sinks?"

"Yes. You see Tom, when Jimmy had his private vault built, he did so in such a way that no one could break into it, even with a bomb. Structurally, if the Hayward Bulk sank to the ocean floor and was completely destroyed, his private vault would still be left safe at the sea bottom. Then, if and when he locates his precious ship, the contents of the vault could be retrieved using a diving hatch, which was designed with an air tight compartment. You know, the kind they use in submarines?"

"Okay, so someone is trying to sink us so that they can steal whatever James Reilly has in his private vault."

"But even if we did sink, it would take months to gain access to the vault. You see, the door is stronger than any bank vault, and would take months to break."

"How does it open under normal operations?"

"He has a secret room onboard and there he maintains a digital fortress . . ."

"A what?" Tom asked.

"A digital fortress. Basically, it works like this. The system constantly transmits a code every thirty seconds to the vault door telling it that everything is okay. If it fails to do so, even once, or the ship stops moving, the door seals shut."

"What if someone destroys the computer?"

"Then the digital fortress fails to transmit and the vault locks. So, you see, it would take a lot more than a terrorist act or accidental sinking of the ship, for someone to steal the contents of James Reilly's vault."

Tom considered this for a moment.

"Was there something particularly important about his last most recent deposit, do you think?"

"Could be. He never tells me, but he had additional security this last time, and he told me to make certain that I arrived four days ahead of schedule, and then left without loading any other cargo until we reached Newcastle."

"Oh shit!" Tom said. "The Hayward Bulk is going to the bottom. Whatever James Reilly has stored down there. It's going to the bottom too, where no one can protect it in this weather."

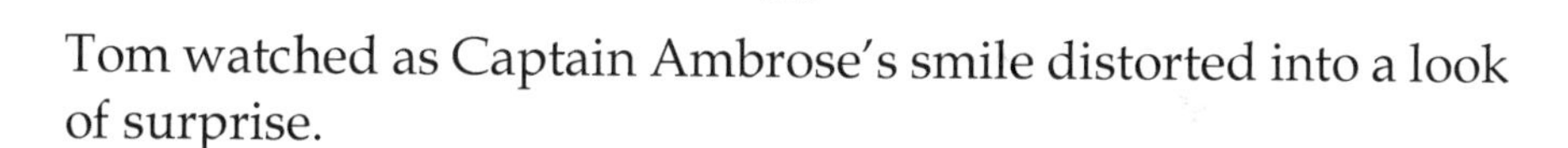

Tom watched as Captain Ambrose's smile distorted into a look of surprise.

"Why in the world would he try to sink us?" The captain was serious when he concluded, "Cyclone Petersham will do that for him soon enough."

"How soon do you think?" Tom asked.

"Four hours, at most."

"So, that's it then. We're all dead men?"

"No, there's lifeboat ready and waiting for us to be evacuated into well before we reach the reef. I've already sent a man out there to prepare it."

That man then came through the door, soaking wet from the

harsh storm outside, his face displaying an emotion far more painful than that of profound fatigue.

"Is the lifeboat in order?"

"No . . ."

"What do you mean, 'no'?"

"I mean that it's missing."

"Shit, where does it normally rest?" Tom said.

"Mid ship, on the starboard side."

"Show me."

The man looked at the captain who nodded his approval, and Tom quickly followed him to where the lifeboat should have been.

The crewman stopped at the spot where the large lifeboat would normally have been secured to the deck, a spot where no wave, no matter how large, could possibly knock it overboard. The mooring chains were all intact and the electronic winch was hanging alongside the railing.

"This lifeboat wasn't inadvertently washed overboard," the crewman said. "Someone has intentionally scuttled it, and has murdered us all in the process."

"Can you see it anywhere in the distance?" Tom said.

"No. Not that it would make much difference. It's not as though we could possibly retrieve it now that it's in the water."

The two of them each tried to spot it with their binoculars, which proved to be relatively useless in the storm. It was almost impossible to see much past the deck railings, let alone try to pinpoint anything on the surface of the turbid sea.

Tom had good eyesight, but in this weather he struggled to locate the missing lifeboat in the violent seas.

Then his eyes caught sight of something.

It was dark, and at first he dismissed it as being impossible. His eyes lost it as the next wave crested, but he managed to spot it again.

This time, he was able to ascertain exactly what he was seeing.

And, what he saw reaffirmed his worst nightmare.

"A submarine?" Captain Ambrose sounded more shocked than anything else.

"Yes," Tom replied.

"But why would it surface here, in the middle of this cyclone?"

"It must take guts to surface a submarine in this weather—guts or desperation. Either way, I think it's safe to say that our saboteur managed to successfully escape from the Hayward Bulk."

"But will he still sink her?" Ambrose asked.

"He wasn't carrying enough equipment on board to sink her. I'm starting to wonder if his plan was simply to stop our engineers from repairing the impeller, and in doing so, force the Hayward Bulk on to the reef. In shallow waters, it will be easier to retrieve whatever he was so intent on accessing." Tom then looked at the GPS and asked, "How are we doing time-wise? Do you think we'll make it?"

Captain Ambrose showed him on the GPS monitor just where the reef would most likely tear open the hull of his ship. It was still 32 nautical miles away, but with the strong easterly winds, the Hayward Bulk was drifting at a rate of a just over 8 nautical miles per hour.

"Four hours? That's the best estimate that we've got going

for us?" Tom checked his math.

"That's correct." Captain Ambrose's face showed that he'd already accepted the fact that he'd would be dying aboard his ship.

"How long do you think it will take them to change the impeller?"

"Under normal circumstances?" Ambrose laughed. "A couple of days."

"And given what's at stake?"

"I have no idea. Even skipping every safety check, I don't see how it could be done in under eight hours."

"Okay, so we need to cut our rate of drag by half." Tom considered the question, as though he were struggling to complete a difficult crossword puzzle. "Surely there's something else we can throw overboard to create a bit more drag?"

"Both anchors have slipped, there's very little we can do now."

"Do we have any more chain?" Tom knew he was being hopeful.

"Every last piece of chain we did have, has already gone overboard."

"Okay, you're the captain, Ambrose, you must have spent years trying to reduce every inch of extra drag to please Global's shareholders. What else might slow your ship down?"

"Barnacles, wind, currents . . ." The Captain started to list all the things which had troubled him throughout his forty year career.

"Okay, so can we recreate any of those things now?"

"No." Captain Ambrose looked at him as if he were an idiot.

"Where is the current going?"

"Away from the coastline, at a rate of half a knot."

"So, then the wind is pushing us at 7.5 knots, is that correct?"

"Yes."

"Can't we simply reduce our exposure to the wind?" Tom smiled, as though he believed that he'd found the solution to their problem, all by himself.

"I don't know if you've noticed this Mr. Bower, but this is a bulker—we hold all our cargo down below. Apart from what's left of your little helicopter, nothing else is on deck."

"I realize that. But when I was flying in, I noticed that we're showing more than sixty feet of freeboard. That's a lot of exposure on the port side of the ship. If we could somehow reduce that, wouldn't it buy us some more time?"

"And how do you suggest we do that?" The Captain's approaching death loosened his tongue and his question was laced with more than a little sarcasm. "Stop at the next port and pick up some more cargo?"

"Can we begin to sink her?" Tom asked in complete seriousness.

"You want me to sink her?" The Captain responded, his lip curling as though he'd just tasted something pungent.

The thought was absurd, but then, failing to do anything at all meant that a lot of people were going to die. What did they have to lose?

Tom shrugged his shoulders, as though it was of little consequence whether or not they all survived the next four hours.

Then, he saw a look of realization on the Captain's obdurate face.

"By God, you're right! We can flood the ship. We can knock off twenty feet of freeboard by filling her with water without actually sinking her! It will make us much heavier and will reduce our exposure to the wind."

Tom sat in the navigator's chair, his feet lazily stretched out on the desk in front. Every muscle in his body was relaxed. He could have just as easily been sitting on his couch, watching the end of a sitcom, for all the effort he was putting in. But instead, he was watching the outcome of a very real drama—mostly indifferent of its outcome.

To a casual observer, cognizant of the situation, Tom might appear to be insane, but he was far from it. In fact, every inch of his body had been taut with stress ever since the Maria Helena left Sydney Harbor. It was only now that he had performed his duty and had no further assistance to offer, that he could begin to relax.

The outcome of the next four hours would determine his fate.

He would certainly prefer to live. He had a lot more to do and see in this world, but he had played his part, and performed his duty well in this maritime drama; now it was out of his hands.

Tom learned long ago that it's only worth worrying about those things you have the ability to change, and to forget about those which you have no control. With that level of indifference, he casually watched from the bridge, as the adventure on the Hayward Bulk was about to reach its final, dramatic conclusion.

Captain Ambrose flicked a number of electronic switches which opened the enormous sea-cocks and reversed the bilge pumps. The reason for such an option on a super tanker baffled Tom, but the Captain explained that the Hayward Bulk often flooded its enormous bilges to maintain stability in rough seas when depleted of its cargo.

To the right of Tom, the instrumentation in front of the Captain's expressionless face, showed a line which portrayed the depth of the ship's hull below the waterline.

Its reading: *forty two feet.*

The line didn't move, and after several minutes, Tom started to wonder whether or not his idea had any possibility of succeeding.

Then. The line moved to forty-two point five.

Once it started to move, it kept moving. Tom thought it was similar to an altimeter on a plane, as it slowly showed the supertanker's descent into the ocean.

"She's moving," Captain Ambrose said tentatively, with just the tiniest hint of a grin appearing on his stubborn face.

"But is it having any effect on our drag?" Tom asked.

The captain looked to his left, where the Hayward Bulk's speed could be read—*eight point three knots.*

"She's slowing down, but not by much." His grin receding.

Next to the speedometer was a GPS monitor, displaying the local geography reaching out toward the northeastern tip of Australia.

The captain clicked an asterisk over the little image of a ship on the map and then placed second asterisk on the nearest point of the eastern edge of the shallow Great Barrier Reef. Instantly, a dotted line formed between the two points and a note popped up—*Time to Destination: 3 hours: 35 minutes.*

The reality of the computation was clear to Tom.

"How long will it take to fill the holding tanks to their maximum with sea water?"

"Perhaps another hour?" The Captain seemed slightly unsure of himself. "It might take as long as two hours, depending on how far we want to take it."

Tom nodded.

Both men were professionals. Neither of them needed to have the simple math explained in greater detail.

They were going to die.

An hour later, the Hayward Bulk had sunk another 20 feet into the ocean. The Time to Destination reading was now: *3 hours: 5 minutes.*

The ship's drift speed had decreased again, but it still wasn't slowing down quick enough.

Those few hours remaining them, had disappeared quickly, Tom noticed, and before he realized where the time had gone, another alarm sounded. It was a loud warning sound, more like an electrical hum than an air horn.

"What's that?" Tom asked.

"That's the sound of our death, Mr. Bower." Captain Ambrose spoke the words with the fatalism of a seaman fully prepared to go down with his ship, rather than suffer the consequences of such a failure.

"That's our proximity alarm. We are no more than a mile away from the reef."

"Then that's it?"

"That's it. There is nothing more we can do, but prepare for the worst."

Neither man was particularly religious; both just sat there and silently acknowledged their imminent death.

Another alarm rang out.

This time, it was the engine room.

"Yes?" The captain asked.

The Captain's facial expression lightened for the first time since Tom had met him earlier that afternoon, and he then placed the handset back on the table in front of him.

"Excellent. Start her up. And Mr. Thomas, skip all safety procedures, there are a lot of lives at stake here."

The entire ship recoiled at the vibrations from the ship's massive engines cranking over. It then settled down to a strong hum.

Tom watched as Captain Ambrose pushed both throttles forward to full speed, and locked the rudder at forty five degrees—the maximum angle at which to efficiently turn a ship. At the front of the ship, he could hear the sound of the electric bow thruster whining.

Tom again looked down at the *Time to Destination* marker. It read: *4 minutes 32 seconds.*

All systems were now back on.

But, did they have enough time for it to make a difference?

The ship started to turn as quickly as was possible for a super bulker like the Hayward Bulk.

It was painfully slow.

Through the large windows on the bridge, Tom could see the white froth of the waves breaking on the reef. Normally, nothing more than a patch of green in an otherwise deep blue water, the reef was now creating a gigantic bombora with the cyclonic waves.

The ship turned as if it were on a single giant axis and then that axis moved at a rate of 4 knots towards the lethal, jagged edge of the Great Barrier Reef.

It was going to be close.

There was no doubt about it. Tom decided that if he survived this, it would be his closest escape from death yet.

The stern of the ship approached the bombora, and Captain Ambrose straightened the rudder. For the first time since Tom landed on the ship, the Hayward Bulk started to make its way forward.

It was at less than half a knot, but it was progress away from their peril.

They had made it.

"I don't believe it." Captain Ambrose finally smiled. "We made it!"

"So we did!" Tom said jovially, and then, removing his feet from atop the table in front of him, where they'd comfortably rested throughout the entire drama, he jumped off the high navigator's stool and said, "Is there any place I can get some food around here?"

"There sure is, buddy."

And then, the entire ship shuddered under a series of detonations.

CHAPTER 5

The series of detonations tore through the ship like a Roman candle. The vibrations in the hull of the Hayward Bulk were strong enough to knock Tom onto the floor. They continued for a couple of minutes, and then stopped.

The ship remained stable.

"Are we still afloat?" Tom asked the captain.

"Of course we are! It would take much more than a few pieces of plastic explosive to sink my ship." He then reached for his microphone and said, "Engine room. Report status."

There was no response.

He tried again, but again, still there was no response.

And there never would be.

A moment later, the Hayward Bulk's enormous hull started to split down the middle.

"My God, she's being torn in two . . ." There was no fear in the Captain's voice, just total shock.

"And you only had the one life boat on board?" Tom asked.

"Yes. It took forty people—more than we've ever had on board at one time."

"Well, that's it then . . . no one could survive in these waters on their own." Tom accepted his fate.

The captain then moved to a large cupboard at the back of the pilot house. Opening it, he revealed four large survival suits. They were designed to keep the wearer dry, and at the same time, to provide the equivalent buoyancy of five life jackets.

"Here, put this on. It might help."

Tom quickly donned his, and then pulled up the water tight zipper until it reached just below his chin. Pulling the hood over his face, he discovered that the suit came complete with a crude mask and snorkel with a small air cylinder.

The captain helped him pull it over his face and said, "Don't take that off your face until you're on the deck of the Maria Helena, whatever you do!"

It was the last thing the captain said to him before the sudden deluge of seawater swamped the pilot house and both men were swept away. Tom never saw the man again.

The water was warmer than Tom expected, and frothier too. He slid out into the water from the back end of the pilot house, and despite his survival suit, he found himself being dragged deep, below the turbulent surface of the sea.

His survival suit was caught on something.

Its buoyancy had somehow managed to become snagged on something in the pilot house ceiling.

Because of his training, Tom managed to maintain his control and determined that he had only three to four minutes to free himself and reach the surface if he was going to survive.

Tom started kicking with his legs, but soon realized that it wasn't making any difference, and that all he was doing was wasting his precious energy and worsening his hypoxia.

A minute later, the Hayward Bulk began to list to its starboard side. Before he could get his bearings, he was freed from the ceiling and floated out the port side of the pilot house, spinning several times, and colliding with some debris before eventually breaking the surface.

At last, he could breathe.

He was alive.

Death, he knew, may come at any time.

As the hours passed, he closed his eyes and drifted in and out of consciousness.

He became conscious a number of times and had no idea how long he'd been in the water by the time he first saw it. The fourth time he opened his eyes, he staring at something bright and shining right at him.

Fuck me – surely they're not coming back to kill me?

It was then that he heard the voice of Matthew, the skipper of the Maria Helena.

"Hang in there, Tom. We'll have you out of the drink in no time."

Climbing the deck of the Maria Helena, Tom could feel every muscle in his body begin to ache—his adrenaline only just starting to subside.

"Tom, you lucky bastard, you're alive!" said Matthew, the skipper, who, despite their differences, looked genuinely pleased to see him.

"Of course I am." Tom shrugged it off, as though his survival should have been expected.

"Old man Reilly's been waiting to talk to you on the Sat phone for the past twenty minutes. He's gonna be mad as hell that you made him wait so long—not to mention, losing one of his ships."

Tom stepped into the pilot house and the Sat phone was shoved into his hand. Clearly the skipper already knew that there had been no uranium on board the Hayward Bulk.

"Tom here," he said.

"Tom, they tell me those bastards sunk my ship!"

"Yeah, so they did."

"How soon can you dive it?"

Although he'd known the old man since he was a boy, Tom still couldn't believe that James Reilly didn't have the decency to at least ask if everyone was still alive.

"Dive it? What are you talking about? We're still in the middle of a bloody cyclone!"

"Of course, but how soon can you dive?" Old man Reilly seemed undeterred by the dangerous weather. "I can only trust you to get me what I need. It's paramount that you get back in the water and that you do so before the cyclone is over."

"Not going to happen for at least a couple days. We're still looking for survivors."

"It'll be gone in days." James Reilly's voice was firm. "You need to be back in the water now."

"What the hell is so important?" Tom asked.

It took James Reilly a couple of minutes to explain. In the end, Tom hung up the phone without telling him that he'd do it.

"What was that all about?" The skipper asked.

"I have to dive the wreck immediately."

Tom quickly exchanged his survival suit for a diving one.

He would have preferred to rest for a few hours and have a warm meal before he re-entered the water, but he now knew that time was more pressing than his physical comfort.

It didn't take long for the Maria Helena to locate the two parts of the Hayward Bulk's hull. It was resting in just 65 feet of water, and even in the middle of a cyclone, the super bulker stood out. Had it sunk vertically, the pilothouse structure would still be visible above the surface.

"Who do you want on your dive team?" The skipper asked.

"No one. It's stupid enough that I'm about to risk my life for it—there's no need to risk anyone else's. Besides, it will be more comfortable under the water than above it."

"It's trying to get you back up out of the water that worries me," the skipper said.

"Don't worry about that. Michael's got a plan to retrieve me. He'll send an anchor to the bottom with plenty of wire on the winch. Once I retrieve what I've come for I'll return to it, connect, and then be reeled in like the ugliest marlin you ever did see. Don't worry about me!"

Tom then dropped into the still vehement waters astride his Sea-Doo.

With its buoyancy set at zero he sank like a stone and in seconds he left the raging storm above him.

His vision was remarkably clear despite the cyclone. In front of him, no more than 300 feet away he could see the Hayward Bulk. She was resting on the shallow, sandy seabed, broken into two separate pieces.

The aft section, which was the one in which James Reilly had installed his private vault, was listing 45 degrees to its port side.

The vault had been built into the starboard side.

Tom turned the throttle of his Sea-Doo and approached it.

He could see the damage to the main superstructure as he rounded the torn midsection.

Whoever was responsible for this damage, must have prepared for it weeks earlier. It looked as though someone had taken a gigantic razor blade and cut through the entire ship. Someone had obviously taken the time to place dozens of small bombs at structurally important points, knowing full well that the water tight compartments and modern pumps would ensure the Hayward Bulk remained afloat, despite multiple disruptions to her hull. In doing so, they'd correctly determined that the most certain way to sink her, was to split her in two.

Reaching the starboard side, Tom maneuvered his craft approximately a hundred feet further aft of the ship, until he reached James Reilly's infamous private vault.

Tom peered inside the door, but he was too late.

The bomb proof door was already wide open and the contents were entirely missing.

CHAPTER 6

Sam Reilly had slept for nearly twenty four hours straight since leaving Hobart.

He needed it after what he'd endured. Every muscle in his body still hurt. He was in this deep sleep when the AIS alarm began to sound.

AIS stood for Automated Identification System and was used to monitor the proximity and direction of nearby ships.

Sam slowly rolled out of his bunk.

The GPS system, located at the end of his bunk, indicated that he was now positioned off the coast of Shoal Haven. His eyes tentatively made note of the fact that he was approximately 2 nautical miles offshore. The depth reader next to the GPS indicated that he was sitting in the relatively shallow waters at 110 feet. The electronic compass showed him traveling along a course of zero degrees, due north. The wind speed had died down to a leisurely fifteen knots, due east, and his speed over ground was just eight knots. Technically, he was sailing at nine and a half knots, but an offshore current was drifting at one and a half knots.

In the background, he could still hear the gentle warning of the AIS alarm in the cockpit.

Something had entered into close proximity with *Second*

Chance.

Sam stood up and stretched his back, his movement more feline in appearance, than a fatigued sailor.

There was no rush.

He'd set the alarm to go off at one nautical mile from a possible collision. He continued to stretch his back, and then went to the front of the boat to use the head.

He then strolled on to the deck.

His eyes scanned the horizon for any immediate threats, and then, having reassured himself that none were present, he went to his AIS monitor. There was one vessel ahead of him, and that vessel had intentionally blocked its name, size and destination from AIS. Reilly wasn't worried. This was a common practice for sailing vessels, whose skippers assumed that by hiding such information, people might give it a wider berth, just in case it was a large container ship. Maritime law and the International Convention for the Safety of Life at Sea require AIS to be fitted aboard international voyaging ships with a gross tonnage (GT) of 300 or more, and all passenger ships regardless of size. There was no requirement for smaller privately owned vessels to provide any information, and he assumed that was what was approaching.

Sam took out his binoculars from a compartment built into the helm.

He scanned the distance where the ship approached.

It looked like an icebreaker that had been modified for experiments or scientific research. It was painted dark blue and had a thirty-plus foot high gunwale, presumably made of steel and designed for breaking through ice as if it weren't there.

Sam couldn't see anyone on deck.

It was the kind of menacing-looking ship which was run

almost entirely by its advanced technology. In fact, it was highly likely that no one was at or even near the helm at the moment, and it was on a collision course directly towards him most probably by sheer coincidence.

The ship was approximately five hundred feet away. It was far too close for the other ship not to have acknowledged that she had been seen.

Although the rules of the sea state that a vessel under motor must give way to a vessel under sail, the law was irrelevant when you're on a little sail boat that is about to be sunk by an icebreaker. Sam loosened the main sheet and turned forty five degrees to starboard so that he would pass the approaching vessel port side to port side.

It was both a common courtesy and maritime law that two ships must avoid a collision at all costs, and if in doubt, both should steer starboard.

He made the simple maneuver with a quick and efficient sequence, since it was a maneuver he had performed many times before on *Second Chance.*

His new course now left plenty of room for the massive motor yacht to pass to his port side without any effort on its skipper's part.

To his dismay, the other ship immediately altered its course to collide.

He sounded three sudden loud bursts with his fog horn.

It was loud enough to wake the dead, the living, and anything in-between.

And still no response!

Sam turned on his engine and increased speed. There was no time to try to reverse his way out of the imminent collision. His only hope was to somehow pass in front of the other vessel's bow by making a ninety degree tack to starboard.

He heard the screech of his 150 horse power Yanmar Diesel engine exceed its maximum RPMs. He then gently pushed the throttle past its highest point and held it there with his hand against its will.

He would have liked to get out a Mayday signal before the collision took place, but there was no time to do so.

One hundred feet, turned into fifty.

Still no change.

Then fifty feet became twenty five.

His bow and the center cockpit passed the other vessel's evil wall of steel.

It was going to be close.

Maybe only a matter of a second, whether or not the other ship would clip his transom, the large butt at the end of *Second Chance,* which housed much of his equipment.

At that moment, he realized there was nothing more he could do. He was going to collide with the larger vessel.

Sam felt nothing but utter dismay at the fact that he was about to be demolished by a stupid rich guy's toy off the coast of Australia, of all places.

Surely it must be a mistake.

Who's ever heard of pirates in Australian waters?

Then it happened.

He knew it would, but the sound of metal and plastic colliding made the most sickening sound he had ever heard.

And then it was over as the larger ship continued on.

Innocently, its enormous propellers kept turning after it passed, without any hint that it had recently been in a collision.

Sam's thoughts were taken to another world.

Accidents like this one never happened in modern times, certainly not with the modern technologies available and required on such large vessels. He struggled to comprehend what had just happened.

At first, he didn't even notice the enormous hole in the stern of *Second Chance,* where seawater was now flooding in. Instead, Sam looked up at the huge transom of the other vessel as it was slowly moving away, like the evil machine it was, totally unaware of the carnage it had just inflicted.

It was painted entirely blue, and it bore no registration number or name on the hull. Located on its aft deck was a small helipad and tied down on it, was what Sam recognized as a black Sikorsky SH-3 Sea King helicopter—the kind most commonly used by the U.S. Navy for anti-submarine warfare.

What's that doing on a civilian vessel?

On the rear of the helicopter, Sam could make out the words, "Wolfgang Corporation."

His curiosity abated when he noticed how quickly his beautiful ketch was taking on water. The entire transom was missing. "Taking on water" was an understatement. In truth, the seawater was gushing in. He'd heard about ships hit by containers out at sea sinking so quickly that its occupants never even realized what had happened. He was about to see firsthand just how such a catastrophe actually happened.

Although *Second Chance* held so much safety equipment on board, Sam had no time to reach any of it. He cursed himself for his distraction. His mind simply couldn't accept the fact that he'd be in a collision just two miles offshore from a holiday town in Australian waters!

He barely had enough time to pop the lid off his inflatable

life raft.

The thing weighed forty five kilograms and required that he pull the emergency tabs and throw it overboard to allow it to inflate properly away from the sinking yacht. Forty-five kilograms wasn't too onerous a weight for a grown man to lift, especially one who is experiencing the adrenaline rush that came from his fight or flight response on a sinking vessel.

Sam carefully tied one end of the safety raft to a cleat on *Second Chance's* bow. He heaved the box overboard. The sodium crystals dissolved in the salt water, triggering the release mechanism, and the box popped open. Seconds later, the carbon dioxide canister deployed and could be heard releasing its gas, instantly inflating the four-man life raft.

Sam felt relieved.

The water was now more than half way up the inside of *Second Chance's* hull.

He considered going back for his radio and satellite phone. Even his mobile phone would have coverage, but since he was so close to land, he decided against it. If the ship went down while he was deep inside it, there was no telling where he'd end up or if he'd be able to escape its bowels.

Sam then pulled the life raft back aboard, so that it rested comfortably against *Second Chance's* shrinking freeboard. He was just about to say good bye to his beloved ship and step into the raft before it was too late.

At that exact moment, he noticed the malevolent ship make an abrupt 180 degree turn. It was, as though either the captain or a crew member finally noticed that they had nearly killed someone.

For the first time since the other vessel approached *Second Chance,* Sam was actually able to see someone high up on the bow of the ship. The man had blond hair, and appeared to be quite large, but otherwise had no distinguishable characteristics at that distance.

He seemed to be waving something at Sam.

Did they have a lower transom or at least a cargo net I can use to climb aboard her?

As the ship returned, Sam was finally able to get a clearer view of the man who was waving to him.

What is that in his hand? Is it a life preserver?

Then it hit him.

The man was holding a weapon.

At this distance, Sam couldn't be certain of the type, but as the man took aim, he its purpose became obvious.

Someone wanted him dead.

The revelation struck him with painful slow clarity as he watched his life raft burst apart as the first round fired. There was a brief pause and he realized that the shooter changed the cartridge before he started firing again.

This time the bullets were shredding what was left of his yacht.

Sam was out of options, so he dived into the now almost completely water-filled hull of his sinking boat. Holding his breath, he swam down and towards the back of the ship. The water was surprisingly clear and he could just make out the location of the hole at the back end of his ship where his transom once was.

He watched the blurred trails of a number of bullets as they whizzed by him through the water, only a couple of feet ahead of him and then cease.

The shooter must be reloading his weapon.

Then the real reason occurred to him.

Sam noticed that his ears were starting to hurt.

Everything had turned black.

Second Chance had reached its critical point, at which it was no longer able to displace the surface tension of the water, and now it was starting its journey to the seabed below.

He felt as if he'd been plunged into a washing machine as he tumbled around inside the sinking boat.

His instinct was to swim out of the hole where the transom used to be. It wasn't far. Perhaps only another fifteen feet away—an easy swim.

And then it struck him.

Someone wants me dead? Like, really dead.

He knew then that they were going to wait until *Second Chance* had sunk below the surface, and then they'd spray the surface with more bullets. He would never be able to hold his breath long enough to return to the surface. Instead, he would have to swim underwater, as far away from here as possible, without first dying from hypoxia.

He tried to remember his ship's last location and the current depth beneath her keel. They were two miles off Shoal Haven heads. There would be less than a hundred feet of water at the seabed.

Sam couldn't accept that he might die with the ship he loved. His mind fought for a solution and then it presented him with one—a very simple one.

The diving equipment was kept at the back half of the yacht. He even had an air compressor built into the transom.

But the transom's gone, what else will be missing?

Sam's hands began to feel around him, searching for some of his equipment.

To his relief, his left hand touched something solid—something cylindrical.

Sam opened the bottle and then closed it again. A gush of air bubbles were released. The bubbles were large enough that he could take a deep breath of air. It was an immediate solution to his need, but without a regulator he was going to be using up his air supply within minutes.

Using his hands to guide him through the hull, he reached for a drawer where he normally stored a number of regulators and dive masks. Sadly, what his hands found were a number of large pieces of splintered wood—the remnants of a broken drawer.

Did the regulator fall toward the transom and then out of the yacht, or did it fall forward towards the bow?

He had no choice, Sam had to assume that one of his regulators was somewhere at the fore of the ship. If he had a mask, he might have easily been able to spot it. As it was, he was nearly blind in the dark, turbulent water inside the sinking ship, which was now more than twenty feet below the surface.

He ran his hand along the internal teak flooring. It was covered in worthless equipment. None of which was of any use to him unless he could find the regulator, and soon.

Just as he was about to turn around and swim back to the tank for another bubble of air, his left hand grasped something that felt like a small hose. It was rubbery, and could have just as easily been part of the yacht's plumbing, but luckily, it wasn't.

He pulled on it and felt for the end.

The familiar emergency octopus valve, known as an Ochy, was in his hand.

His head was spinning. It might be from hypoxia, or it as a result of the sudden increase in pressure, while the atmospheric pressure doubled for every thirty three feet of water above him.

Sam flicked open the air tank four more times, releasing enough air bubbles so that he could catch his breath. He then attached the first stage to the air tank, and turned the tank valve so that it was completely opened.

Depressing the blow off valve on the primary regulator, Sam watched as a huge gush of air bubbled out from the valve opening, as water was cleared from the piping.

He then placed his mouth on the primary, and inhaled.

It felt like coming home.

This was his normal environment. He was safe. He'd done this a thousand times before.

He scrambled to see the depth gauge at the end of the console. Its reading was, 80 feet. Sam remembered that he'd been sitting in 110 feet of water.

His next concern was what was going to happen when his ship struck the seabed?

Sam didn't plan on waiting to find out.

He carried his tank, regulator and weight belt to the back of the now-open transom and swam outside.

Immediately thereafter, he watched the seabed erupt as *Second Chance* collided into it.

He waited a minute for the debris to settle. It would have been nice to have the luxury of giving it more time, but that wasn't going to be possible. He was sitting at 100 feet below the surface. His air supply was going to run out pretty quick, and his maximum no-decompress time would be over even faster.

Sam checked his dive watch. He always wore it on his left wrist, a trusty companion that was always with him. It read 100 feet. Then at the dive tank, which was at—210 bar. His mind rapidly made the calculations, as only someone who has spent a life time diving could—somewhere in the vicinity of 15 minutes.

Either way, he needed to return to a lesser depth if he was going to remain submerged long enough to escape his enemy.

Whoever he is?

The air was still hissing out of the end of the low pressure hose, which normally would be attached to a buoyancy control device, known as a BCD. He needed to get down to the wreckage and find one quickly, or his 15 minutes would drop to 5 minutes very soon.

Fortunately, the ship landed the way she had sunk—keel down. Eerily, Sam noted that her sails were still up, and she was standing upright on the seabed, looking as though she had continued sailing on the bottom of the sea.

He struggled through the wreckage to get to the center cockpit.

His eyes stung as they tried to orient himself in the dark, murky water. He couldn't see much at all; but there, right in front of him, about twenty feet away, he could just make out the faint red glow of the navigational instruments behind the helm.

He reached the helm and then felt around for a plastic compartment on his left—*no, it's not in there.* Then he felt for the one to the right of him. It opened easily. The BCD began to float. Sam's fast reflexes managed to catch it before it disappeared toward the surface.

Next, he continued to feel his way along, until his hands finally grasped the glassy frame of his dive mask.

He pulled it over his head, then placed his hand over the top half of the mask, as he leaned forward and exhaled to clear the mask of water, so that he could once again see.

He checked his watch.

The little symbol of a frog could be seen swimming on its face. Next to it was the number 07:28 indicating that he had now been underwater for almost seven and a half minutes, and was now at a depth of 91 feet. The NDT reading, short for No Decompress Time, was eight minutes.

His eyes quickly glanced at the console.

It now showed that only seventy bars worth of air remained in the tank. *Where had he miscalculated the rate of air usage?* Then the answer came to him. Without the BCD attached, the low pressure hose had been constantly hissing out air. However, recognizing the cause of miscalculation provided him with little in the way of solutions to his problem.

Now what?

He could now see a little more clearly, and felt as though he'd gained just a little control over his rising panic, now that he had regained the use of one more of his five senses.

Sam resisted the urge to instantly begin the process of resurfacing, which would be a death sentence. Only in James Bond films did the bad guys ever leave immediately after thinking they'd killed the good guy.

Then the answer to his predicament suddenly came to him—he was going to test his new Sea Scooter!

Sam made his way to the back of the center cockpit, where a large storage compartment rested. Undoing the hooks, he found his Sea Scooter 120—an experimental version, capable of traveling at a speed of 20 miles per hour.

After mounting the sleek scooter, he pressed the red start button.

For a moment, Sam worried that seawater may have gotten into its electronics, but of course, it was designed for diving and it started right up.

The Sea Scout's little electric engine started to whirl within the confines of its protective mesh, which was there to prevent a diver from accidentally losing any limbs or digits.

He then opened the two air cylinders already attached to its frame.

A soft, red light illuminated the computer screen, located between the handlebars, just the same as those which would be on the dashboard of a motorcycle.

On the top of the dashboard there was a sonar image of the seabed, reaching up to 500 feet ahead. Below, were three instruments. The one on the left was a simple compass. The middle one displayed the current battery power, and like the markings on a fuel tank, it showed a number of boxes up and down, and right now, it showed all the boxes as filled in green, indicating that the tank was full. The last gauge showed the air supply in BARs, at 920.

That was another huge relief.

Sam had already exceeded his maximum no-decompress time, but with that much air in his tanks, he could take his time to resurface ensuring that he would be able to incorporate enough decompression stops along the way to release the nitrogen build up in his bloodstream, a necessary step in order to prevent getting the bends.

Pointing the Sea Scooter so that the compass arrow indicated due west, Sam turned the throttle in his right hand, and the little electric motor started the propeller whirling beneath him. He planned to head straight for the shoreline.

This one is going to be hard to explain to the insurance company.

The trip took less than twenty minutes to reach the shoreline, and another thirty minutes for him to eliminate his risk of decompression illnesses.

Sam then powered the Sea Scooter all the way up onto the sandy beach.

Taking off his dive mask, he noticed that he'd reached an almost-secluded beach. To the south, the point was creating a beautiful break, one that today, had been forming into barrel waves, which then broke about fifty feet from the beach.

It looked like a nice place to surf.

A tanned blonde girl in a purple bikini flashed her sparkling blue eyes and with a friendly smile, asked, "Hey, where did you come from?"

Sam's mind returned to the present.

"I've been diving a wreck," Sam replied, looking back at the waves breaking on the beach. "It's pretty choppy out there today. How's the surf?"

"Really? Where did you put in at? I've been surfing here for the past couple of hours and I thought I had the break all to myself." She sounded rather suspicious for a girl who'd just spent her morning surfing in what could only be described as a surfer's paradise.

"There's a wreck dive out there and a beautiful sunken ship." He then glanced over at the malicious dark blue structure, which was still visible at more than two miles out to sea. It looked like it hadn't even moved. They were taking no chances, that's for sure. "It's a long way out, I wouldn't recommend it."

CHAPTER 7

Aliana looked at her Cartier wrist watch.

The elegance of its solid sapphire bezel on its stem seemed oddly out of place on the wrist of a woman who'd arisen early to see if she could catch a wave.

It was already 9:30 a.m.

She would probably make it back to her hotel in time if she left now. Besides, the winds had started to pick up and were ruining the surf.

It had been a nice morning so far. Cyclone Petersham, to the north, had now dissipated, however, more than two thousand miles to the south, the result of its passing was an enormous, continuous swell.

It had turned an otherwise average surf beach into one bordering on perfection. But, now that the wind had picked up, the surf had become much choppier.

She tossed her short board onto the back seat of her Jeep, where it nestled along her roll bar, climbed into the driver's seat, and then made her way back into town.

It had been a nice morning for surfing.

Her phone, which she'd left carelessly inside the glove compartment, showed a new message from her dad.

I've completed my work in Australia and will be leaving today. Will you be flying home with me, or are you planning on staying longer?

She thought about it for a moment.

She'd enjoyed the Australian coast and was happy to stay for another few days. Then, she responded with, *Think I'll stay until the end of the week. Will try to and see you again before returning to college. I've had fun. Thanks. Aliana.*

When she turned the car key, the powerful, limited edition 6.2 Liter engine kicked into life, and she started making her way back into town.

She still couldn't shake the image of the man she'd seen coming in from a dive earlier that morning. There were many good dive sites in the area, but she'd never heard of or seen one out near the point. Not that she knew the area all that well, having stayed there for barely a week. Still, there was something about him that seemed wrong—she just couldn't figure out what it was.

She shook the thought from her mind as irrelevant and continued driving.

Her father had said that his work in Australia would take about three weeks. It was rare these days for her to follow him on these expeditions, but since she was on vacation from her studies, she'd decided to join him.

Aliana and her father had never quite seen eye to eye, but she knew that he loved her. He was driven by the power that accompanied the fortune he'd amassed, and consequently, he worked hard to maintain it. For Aliana, it was different. She became a microbiologist for two simple reasons, first, the science was fascinating, and second, it was a way to genuinely help people. At times, she wondered if her father even liked the fact that his discoveries had improved the lives of millions of people around the world.

Driving on, her thoughts returned to the man on the beach. She recalled his blue eyes, his kind face, and his disarming smile.

There was something about him that intrigued her. He certainly wasn't there for the reason he had given her—of that much she was certain. A part of her felt ashamed to automatically discredit his story. The man had appeared to be friendly enough. He certainly hadn't meant her any harm. The two of them had been the only two people on the beach. Upon reflection, she thought that she probably should have been at least a little frightened by him.

It might have been the scientist in her, but if she was going to be honest with her self-analysis, it was quite possible that her own father had fostered such distrust in her, not just because of the way he'd treated her mother while she was alive, but because her father had raised her to try to understand people, and people, she knew, were the most self-serving creatures on the planet.

Despite her mistrust, Aliana thought that she would have liked to get to know the man on the beach a little better.

She again wondered what it was about his story that just didn't ring true.

Then it struck her—*the man hadn't been wearing a wetsuit.*

At the age of sixty-seven, John Wolfgang showed little sign of aging. He had always been healthy. Despite growing up in socialist East Germany, his father had often told him that he came from good German stock.

John was finally back in his office, and wearing a $15,000 tailored suit—one of more than a dozen made specifically for him. He felt comfortable in it. He was much happier to be returning to his lavish lifestyle rather than being out on some ship investigating a new microbe that one of his scientists had recently discovered in an iceberg which had broken off from the Antarctic shelf. He was even happier to have returned from his other project, which Cyclone Petersham had delivered.

When he had boarded the long-haul return flight to Massachusetts, where his company Neo Tech was based, John had a number of important business calls to make, and one important call to receive. Although he was the sole passenger aboard his private jet, he was still dressed as if he were at sea, and he felt it impolite to do business in anything other than business attire. Now, after having a hot shower, he was comfortable in his familiar office, and in his perfectly-fitted suit; after a week out at sea, it was nice to feel clean again.

John felt that he was now ready to receive those important calls, while sitting at his desk in the largest room of his luxurious Lear Jet G6. Its accoutrements looked far more like they graced the office of a Wall Street billionaire than the inside of a luxurious Lear jet.

The room was simple but performed its purpose well. State of the art sound proofing allowed him to forget that he was on a plane. An imperial oak desk, a secure satellite phone, two separate computer monitors were all that made up his office.

A single painting graced the wall—an original Monet, depicting water lilies on a lake. It was the master's first attempt, which he'd thrown out having been displeased with it for an obvious technical mistake in the method he used to depict the water lilies. Having been retrieved by a neighbor, and given to a cousin in Germany, it had adorned the Wolfgang family room for three generations, under the assumption that it was an imitation. Two years ago, the real origins of the painting had become known, and it became the most valuable Monet still in existence. Before reaching auction, it had been stolen.

It was only after its loss, that John had discovered the real value behind the great painting, which made it far more valuable than the 80 million dollars that the assessor suggested it could fetch at auction.

Only after the efforts of a billionaire and luck of the impending catastrophe of Cyclone Petersham, was John able to reacquire the painting.

John stared at it for a moment.

He cared little for the artwork itself, and wondered what his father would have said if he'd known what he'd hid, in plain sight, for most of his lifetime. Either way, it was on its way home now, and John only hoped that it wouldn't destroy the world.

He let the phone ring once only, then picked up the handset.

John was expecting the call. Dreading it almost as much as he longed to receive it, so that it would finally be over.

He noticed the small tremors on his otherwise still hand.

That's new, he thought.

"John, is this line secure?" The man spoke English; the tone of which could only be mastered by one the British aristocratic elite. An accent acquired at Oxford or even Cambridge, he guessed. It was a voice that betrayed the speaker's lavish breeding. It had been years since he'd actually heard this man's voice, but despite that, he recalled it as though it had been only yesterday.

And, after the information he received yesterday, he had no doubt that the man would contact him today about it.

"It is." He said, unwilling to say more.

"Have they been taken care of?" The man on the phone sounded displeased.

"Yes."

"All of them? Are you certain?"

"Yes. I took care of the last person myself." John was unused to being questioned like this, by anyone, even the man on the other side of the phone.

"Now, how long before we have it?" The man's voice was coarse, sounding like that of someone in their eighties, who had spent a lifetime, smoking tobacco.

John nearly choked on his 30 year old Glenfarclas whiskey. Terrified, he looked up at his recent acquisition on the wall, terrified that this man knew about it already.

But how could he know? I didn't even know its value until three months ago?

Suddenly remembering exactly why this man had called, John responded with his prepared response, "The thing's been missing for seventy five years. It may still take some time before it's found. Things generally are when they wish to remain lost. And this, was supposed to disappear forever. It's a hard area to search, but we've already got people over there. Once they find her, we'll send in our own team to retrieve it. It's not like we can send in a team of mercenaries without anyone noticing. We have to be extremely careful exactly who we do send to do this, and we must be discreet, otherwise we'll have every treasure hunter after her."

"Do I need to remind you of the consequences if you fail to deliver it?"

"Fuck you!" John was done being servile. The man on the other end of the line might be his master, but he was long past his willingness to be treated like a dog by anyone. "I'm well aware of the outcome if I fail. I know exactly how dangerous this thing is."

"Good. Then at least, in that, we are in agreement." The man coughed and then said, "I will call you in a week to see how you have progressed."

"No, you won't. I'll call you when we have it, and if you'd like to be the first to have her in your possession, you will remember to permit me to do my job."

John hung up the sat phone, ending the call.

On the desk in front of him, there was only one photo. It was a picture of him and his daughter at her graduation after she had completed her undergraduate degree at MIT. She had a big smile on her face, and you could see the pride on his own face from a mile away.

He studied that picture for a moment.

What have I done?

John Wolfgang had more phone calls to make.

His business was worth a fortune and he rarely slept for more than a few hours at a time these days.

The company, which was started by his grandfather before Hitler lost the war, had a prolonged moratorium after his grandfather lost all credibility and financial support. John took over the family business shortly after the Berlin Wall came down. Since then, he had immigrated to the U.S., where his scientific acumen could take him further. His pharmaceuticals had saved millions of people worldwide, not to mention winning him the Nobel Prize for medicine.

John placed the graduation photo back on his desk, his determination visible in his eyes.

He was committed now and there was nothing he could do to change that.

He knew when he first accepted the man's help that it would be difficult to say no to him when it was time to return the favor. To fulfill this obligation would be unconscionable.

However, failure to do so now, was unthinkable. It all seemed so far away at the time, that John secretly believed that it would never be found, or that he would be the one to release its horrible wrath.

All that he had worked for would be lost, because they had maintained control over him and over everything held dear.

As painful as this was, John would have been more than willing to suffer it all alone, the blame landing squarely upon his head; the price of fulfilling this obligation was too terrible for the world.

Before he was even given a chance to falter in his obligation to the man he'd never met, a package arrived.

We own you – don't falter.

Those were the only words displayed on the outside of the brown package. They were handwritten, in the carefree scrawl of someone who knew, without a doubt, that John would never go to the police.

Its contents confirmed what he already knew, there was no way he could get out of this.

It was a picture of his daughter. She was in her pajamas, having breakfast alone. John recognized the room. It was the 32nd floor penthouse he'd bought for her while she was still studying at MIT. It was a secure apartment, and he had taken steps to ensure that few people knew where she lived.

But somehow, they'd found her.

They always would.

How can a father bring himself to choose, between the well-being of billions of people, or the life of his only daughter, the one thing he'd managed do right in his entire life.

Mathematically, the equation appeared simple.

To a father, the mathematics were irrelevant.

He considered killing himself. Some part of him wished that he'd simply have a fatal heart attack or some other form of death over which he had no control. He knew that if he died, he'd fail to complete his obligation, and, as a result, his daughter would die, so killing himself wasn't an option.

No, he would go through with it, as he'd agreed to do all those years ago.

John Wolfgang leaned back in his lounge chair, staring out the window of his Lear Jet, more than forty thousand feet above the earth, over whose very existence he held so much power.

It went all the way back to the start of the Second World War.

To a story that he'd heard from his father many times during his childhood, as the only child of a poor family living in post-war Germany.

Walter Wolfgang, John's father, had been a promising young microbiologist, who had been pursuing a PhD in viral adaptations to change. His supervisor, Professor Fritz Ribbentrop, immediately saw the promise of such research, and its potential danger to humanity.

Walter had worked hard for three years on his project before discovering the strange mutation. It had been well established that viruses, such as influenza, naturally mutated, from time to time, often becoming more easily transmittable. The virus's undesired result of some of these mutations might often result in the death of the host.

In theory, a virus wants to be symbiotic—living on or within a host organism, without draining its host of its strength and vitality.

Often, these changes occur every decade or so, to keep up with their host's immune system, which is constantly adapting to better protect itself from the virus. Every now and then, something strange happens, and the new viral strain leaps ahead of its hosts ability to protect itself, perhaps jumping ahead by two or three decades worth of random mutations, and becoming stronger than the hosts natural immune system.

One such strain that springs to the mind of any microbiologist is the Influenza H1N1—AKA, the Spanish Flu pandemic, which occurred in the early twentieth century, which decimated more lives worldwide than the First World War. This type of event generally occurs only every couple of centuries, or so.

What Walter discovered, while attempting to speed up the rate of viral mutations in a controlled environment, was the genesis of a strain of influenza which had made several hundred steps towards evolution. The type of anomaly that would only occur once every couple of millennia, under normal circumstances.

It had evolved such that the longer it remained undetected, the safer it would be, and therefore, the greater would be its chance of propagating. In one study, Walter learned that its host would not display any symptoms whatsoever for an entire month after infection, and then result in an astonishing 80% mortality rate.

The implications of such a prolonged incubation period in a virus with such a phenomenal mortality rate were immediately obvious to him.

It could wipe out 80% of the planet's population.

He brought this discovery to the attention of his mentor and friend, Professor Fritz Ribbentrop.

Walter's original thought was that he should destroy it immediately, but Ribbentrop had a different viewpoint. What would happen if this anomaly occurred naturally at some time in the future? Could their investigations now possibly save the entire planet from what might prove to be the worst plague ever faced by mankind in recorded history, at some future date?

In the minds of scientists, who had no loyalties to either good or bad, but only wanted to further man's knowledge, such a discovery could only be viewed as a good thing.

The next day, the riots began and ended with the raids on Jewish families, heralding the rise of Hitler's Third Reich and start of World War Two.

Professor Fritz Ribbentrop was the first to point out what these events might mean for their discovery. "Do you understand the consequences of your discovery, given that the world is about to be plunged into the depths of a war?"

"I will have to put my experiments on hold so that we can work towards the Fuhrer's goals for Germany."

"No, it is far more sinister than that."

"It is?" At such a young age, Walter failed to understand the harsh realities of where the world was headed.

"You must now decide. On one hand, you have the key, which will almost certainly provide the Fuhrer with the means to win this war, but on the other hand, in so doing you may end up destroying more lives than would be lost in a hundred years of fighting."

"Is that really the right question to ask?" Walter, even in his idealistic youth, was not wholly immune to the loyalty and might of the Fascist movement.

Professor Ribbentrop watched him carefully, without betraying his hand. "Go on son, what would be the right question to ask?"

"How can we protect our own troops from this virus?"

"Yes, of course," the Professor continued. Only the slightest hint of hesitation could be detected in his voice. "Prepare your viruses. Tomorrow, we start developing a vaccine. Collect your notes, and I will send them on to the Fuhrer himself. He would want to be personally informed of a matter of such this importance."

John made a copy for himself, and then sent his original notes to Professor Ribbentrop, who had assured him that he would personally bring them to the attention of the Fuhrer.

Two weeks passed, yet Walter had still not received any message from the Fuhrer.

He talked to Professor Fritz Ribbentrop about it, but the man seemed undeterred, and reminded Walter that the Fuhrer was a very busy man.

At first, Walter assumed that it was their academic professionalism which was causing the friction, but as time went by, he started to doubt Fritz's loyalty. The problem was, he had no idea how to create a vaccination against the horrid virus. Fritz was possibly the only man alive who had the ability to develop it. Besides, it was ridiculous of him to question Fritz's loyalty. The two of them were ardent supporters of the Third Reich, and Fritz specifically had supported and was a strong ally of his friend, Adolf Hitler.

At the end of the two weeks, Walter decided to send a secret letter to the Fuhrer, containing his findings and their potential in the field of biological warfare.

The next day, Walter was picked up by the SS Police, who took him to a secret location, where Adolf Hitler himself greeted him warmly. Hitler reassured him of Fritz's loyalty, but pointed out that a matter of such great importance required redundancies to ensure that the plan came to fruition. The Fuhrer also reminded Walter that he was counting on him to make sure that Fritz maintained the undying loyalty he had always displayed to Germany.

Two weeks after that, Professor Fritz Ribbentrop disappeared.

All traces of the virus with him.

When the Gestapo told Walter that Professor Ribbentrop had boarded an airship and escaped, he was certain that Germany would now lose the war.

As a punishment for this failure, he was conscripted and given the rank of private in the infantry.

It was a death sentence, and a total waste of an intellect such as his, which could have been put to better use in so many other war efforts.

Despite the punishment, Walter remained true to the regime's core values, proudly believing that he was doing his part to win the war for Germany.

Despite the highly improbable chances of his survival, Walter did succeed in living through the war, but, unfortunately, a remaining high-ranking official leaked the information that Walter's mistake had resulted in Germany losing the war.

In the starving depression of postwar Germany, Walter was treated with contempt, and he was unable to gain employment as anything better than a common street cleaner. His wonderful mind was utterly wasted for the second time by Germany's remaining leaders.

In spite of everything that had befallen him, Walter married a woman in 1950, named Alda. Notwithstanding living in socialist Eastern Germany, and although they were both poor and famished, the two were happy, and their son, John was born in 1952.

Despite it being a new world, many members of the East German leadership still blamed Walter for his part in the loss of their pre-war living standards. He found it hard to get a job, and harder still to keep one. In 1962, when John was age 10, his mother died during a particularly bad winter.

John asked the question that his father had been dreading.

"Why are we hated so?"

Walter then told him the story about the missing Magdalena, which he discovered had never made it to her destination in Switzerland. He explained that if they could just find the Magdalena, he could forever change the course of their lives.

In 1961, East Germany had become so frustrated by the mass exodus of its citizens to the west, they erected a wall between the two in order to prevent people from fleeing into West Berlin. Walter became infatuated with the dream of discovering the resting place of the Magdalena, and consequently, the virus, which he still saw as being the source of all of his misfortune.

John, on the other hand, excelled at all his studies and dreamed of becoming a scientist someday. He ended up working at Humboldt University. It was the one bit of good luck the family had had since Walter discovered the virus.

When the Berlin Wall came down on the 9th of November, 1989, John was 38 years old, and had become one of the leading microbiologists in the world, with little chance of achieving any financial security.

He wanted, more than anything, to rekindle his father's pharmaceutical company, but it would be another five years before he was given the opportunity to do so.

In 1994, five years after the Berlin Wall came crashing down, a man approached John. He appeared to be of Mediterranean descent, but he might just as easily have been from England, based on how perfectly accented his English sounded. The man offered him five million American dollars, a fortune, to support the development of his pharmaceutical company on behalf of his client, if John would be willing to help his boss find the Magdalena, and provide him with a usable virus. His boss remained the legal owner of the company on secret papers, but all profits were John's to keep.

It seemed so simple at the time.

A deal with the devil, perhaps—but what a deal!

Why not take the chance? If the Magdalena, and the virus she carried hadn't been discovered in 55 years, why would it be discovered in his lifetime?

Since then, his business had exceeded his every dream. He was rich, he had married a movie star, and they had produced a beautiful daughter. His wife had left him once she'd extracted enough of his money, but she left him with his daughter, so what did he care? His professional dreams were achieved when he won the Nobel Prize.

He never once heard from his benefactor.

There was never a request for a dividend or repayment of any kind.

Until a week ago, he had all but forgotten about his humble beginnings and about his deal with the devil.

When he was greeted by a much older man with olive skin and a pompous English accent, he didn't immediately recognize the man. It was his accent that sounded completely out of place, which finally triggered his recollection.

The Lear Jet banked to the left, and John settled in for a landing, dragging him out of his memories.

A long time ago, he had indeed made a deal with the devil himself.

Might a deal with another devil save me?

John considered the question which he had turned over repeatedly in the past seven days, and for the first time, reached an answer.

Yes. But to do that, I'll have to be the first to find it.

CHAPTER 8

Sam Reilly had discarded his Sea Scooter in the shrubbery and started the long, painful walk into town. It had been years since he'd been to Shoal Haven. He couldn't quite remember how far it was to town, but he knew it wasn't a long drive.

Half an hour later, the adrenaline rush had worn off, and he now realized just how exhausted he felt as a white Jeep pulled over alongside him.

"You want a ride?" It was the beautiful blonde girl from the beach.

"Sure would. Thanks."

"Where are you headed?"

"Anywhere in town would be nice." He didn't have much strength left for lies.

The Beatles were playing in the background.

She turned the radio volume down and said, "So, what's your story? I mean, you clearly weren't out for a reef dive."

She had a mostly American accent with just the slightest hint of a European background, which he couldn't quite place. She'd probably studied at some swanky Ivy League college and had spent years trying to eliminate her original accent.

"I don't know what you're talking about?"

She skidded her car to a stop.

"Listen here. I've done some wreck diving myself over the years, and I'm not a bad skin diver, but I've never seen someone dive wearing their normal clothing." She looked as though she might throw him out of her car. "And, for another thing, where's your dive gear? What'd you do with it . . . throw it away after you had your one and only dive, or was it just too hard to carry home again after carrying it all the way here without a car? You can tell me the truth or you can get out of my car right now."

Sam considered stepping out of the car and walking away, but decided that he was better off telling the truth to a complete stranger.

"I was out sailing, and . . ."

Understanding dawned in her eyes.

"So you sunk?"

"Yes."

"What? Like for an insurance claim or something? Is that why you're so secretive about it?"

He laughed out loud at the very idea.

"No, insurance is the least of my worries. Actually, my boat has been sinking for a number of hours, and I've been too embarrassed to do anything about it. I'm far more concerned about what my father's going to do when he hears that I was so careless."

"Jesus, are you all right?" He thought he saw some sort of understanding in her eyes. She'd been the recipient of enough prejudice from her own father.

"I'll be fine. Hey, do you mind if I use your phone?"

"Sure, go for it." She had a kind smile, Sam decided.

He bent down to pick it up off the center console. Sam noticed that she hadn't bothered to change her clothes, and her long tanned legs could be seen in their entirety. He struggled not to stare, sat up, and dialed the number.

"I'm surprised you can still remember anyone's phone number by heart."

"This guy's been my best mate since I was a kid. His is just about the only phone number I've ever bothered to memorize."

The ring tone ended as someone picked up.

"Tom, it's me."

"Hey Sam, where are you? James is still pretty pissed that you refused to answer his calls, given the whole Cyclone Petersham thing. You won't believe what we did . . ."

Sam cut him off short.

"Hey, I'll hear all about it soon. It's a long story, but I need you to pick me up from . . ." he looked at the beautiful woman sitting next to him who mimed the words "Shoal Haven." I'm in Shoal Haven, he recited. I don't have my phone, wallet or anything else with me. Can you be here in about an hour? I've got a few important things to do."

"Sure, I'll bring the helicopter."

"Good, I'll see you shortly. Thanks pal."

He handed the phone back to her. "Thanks for that . . ." He stopped short. "I'm so sorry, I don't even know your name. I'm Sam Reilly." He said, shaking her hand. It was firm, more like a man's handshake than a woman's, but without the intent to prove who had the strongest grip. It was the handshake of someone who had spent years doing business with men and treated them equally.

"Aliana," she said, and he noted that she'd withheld her

surname.

She had a beautiful smile, and he wished the drive into town was longer.

"Pleased to meet you," he said.

"Where's your friend coming from?"

"Who?"

"Your best bud. The guy you just called, who's just going to drop whatever it was he was doing to come and pick you up?"

"Oh, Tom? He's in Sydney."

"What, and he's going to get here in an hour? It's about a four hour drive. I know, I drove it just last week."

"Yeah, well I told him he could take the company's helicopter."

"Your company?" She sounded surprised.

"No, I just manage a section of it," he admitted.

"You must be pretty important to the company if you have a helicopter to come pick you up. What do you do?"

"I work for a company called Global Shipping, but I manage only a very small part of it, involved in Special Operations. We're involved in some salvage stuff, but mainly we work on consignment to various government agencies around the world. We do outside investigations into water quality, environmental issues, and stuff like that."

"You work on the ocean?" She asked, sounding surprised.

"Yep."

"And you just sank your own sailing yacht?"

"Yeah, well . . . now you can see why I'm being so coy." Although unaccustomed to it, Sam feigned embarrassment as best he could.

She shook her head in amazement.

About five minutes later they arrived in the center of Shoal Haven. It was a little coastal village with a coffee shop and a couple of cafes, which were the only things open this early on a Sunday morning.

He got out of the car and thanked her again.

She was about to drive away when he stopped her.

"Say, can I buy you a cup of coffee or something?" He smiled. It was a hopeful grin and then he added, "My flight is still going to take a while to get here."

"Do you have any money on you? I thought you lost everything?" She said, her smile teasing him.

"You're right. Can you buy me a coffee, and I'll pay you back when my ride gets here?"

"Come on." She smiled back at him comfortably, like a girl who doesn't normally get involved in other people's problems. "I'll spot you."

At the end of the deck was a place called "Café de Pacific." It had an outlook over the ocean in the distance. They seated themselves and ordered, and Sam asked for a large jug of water, which he drank down the second it arrived at their table.

"So, what's your story?" he asked, genuinely interested in hearing it.

"Mine?" She smiled again. Sam thought that he could get used to watching her smile. "I'm studying Microbiology at MIT."

"No kidding? I have a Master's in oceanography from MIT."

She gave him that look which he translated to mean, "Sure, like you could afford MIT as a tugboat driver."

He ignored the look and said, "So, do you come from old

money too?"

"Oh yeah, that's my family." She said sarcastically. "My dad's forever trying to send me my own helicopter."

Sam laughed at that. More from his understanding and his past experiences than he would ever let her know.

"No, I'm there on a scholarship, actually."

"Hey, good for you." He'd already picked up that she was bright. "What . . . like a Rhodes scholarship or something like that?"

"Yeah, something like that . . ." she replied. Still, that smile seemed to become even cuter, as though she was deciding whether or not to keep hiding something.

"Oh, shit. You're serious! You are a Rhodes Scholar! You must be really bright." *Good looking and bright. Maybe I should just ask her to marry me now.*

She laughed, but behind it, he could see that she was mildly embarrassed, as though she was used to being treated differently by boys.

"My dad's the bright one, she added. He's a microbiologist as well, and after my mum left him, I suppose the only thing he could do right was to teach me about science. I don't think I'm necessarily any better or brighter than anyone else. You see, it was just what we sort of did as a family."

"You don't get on with your dad?" Sam asked.

"No, of course I do. I mean, he still treats me like I'm sixteen and his little girl, but I know he loves me. What makes you say that?"

"You've made a few comments about him stifling you. Don't look upset. I have the same problem with my dad. We love each other, but I wouldn't want to live anywhere near him, or see him too often."

"Yeah, I suppose that's true of my dad, too," she admitted.

"And your mum?"

"No idea. She left my dad years ago."

"I'm sorry," he said.

"Don't be. It happens."

They continued talking for about half an hour, and the time went by too quickly. Then, he saw a large, unfamiliar Jet Ranger hover overhead, circle and then land in the parking lot at the end of the street.

"I guess that's your ride," she said.

"Guess so, but it isn't one of ours."

"It's been nice talking to you, Sam."

"Thank you. It's been a pleasure talking to you too, Aliana." He then wrote down his phone number. "I have some work to do in Europe, but I travel a fair amount. If you would ever like to have lunch with me, I'd love to see you again—anywhere, anytime."

Sam meant it too. He would happily make an excuse to visit any part of the world just to spend a short amount of time in her company.

She took it, kissed him on the cheek, and then said with a grin, "Maybe I will."

"Boy, am I sure glad to see you, Tom," Sam said.

"You look like crap. So, what have you done this time?" There was laughter in Tom's voice, but he spoke with genuine concern too, combined with a touch of reproof.

"It's a long story," Sam said, as he looked up at his friend. "You look like you've had a rough week at work. Where's my

Sea King, anyway?"

"About that . . ." Tom stopped short.

"I get it. It's going to be a long story."

"You go first."

It took the entire flight back to Sydney harbor, where the Maria Helena was at its temporary mooring making repairs, for Sam to tell his story, filling in all the parts about the gold, the brutal attack, and at last, about the girl that he'd met.

After they landed on the back deck of the Maria Helena, Sam looked across at his friend, and said, "So Tom, what did you do while I was away?"

"Well Sam . . ." Tom wore his usual grin as he pressed the collective all the way down, letting the rotary blades wind down, through their natural whine, and then patted Sam on his shoulder and said, "While you've been out playing, I've been busy working. I flew the Sea King through the eye of a cyclone in order to save one of your dad's super bulkers in an attempt to also save the lives of all the sea, as well as the lives of millions of Queenslanders, in the process."

"No shit?" Sam's eyes showed that he was impressed, and that he believed what Tom had just told him. Had it come from anyone other than Tom, he would have called them a liar.

"Yep."

"Did you save her?"

"Nope, she sank just before reaching the Great Barrier Reef," Tom admitted.

"Wow, I guess my dad was pissed about that."

"Sure was," Tom replied, "but not so much about losing his ship."

"What then?"

"He was more upset about the loss of the contents of his private vault."

"Bet he asked you dive for them during the cyclone, didn't he?" Sam asked. He knew all about his father's private vault, and he had a good idea of just what he was transporting inside.

"Right again."

"And, I'll also bet that you told him where to go."

"No. When he told me what was at stake, I had to do what he wanted."

"What was inside it when you opened the vault?" Sam asked, only mildly curious. He and his father generally kept out of each other's secret lives.

"Nothing."

"What do you mean? Had it been destroyed?"

"No, just stolen."

"Really?" Sam said, his eyes brightening as though the news had made his day. "Someone stole something from my father while his ship was stranded in a cyclone? That would definitely have pissed him off. So, what's his next move?"

"He didn't say."

"I wouldn't want to be in the shoes of the person who stole whatever it was. My dad can be quite persistent when he's out for revenge."

"I don't doubt it." Tom said. "Now, what are we going to do about your problem?"

"I'm going to take a shower, put on some dry clothes, and then we'll work out what we're going to do about the Wolfgang Corporation."

Twenty minutes later, Sam sat at the end of the operations room, with his laptop computer open. There was a fatigue that went with surviving the past few days of his life, but the shower had made him feel human again.

He looked at the laptop screen before him and typed the words, "Wolfgang Corporation" into google.

A long list of pages relating to the infamous Wolfgang Corporation came up instantly. Its president was a Mr. John Wolfgang, a microbiologist with a number of accolades to his name, including a Nobel Prize for Medicine in 2012.

Sam scrolled down, and discovered that John Wolfgang appeared to be a well-respected microbiologist, as well as a wealthy businessman. His father, Walter Wolfgang had also been a brilliant microbiologist, who had founded the company in 1935, while working on his PhD, but had struggled to succeed in it after Germany lost the war. He ended up living in East Germany, which entirely strangled his operations. After the Berlin Wall came down in 1989, John rekindled the family business by finding financial backing from an unlisted source. Since then, the company had moved to the U.S., where it now thrived, and became one of the leading pharmaceutical companies involved in stem cell research.

Sam made a mental note of the company owner's name, and decided that he would have to give the company's past history a closer inspection at a later time.

Next, Sam opened up his last email from Kevin Reed. At the end of it, there was a note with the name "The Summit," a bed and breakfast, located in the Alps, where Kevin was staying. Below that, was a note with his contact phone number in case he discovered anything interesting about the gold bar.

I don't have anything to tell you about the gold, but I sure hope you can answer some of my questions – Kevin.

With that in mind, Sam dialed the number.

"Hello. Summit."

"Hello. I was given this number and told that I might pass along a message to a friend of mine who has been staying with you over the summer."

"Yes, certainly. What is your friend's name?" The tone was not unfriendly, but the man's thick German accent made it difficult for the man to hide his formality.

"A Mr. Kevin Reed." Sam said, and then added, as if to clarify: "He and his wife have been climbing in your region for a number of months now."

The line went silent. Sam wondered if he had been cut off.

"Hello, are you still there?"

"I am sorry sir. I guess that you haven't heard?" The man's voice sounded more surprised than concerned, that clearly Sam was unaware of recent events.

"Heard what?" Sam's heart missed a beat.

What now?

"I regret to inform you that Mr. Kevin Reed and his wife had an accident on the mountain earlier today. His rope broke, and tragically, both he and his wife fell to their deaths."

"Oh my God!"

"I'm sorry, what did you say your name was?" The man asked.

Suddenly, the realization of how serious this was hit Sam like an avalanche. It was his fault that his old college acquaintance and his wife were now both dead.

Someone had been after him because he'd found out about the gold. *But how did they know?*

"Thank you for your help."

Sam hung the phone up before he made the mistake of letting them know he was still alive.

He then sat there, looking blankly at the computer screen, which was still displaying a picture of the head of the Wolfgang Corporation, a blond man with a rigid face, but a kind smile, staring back at him.

What did you have to do with this?

He struggled to recollect the chain of events that had transpired since the discovery of the gold's existence. His friend, Kevin, had discovered the gold and now he was dead; he himself had made some inquiries about the gold, and now someone had made very serious attempt on his life, too.

Who else knows about the gold?

Then he remembered, Blake Simmonds, his father's friend.

Simmonds had said that he'd spent years fascinated by the story of the Magdalena and her disappearance, which was why he had called as soon as he'd seen the picture of the gold, with the G & O emblem clearly marked.

Could Blake have betrayed me?

No one else knew about the discovery. It was certainly possible. His father's friend might have deceived him. Even the best of friends may choose betrayal if the reward was high enough, except that in this case, he'd never even met the man.

Someone else must have been searching for this gold for quite some time in order to be willing to commit murder to prevent anyone else from getting to it first.

That thought sent a shiver down his spine.

At that point, the door opened and Tom walked in.

"Tom, I just spoke with Mary in Human Resources. You have four weeks leave owing?"

"Yeah, that sounds about right. Why do you ask?"

"Because I've just told her that you've decided to take them starting tomorrow." Sam said.

"Tomorrow?" Tom's patient, smiling face looked back at him with surprise.

Sam had seen that look on his friend's face before. It said, *what have you gotten me into this time?*

The friendship between Sam and Tom went back years, well before they'd decided to join the Marines together. Over the years, they had dragged each other along on some pretty crazy adventures. It was a wonder that either of them were still alive to tell the tale.

"Yep. Tomorrow."

"Why would I do that? I'm planning to go surfing at the big wave contest in Oahu in September!" Tom protested.

"Don't worry about the surf. It will still be there next year."

"What do you mean, don't worry about the surf? I've been looking forward to this for three years running!" Tom complained.

"Now, we're going to Europe instead."

"And why the hell are we doing that?"

"Well, buddy . . ." This time it was Sam's turn to look at his friend, with an expression he had seen many times before, which said, *Believe me, this will be worth it,* " . . . because we're going on a treasure hunt."

Sam scrolled through the priority list on his satellite phone, and clicked on the words: "The Old Man."

He didn't have a particularly close relationships his father. They had never been the typical American immigrant family, who maintained their close family ties. It wasn't that he didn't like his dad, and he certainly respected him. After all, the man was exceptional in his field, and in any other in which he had to deal, for that matter, that much was certain.

Sam only spoke with him two, or sometimes three times a year, and it was rarely for personal reasons. Today was different. He needed help. He was in trouble and his dad might just have the right connections to help him out.

He had no doubt that his father loved him. In his own way.

The phone never even got the chance to ring, "Yes?" His dad didn't waste time with unnecessary terms such as "hello."

"Hey, Dad."

No response.

He was waiting for Sam to make the next move, as though their conversation was an intricate chess battle.

"I'm in trouble."

"Yes, I heard that you refused to return to your post because you were off chasing some perfect disaster of a storm, instead of performing the task that you were paid for, and as a result my ship was sunk—and even more importantly, something of tremendous value was stolen from me."

I was on bloody holiday!

Sam knew better than to get into this argument with his father. Besides, given what had happened, the point was moot.

"This isn't about work. This is serious!" Sam said. "Someone tried and very nearly succeeded in killing me."

"Really?" His father sounded interested, or at least somewhat amused—certainly not concerned in the way a reasonable parent would be, but rather in the way that a rich man might enjoy hearing a good anecdote.

It took Sam several minutes to relate the entire story to his dad, omitting how he survived by using his dive equipment, and focusing on the fact that someone wanted him dead. He also included his opinion that at this stage, his only guess as to the reason why, was because he'd discovered the possible resting place of an old WWII airship filled with what he assumed were Jewish treasures. He concluded with the name on the back of the helicopter, which had been aboard the offending ship, Wolfgang Corporation.

Sam's father didn't interrupt, and allowed him to finish the entire story.

"Oh, by the way, I met a beautiful girl when I got back to shore," Sam said. "I don't know if I'd ever welcome another near death experience just to meet her, but she seemed pretty great to me."

"A girl, hey?"

Sam knew that his father would be far more interested in hearing about her than he was in hearing the rest of Sam's story.

"What's her name?"

"Aliana."

"Nice name. So, what are you going to do about all this?" His father was always direct.

"Tom and I are going to Europe to see what we can find, and where it leads us."

"And the Maria Helena? What about your responsibilities there?" his father asked.

"We're finished in Australia. Matthew is transferring her back to San Diego. She needs an overhaul anyway. I won't be missed, and Tom is owed leave." He then paused for a moment, and asked, "Dad, have you ever heard of the

Wolfgang Corporation?"

"No, should I have?"

"I don't know. It's the only name I have to link to the man who attempted to kill me." Sam paused, and then said, "Dad, I need you to look into the Wolfgang Corporation for me."

"I understand." His father had many connections, and they went just about as high up and as low down as could be imagined.

Sam knew that his dad had sunk large amounts of money into Obama's election campaign in 2008, and, ever since the man's presidential success, the two men had maintained a close relationship. As a result, his father had been appointed a senior financial advisor to the Obama administration. The President would have been pissed as hell if he ever learned that Sam's dad had also poured money into John McCain's campaign coffers. Sam doubted that his father would use any official channels to conduct this search. His father kept a number of mercenaries around the globe who provided very specialized services. Some of them were legal, many were questionable, and others were utterly, outright, illegal.

In this case, Sam was entirely indifferent as to the method his father would use, but he was certain that his father would be able to get him some answers without revealing the fact that Sam was still alive.

His father was an immensely intelligent, mostly self-centered, megalomaniac, who had spent his entire life satisfying his own appetites, but in the few rare times that Sam had needed his help, his dad had been there for him.

"Thanks, Dad."

"Take care of yourself, son." As an afterthought, he added, "Say hi to your mom for me, will you?"

"Will do, Dad."

"By the way, how was your sailing trip? Did you find what you've been looking for?"

Sam thought about it for a while.

His mind flashed back to the terrifying night with his brother, and then to the more recent night, when he sailed through Bass Strait while it was squeezed between a catastrophic high and low convergence.

The night was rough, that was for sure, but no, it wasn't the same.

"No, not yet."

CHAPTER 9

Blake Simmonds walked out of his office on the afternoon of the August 26th and strolled up Waldorf Street, in the heart of Berlin. Standing at a height of six foot, five inches, he had always been tall, and found that as he'd aged, it became harder to disguise the fact that he walked with a limp.

At the age of 68, he had begun to hope that he would be long gone before his current problem came to the light of man.

He caught a taxi to a place where he'd worked hard to forget for many years. Before reaching his destination, the taxi slowed to a halt near the site of a recent accident. Paramedics were still at the scene and were attempting to free an injured man from his vehicle.

"I'll walk from here." Blake said, as he rapped on the divider which separated the driver from his passengers.

The man pointed at the fare owed, and he paid it in full, without adding a tip.

As he began to walk along the footpath, his cell phone rang.

"Good morning," he said.

"Blake, its James Reilly here. Can you talk?"

He almost laughed. James never asked for anything, he only ever commanded.

Something's up.

"Of course," Blake said. "What I can I do for you?"

"John Wolfgang just fucked me good. He's stolen it from me, and after we had made a deal! I want it back, and I want him to suffer for his impudence. I don't care what it costs—just make it happen."

"Really?" Blake Simmonds kept walking; a broad smile appearing on his face. "Yes, of course. I will fix this for you."

"See that you do."

The phone went silent.

It was turning into a much better day than he'd anticipated.

With his cane in his left hand, he walked the three blocks until he reached the new Remington building, and without pausing to admire its futuristic architecture, he entered.

He looked at the receptionist.

Now in her late forties, she had lost none of her youthful looks. She'd been there since the first time he'd been there. She had fair hair, blue eyes, and a slim figure. She was beguiling. Her fingers didn't pause for a second, he noticed as they danced over the keyboard on one of those old-fashioned typewriters. Her master, Blake knew, was a cautious man by his very nature, and would never allow company records to be placed on anything that a fifteen year old computer whiz could hack into in a matter of minutes. The information collected in this building was far too valuable for that.

She smiled politely at him without saying anything, as if she'd expected him to show up today.

Blake walked past her without saying a word, entered the room behind her, and then closed the door.

The man in front of him didn't bother to stand up or greet him. His skin was relatively dark, and gave him the appearance of someone of Mediterranean or even Middle Eastern descent.

It had been a long time since Blake had seen the man.

The man sighed, and then finally spoke to him, "We both knew this day would one day come."

"Yes."

"Now, what are we going to do about it?"

John Wolfgang looked out the window of his Lear Jet.

It was a never-ending desert in all directions. Then, as the pilot made his approach, and softly set the jet down, until it lightly touched Sheik Abdulla Azzama's private runway, he noticed a large, luxurious building, with an enormous pool surrounding it as if it were an island, like a mirage up ahead in the distance.

He could already see the man's armored Bentley drive along the runway towards them.

The pilot had stopped the plane, but its engines could be heard idling in the background. He watched as several men rolled a gold-plated set of stairs towards his aircraft. Then, Sheik Abdulla stepped out of his vehicle. Confident from any threat in his own land, he alone walked toward the plane.

John had no love for the man or for his damn holy wars, for that matter, but as he admired the gold-plated stairs, he had to admit that nobody could pay like the oil-rich masters of the Middle East.

Abdulla was escorted into John's luxurious board room, which was big enough to seat more than a dozen people. Today, it was to be the meeting place of just two men. In so doing, it provided both he and Abdulla a private place to converse with the absolute certainty that no one else was listening.

John had already guessed that a number of intelligence agencies had captured the image of his jet setting down on the Sheik's runway. He wasn't worried. There was nothing illegal about that in itself. By all openly accepted and provable facts, the man he was here to meet was simply one of the region's wealthy Sheiks, but it didn't take a genius to see where his money flowed further downstream. As far as John was concerned, it didn't matter. By the time they completed their terrifying plan, the most powerful nations in the world would be crumbling and would be unable to harm him.

The man came up to him and shook his hand, warmly.

"So, the Magdalena's vault has been found?" Abdulla spoke quietly, and animatedly.

"Not quite, but we have the closest thing to a lead which seventy five years of searching for her has ever produced." John said.

"But, it gives us hope that it really did exist, and after all, hope is all that any of us can ask for?" Abdulla sighed. "It is proof that the Nazis never got their hands on it."

"Yes, if they'd made such a discovery, the world would have known about it. That's for certain."

" And, you believe that you will be able to find her?" Abdulla stared at him, trying to discern whether or not John could actually provide what he had offered.

"Yes, I'm certain of it. We have our best men on the job."

"But, will it have survived intact, after all this time?"

"Yes." John wrote something on the small piece of paper before him with his gold tipped Biro and then said, "Influenza A1W5 was designed to survive in environments that would destroy all other microbes, whether: viral, bacterial or fungal. It doesn't require oxygen to survive, and consequently, it is completely viable in environments where other strains of virus wouldn't survive. It spreads rapidly through both air and liquid vectors, but has an incubation period of up to three months, followed by an 80 percent mortality rate. With such a prolonged incubation period, the disease will spread globally before the CDC or WHO even knows that it exists. By the time the first horrified scientist examines it, the entire world will be infected."

"How long will it take them to combat it?"

"I have no idea, but I am certain that someone will eventually be able to beat it," John said. "But, by the time someone does, the world will have changed so much that who knows how many people will be left alive."

"How can you be so certain that a cure for the virus will ever be developed?"

"Because my father created such a vaccine," John replied.

"Where is that vaccine now?"

"Destroyed." John lied, "Many years ago. Along with the life's work of my father before the Berlin wall was finally demolished.

"And the price?"

He then slid the paper slip of paper over to him.

The sheik smiled as he looked at the price tag.

"Twenty billion dollars is a lot of money." He looked as though he was considering the price of a pound of fish, and then he said, "But then resetting the key players in the world is worth it."

"I'll need half the money now and the other half on delivery."

"But, of course. My men will take care of the transfer of money to a bank of your choosing."

With no further discussion, Abdulla left the room, walked through the narrow passageway, down the stairs, and climbed into his car, closing the door without looking back.

John heard the jet engines power up to full.

The entire aircraft shuddered under their force.

Once airborne, John placed another secure call on his Sat phone. It rang a couple times before someone answered. This time, it was a woman's voice on the line.

"Yes?" She said.

"I've done it," he said. He then disconnected the phone and looked out the window once more, at the desert below.

He would be glad to leave this desolate place.

Aliana was worried about her father.

He had sounded more concerned than normal over the phone. Something was wrong. She was certain of it. The more she thought about it, the more she realized that she would have to fly to Europe and meet up with him before returning to her studies.

She had three weeks left before she had to return to her university. Aliana's thoughts instantly turned to Sam Reilly, the unique man she'd met in Australia. He'd said that he wanted to meet up again if she was ever free, and their lives crossed paths.

And it appeared, that they just did. She would be in Europe the same time as him.

Aliana looked at the phone number that Sam had given her. She could do with some fun, but she'd only make the call if there was time.

Her father, she realized, often worried about a number of

things which mattered little to her–money, younger women, expanding his already enormous wealth, and most of all, beating his father in the world of medicine. Her father's recent Nobel Prize went a long way toward improving his self-esteem, but like all great men, he needed more.

When she'd spoken to him today, it was different. All those things, the money, the women, they were simply games to a man at the top echelon of a life filled with politicians, rich tycoons, and world-changing scientists.

Something had rattled him.

Whatever it was this time, it was different. It had really frightened him.

Obviously, he wouldn't talk to her about such things. He never had. To him, she would always be his 16 year old girl, despite her pursuit of a PhD in microbiology at MIT.

That night, she made the decision to stop in at her father's Berlin office before returning to Michigan. The next morning, she changed her flights, and 18 hours later, she was standing in front of his office building enjoying the warmth of a mild German summer.

"Hey Dad . . ." she called out to him, as he came through the revolving door in front of his building.

He stopped walking immediately.

Aliana was happy to have genuinely surprised him.

"Aliana." He bent down to kiss her cheeks. "What are you doing here?"

"I was worried about you."

"Me? Why would you worry about me?"

"Come on, Dad. You can take me to dinner and tell me all about it." Aliana said, knowing that her father would never betray his feelings out in the open.

He took her to the Lorenz Adlon for dinner, located in the heart of Berlin. The two spoke about simpler things—how her studies were progressing, the growth of bacteria off the coast of Antarctica, and the effects of the further stabilization of the American dollar. After dinner, they walked back to the penthouse he kept in Berlin.

Aliana was about to go to bed when she turned towards her father and said, "Dad, really . . . is everything all right?"

"Yes, of course it is. Work's just been keeping me busy, that's all." His words seemed sincere, but she noticed that he avoided meeting her eyes as he spoke.

"Okay, then." She kissed him on his cheek. "I'm going to bed. I just want you to know that I'm not a little girl anymore. If you need me, I'm here for you. I don't start classes again for another two weeks."

"I know, but you will always be my little girl."

A half-hour later she heard a gentle knock on her door. She'd been reading a new thriller to take her mind off things.

"Yes?"

"Are you still awake, my love?"

It was her father.

"Yes," Aliana replied as she met him at the door.

"Would you like a hot chocolate?"

Years ago, the two of them would stay up chatting for hours, while sipping their rich hot chocolate. Real hot chocolate, the kind that only the Europeans believed in. None of this watered down, milky stuff they made elsewhere in the world.

"Yes, I'd like that."

She followed him downstairs to the kitchen and watched as he added rich, cocoa into a flame-lit saucepan, followed by several blocks of solid chocolate, and stirring it slowly until it turned into a molten goo of chocolate.

He then added several drops of rich liqueur.

The two moved to the couch and sat alongside one another, sipping their hot chocolate for a few minutes before Aliana finally spoke.

"Dad. What's wrong?"

"When you were very little, do you remember when I took financial backing from a man so that I could finally get your grandfather's company back off the ground?"

"Yes, of course. For years the newspapers questioned who your backer was, and why, even though you own fifty percent of the company, the other half has never been seen."

"For more than twenty years I have not heard so much as a single word from that man, not until a week ago."

"What did he say to you?"

"He told me that it's time for him to collect."

CHAPTER 10

Sam read a book during the long flight from Sydney to Munich on Lithuanian Airlines. After years of working in and out of helicopters, and after having flown aboard a number of fixed wing and rotary aircraft, one might assume that he was comfortable aboard the enormous Airbus A380.

Yet, somehow he didn't trust something quite so large in the air.

Tom, he noted, hadn't woken since their departure. Like a cat, he could sleep anywhere. He nudged Tom with the sharp point of his elbow.

"Everyone's starting to deplane."

"Oh yeah?" Tom feigned disappointment. "I said wake me when the food comes around!"

"Yeah, well I decided you weren't hungry, and ate your food instead."

"Some friend, you are!" Tom said, looking aggrieved.

At Munich's International Airport they were met by a man named Dietrich. He was who had arranged for the delivery of the equipment they had requested, and also for a Robinson 44 four-seat helicopter to be fueled, waiting, and ready for them to board.

They loaded their luggage into the back of the Robinson 44.

Tom started the onerous job of ticking off each item on the pre-flight checklist. It had been a while since he'd flown such a small helicopter. It felt strange to him in the same way that an airline pilot would feel at the unfamiliar controls of a Cessna 152.

He entered the GPS coordinates for the lodge in which they had made reservations, located at the northern end of Ötztal. It was a little over forty-five minutes by air, which they started immediately.

Sam noticed as they flew over them, that the Southern Limestone Alps lived up to their reputation for sheer beauty. The enormous, limestone mountains were made of the lighter and more porous rock. In addition to limestone, they contained dolomite, marl, sandstone and other minerals, rather than the dark granites of the more familiar Alps.

A number of alpine lakes could be seen from the air. Their distinct turquoise-aquamarine color showing the lime content in their makeup.

Tom pointed below and said, "Any one of those lakes could hide the Magdalena."

"I doubt it."

"Why?"

"Because they're crystal clear. If she were down there, someone would have seen her over the past seventy five years."

They continued flying, the hum of the Robinson 44's engine providing a constant background noise.

Flying over the highest peaks on their way to Ötztal, Tom looked at Sam and pointed at the altimeter.

Its reading was at 13,000 feet, and they were barely a

thousand feet above the peak.

"I doubt that any airship could have made it past here."

"Neither do I," Sam agreed. "We'll start by searching the area to the north of here. We know the Magdalena left Munich, and that the single gold bar was found at Innsbruck, approximately twenty miles to the north of here. It's a big area, so she could be anywhere. I'm with you though, there's no way that she could have cleared the high Ötztal Alps."

Within a few minutes the alpine town of Ötztal could be seen ahead of them.

In its alpine valley, located in Tyrol, Austria, Sam could see the Ötztaler Ache River flowing in a northern direction. The Ötztal, separates the Stubai Alps in the east from the Ötztal Alps in the west. Looking at the map, Sam noted that the valley was 40 miles long, and surrounded by the confluence of the Ötztaler Ache and the Inn rivers in the east. The southern end of the valley, called the Gurglertal, terminated at the Italian border. The valley was formed by the main chain of the Alps, with many glaciers and high peaks, including the Weißkugel and the Similaun.

Sam drew a line connecting the three edges of the alpine ranges to form a small triangle, and placed an asterisk at the top to represent Munich, from where the Magdalena was known to have departed in 1939. At that time, coming in an easterly direction, was neutral Switzerland. Due south lay Fascist-ruled Italy, and to the east, German-ruled Austria.

He then looked at the area to the north of the Ötztal River, to a place called Bahnof, where his old friend had discovered the single gold bar, and Sam marked the spot with another X, as in "X marks the treasure."

Tom started to make their descent and Sam put away the map.

He wondered if the pilot of an archaic airship, possessing negligible navigational abilities could have successfully flown through the narrow Ötztal valley, thus crossing the Southern Limestone Alps, without ever raising his aircraft more than a couple of thousand feet.

He shook his head, realizing that the thought was sheer foolishness.

Sam Reilly woke up early the next day.

The air was crisp, and although the sun had not yet pierced the peaks of the distant mountains, it wasn't quite uncomfortably cold. When Sam looked at the mist ahead, he felt that it mirrored his sentiments on the vast endeavor of the search ahead of him. He watched as Tom finished making their coffee.

How could something a hundred and fifty feet long disappear for seventy five years?

He then considered the more important question, *and how am I going to find it?*

Despite the enormity of the challenge, Sam was happy to be in Europe again.

It had been years since he'd been to central Europe. He had once dived the canals of Venice, and had promised himself to do so again. So much history could be discovered there, but so far, he had found little reason to take Deep Sea Expeditions there.

It was summer, but not overly warm.

Europe never was, he decided. He'd rented a log cabin that rested at 3,500 feet. It was located in a pass that overlooked the Tyrol River.

He had chosen the place because, unlike the rest of the

Tyrolean village, which rested on the valley floor, it was perched high up in the mountains, thus saving them hours of both climbing time and fuel during the many flights that they would take over the next few weeks.

He looked at the Robinson 44, which was perched precariously on a purpose-built helipad that rested on the edge of the mountain. Sam had half expected to discover that a strong wind had knocked it off its perch over night, but there it was, still as graceful as ever.

It was not a very large or powerful vehicle, but it would serve their purpose well.

He had considered hiring a Jet Ranger or a Skyhawk, but both were so rarely seen there that people were bound to comment. The Robinson 44's were the helicopters of choice for sightseeing use by tourists. No one was going to take notice of yet another one above the Alps.

They'd landed yesterday afternoon, but had decided to take the time to relax and recover from their jet lag before starting in earnest.

Tom walked in just as the kettle on the stove began to boil.

"Morning, Sam."

He noticed that Tom, unlike any other traveler he knew, had actually caught up on sleep during his long-haul flight, and today, was looking even more relaxed than he had seen him for quite some time—if that was even possible.

He would give anything to be able to sleep like that.

"Morning, Tom. You look well rested."

"Thanks, I was up early."

"Really?" Sam was surprised.

"So, I've looked into the Magdalena for you. She was supposed to be carrying the following well known families: the

Goldschmidts, who were linked by marriage to the Oppenheimers. They were involved in gold bullion and diamonds; the Rosenbergs, as in the private banking Rosenbergs, who, rumor has it, funded a number of crime syndicates in the 1930s. This is what we know about them: the Goldschmidts would have been carrying large amounts of gold; the Rosenbergs may have been in possession of the Rosenberg Diamond, which was rumored to be in excess of 50 carats, cut in a perfect emerald cut. The last was a professor, about whom we know very little. What we do know is that he was a recluse, and an avid fascist, who had been working for the Nazi movement. How he came to be on the Magdalena's manifest, no one has yet been able to figure out."

"What were you doing on that flight Professor Ritztroben?" Sam asked, thinking out loud.

"It's clear enough that the ship was carrying a fortune in gold and jewelry. Whoever is after it has already shown their willingness to do anything to prevent someone else from getting to it before they do."

"Any more news about the Wolfgang Corporation?"

"Not yet. I'm still waiting for my Dad to get back to me with whatever information he's been able to discover about our new friends."

Tom sat down, and set the two cups of coffee on the table next to the topographical map, in front of him.

"What's our plan?" Tom asked.

"I was thinking that we'd start with where my friend found the single bar of gold bullion, and fly an aerial reconnaissance first. Perhaps the answer will present itself from the air?" Sam said.

"That's pretty optimistic, my friend."

"You never know. We both know how much clearer these

things are from the air."

"And you don't think your friend might have already hired a helicopter to do just that?" Tom was quick to point out.

"Maybe he did and that's what got him killed, but there's only one way to find out and at least it's a start."

After breakfast, Sam loaded his daypack and some rope into the chopper, while Tom prepared it for the day.

They took off just as the sun penetrated the valley deep below. It looked beautiful as the rays of sunlight reflected off the snow-capped mountains.

It was only a little over fifteen minutes flight along the Tyrol valley until they reached the northern entrance, where Kevin had first come across the gold bullion, which had started this entire treasure hunt.

About a thousand feet above the place, Sam examined the location.

It was a steep wall of limestone, which made the face of the mountain, below which was a slight saddle through which another could be seen, and far below that, lay a small lake. Dotted along the mountain face, about halfway up, were thousands of enormous pine trees.

Kevin, he recalled, was an avid free-climber. Someone who still believed that the mountains were sacred places, which should be reserved for those few whose skills allowed them to ascend without ropes. Looking at the rocky slope below, Sam imagined that only a few rock climbers had ever scaled this mountain's walls in the decades since the Magdalena had first left Munich.

He found it virtually impossible to think that the mystery of the Magdalena had remained hidden for so long, simply because no one had bothered to climb this particular mountain, especially since it was located so close to the entrance of the popular Southern Limestone Alps.

Tom made the decision to broaden the search area, and began to fly in increasingly wide circles around the location.

"I can understand how a single gold bar managed to remain hidden for so long up here," Sam said.

He was about to continue when Tom interrupted, "But you've no idea how a 150 foot dirigible could?"

"Exactly," Sam laughed. The two of them were still thinking the same as each other.

As the circles widened, Tom said, "I can't see any place down there where such a large airship could have set down and yet remained unseen from the air. I mean, there's the river down at the very bottom, but it's nowhere near large enough to hide such a craft."

They continued their reconnaissance from the air, until the helicopter needed to be refueled.

On the way back, Sam figured out how they would find the lost Magdalena. They had been coming at the problem from the wrong angle, but starting tomorrow, he would rectify that.

That night, while sitting before the warmth of the fireplace, Tom poured Sam and himself a snifter of rich cognac.

"Look at us, Sam," he said, while pouring.

"What?" A grin came across Sam's face.

"Two old men, sitting here in front of this fire, drinking cognac, the rich stench of expensive cigars scenting these leather seats." Tom laughed, his white teeth reminding Sam of the Cheshire Cat. "Are we getting old, my friend?"

"I don't know what you're talking about," Sam sighed as he took another small sip of the expensive drink in his hand.

"We're only just entering our thirties."

"I mean, it wasn't all that long ago that we would have camped on the mountains and climbed our way through them until we discovered our lost Magdalena."

"That's true, but I bet we wouldn't have found her," Sam was quick to point out.

"Yes, well buddy, after today, I'm not so convinced that we're going to be the ones to solve this 75 year old riddle, anyway."

"Oh, let's not write this thing off just yet. We've only just begun," Sam replied.

Tom had seen that same look in Sam's eyes many times before. It was a look that said, *fuck the odds, I'll have it my way.*

"We'll see."

"Tom . . ."

"Yeah, Sam?" Tom filled their second glass.

"Don't forget, we're still having one hell of an adventure."

"That we are. And, as I hope will always be the case, I will join you on your crazy escapades." Tom drank more of his cognac, and then asked, "So what's our next move?"

"Okay, so I've been thinking about it and this is what I've come up with," Sam said, handing Tom the grid map of the western side of the Alps. "There's little point in trying to fly over every single point on this grid, because for the majority of it, an airship would have been clearly visible from a helicopter."

"I agree." Tom looked dubious. "So, where are we going to search for her?"

"We're going to do a reconnaissance of the area within this grid, of course. But we're not going to be looking for the

Magdalena."

"What are we going to be looking for?"

"Any areas where such an airship could conceivably disappear for three quarters of a century."

"There must be hundreds of places to hide something in these mountains." The wrinkling of Tom's brow showed that he expected Sam to come up with a better plan than this.

"Not hundreds capable of concealing the 150 foot canopy of the airship."

"No?" Tom still looked doubtful.

"Just five."

"Five?" Tom was incredulous.

"Yep, just five."

Sam handed Tom a second version of the same topographical map. Superimposed over this one, he had highlighted places where something as large as the airship could potentially have been kept hidden for years.

Tom's pale green eyes scanned the markings on the map.

There were a number of rivers and lakes, and the constant erosion of the predominantly porous limestone rocks that formed the mountain range would, in all probability, have created numerous limestone caves. A quick study of any topographical map would inform you that only a few of them were large enough to hide something as big as the Magdalena.

In fact, there were only five places on this side of the Alps that were even worth considering.

Three of these were large caves, and two were covered by deep sections of snowpack, which wouldn't thaw out in a thousand years. Although large portions of the mountain were covered in snow, there were only two locations where the snowpack remained virtually unchanged year round. All of the lakes, although certainly large enough for an airship to disappear into, thawed out in the summer, and were too clear and unspoiled to obscure anything beneath their waters from above.

"I think you're on to something, Sam," Tom said. "That is, unless the entire Magdalena has been concealed by seventy five years' worth of tree growth."

"These are predominantly pine trees which cover these mountains. A thousand years of their growth would have trouble concealing the crippled remains of the Magdalena."

"I hope you're right."

"I'm right. And I'm going to prove it," Sam said, with his signature certainty.

And I sure hope you do . . .

CHAPTER 11

Tom conducted a number of flights over the course of the next two weeks. But with each new day, he confirmed what he'd believed from the start—*a ship that wants to stay hidden, will.*

The available landing sites were generally pretty poor, but the Robinson 44 was capable of landing on the even the smallest locations.

There were many large caves, tunnels, and snow fields, but none of them were quite large enough to hide the Magdalena.

Despite the constant hum of the engine and the whine of its rotary blades, there was a melancholy quiet inside the cockpit on their return. Both men knew that they had exhausted their initial theories, and that their subsequent ones had come to nothing.

In truth, Tom realized that they still knew very little about what they were looking for. Their specialty was in sea-related searches, not in treasure hunting in the Alps.

Sam was the first to break the silence.

"What about a lake?"

"What about it?" Tom looked at the glassy lake below, and he could see the reflection of the helicopter on its clear surface. "We've already discussed lakes. They're too clear."

"Might it have sunk into any of these lakes?" Sam was serious.

"Are you kidding me?"

"No. Why?"

"Look down at that lake there, Sam. What do you see?"

"I see giant rocks, holes, and even some fish. What do you see?"

"That's exactly what I mean, Sam. If there were an enormous airship in that lake, or even something the size of one, in an area which is frequented by so many tourist choppers, it would have been spotted long before now."

"You're right, Tom. It would have been impossible to lose the Magdalena on this side of the mountain for any prolonged period of time," Sam said, as though Tom had been agreeing with his train of thought, instead of disputing it.

"So, it was never here, then?"

"No, I didn't say that. I believe it definitely passed over this area; the location of the gold Kevin found confirms that." Sam's confident grin returned as he spoke.

"Then where did it end up?"

"I have an idea Tom, and I think it's time to take this search elsewhere."

Sam dumped the topographical map of the Southern Limestone Alps in front of Tom.

"Okay, so let's just say that they were trying to clear the range. The gold bullion my friends found was . . . here, he said, pointing to the spot. But there is no other evidence of the Magdalena anywhere around this place. Perhaps they were trying to lighten their load in order to clear the mountain top,"

Sam suggested.

"That's nuts," Tom replied. The zeppelin had a maximum ceiling of 650 feet. There's no way these guys were ever going to get over that mountain, and they must have known it. My bet, they turned around somewhere, and put her down on this side of the mountain—possibly hundreds of miles further north?"

"Then our previous list of five places to hide her, would increase to thousands," Sam didn't sound convinced. "But, what if they knew precisely where they were and thought that they could fly her through the giant mountain passes?"

"You mean, weave her through the Tyrol Valley?" Tom asked, incredulously.

"It must have been possible." Sam said.

"But very unlikely."

"Well, clearly they didn't make it."

"There is that," Tom conceded, and then went on to say, "Besides, what were they even doing there in the first place?"

"What do you mean?"

"Okay, say you wanted to escape Hitler's stranglehold—where would you have flown from Munich in order to escape?"

"Switzerland, of course," Sam answered immediately. "It was the only neutral country located nearby."

"Of course it was. So, why did the Magdalena fly due south, towards the Southern Limestone Alps and towards Italy? Mussolini had already partnered with Hitler. If they'd somehow managed to clear the Dolomites, they would still be within Hitler's grasp. It doesn't make sense."

"Unless they simply didn't realize where they were?" Sam commented.

"There is always that possibility. GPS was nonexistent in the 1930s."

"Perhaps someone on board was a traitor? Or there's always the possibility that one of the passengers or crew might have been coaxed to take the treasure-laden ship somewhere else entirely?"

"Anything's possible," Tom said. "The other thing that troubles me is this, if the Magdalena really has been resting somewhere on the southern side of the Alps, don't you think someone would have noticed her remains by now? I mean, the biggest climbing haven in the world runs throughout the Dolomites; skiers in the winter, paragliders and base jumpers in the summer, and helicopter joy flights all year round. I'm sorry to say it, pal, but if she was on the other side of the Alps, someone would have already found her!"

"When all the likely causes have been ruled out, the only natural course of action is to investigate the unlikely ones. Now, you have to remember that the Magdalena wasn't a zeppelin, per se. She was a dirigible, built by Peter Greentstein, a very rich, former employee of Zeppelin Enterprises. He himself had seen the decline of the era of the great airships after the Hindenburg disaster, and he had decided to reinvent the glory days of airship travel. Is it not possible that he built the Magdalena to make this journey? One of the greatest problems with airships in Europe at that time was its impassable mountain ranges. Had he discovered a way to overcome that?"

"I don't buy that theory at all. Perhaps, if the mountain rose to a height of only two, or even three thousand feet, it might have been possible, but we're talking about almost ten thousand feet! No, my money says that they turned around and went back the way they came. We'll find them on this side of the mountain, if anywhere at all."

"Okay, show me where on the map, on this side of the

mountain, where you think you could possibly hide a 150 foot airship for 75 years?"

Tom's intelligent, hazel green eyes scanned the topographical map for almost five minutes.

Then, he studied Google Earth on his laptop for another forty five minutes before saying, "It couldn't be done. Not there. Someone knows where she is. Maybe the Nazis already discovered her, took her apart in pieces, and never acknowledged it, just as they never acknowledged so many of their other war crimes?"

"Now it's my turn," Sam said, "to say, I don't buy that story. If someone successfully shot her down, and captured the sort of prize she was carrying, someone would have heard about it by now. War crimes or not, these stories have a way of getting out." Sam stated, confidently.

"Okay, so hypothetically, if this ship actually did somehow succeed in making it over the mountains, then where the hell did she end up?

"Somewhere on the southern side of the mountains," Sam grinned, his all-knowing, I'm about to show you my winning hand, smile. "Have a quick glance here, and tell me, as a pilot, where would be the first place to come to your mind if you had to put an aircraft down quick."

Tom's eyes scanned Google Earth's map of the other southern side of the mountains. He smiled, when he saw it, "Oh, you mean here?"

CHAPTER 12

Sam studied the lake pictured before him.

Lake Solitude.

It was perfect. As huge as it was remote, inaccessible to all, with the exception of mountaineers and helicopter pilots. It was also known to remain frozen for most of the year. Its elevation being 8,500 feet.

Measuring more than six miles long by five miles wide, and perched near the top of the mountain, Lake Solitude would have been more than adequate to hold such a large airship. Who could even guess how deep the lake could possibly be?

He imagined the Magdalena somehow clearing the mountain peak, and then making her descent. Something must have gone wrong and forced them to land. To the pilot, in the middle of winter, the rocky, tree lined mountainside must have looked like a nightmare; its jagged rocks resembling giant teeth, and then, seeing a perfect clearing up ahead. Blanketed beneath the thick covering of snow, it could have just as easily appeared to be an open field, cleared for farming.

What happened to you, Peter? What were you thinking?

"She's here, I know it is." Sam stated, fervently.

"I hate to burst your pride bubble and all, but, the last time this lake reportedly thawed out in winter was before the turn of the nineteenth century."

"Or, was it on the night of the September 24th 1939?"

Tom tapped the keys on his laptop a few more times, and then looked over at his friend.

"You're wrong again. Wow, I'll bet you wish you never invited me along for the ride. The night in question was particularly cold. There was no way this lake would have thawed."

"Okay, I have another idea. What if they somehow clipped the top of the mountain?"

"And if they did the clip the top of the mountain, then what?" Tom asked.

"We all know that it was nearly impossible for them to have any chance of clearing it in the first place. What if they didn't quite make it, and instead clipped some of the rocks off the top of it? Is it possible that such a collision might trigger a landslide of some sort—something that just may have been enough to at least crack the ice covering the lake?"

"That's possible. At the start of the war, no one would have been at all interested in a landslide that affected an alpine lake, especially one accessible to only the best mountain climbers of the time."

Tom zoomed in to the western face of the mountain, depicted on Google Earth, and then grinned, mischievously.

"Does that mountain look like it's missing something?"

"It sure does to me. Can you find an earlier image—anything before 1939?" Sam asked.

"Here we go." Tom brought up a picture of the mountain peak taken in 1920. It showed an Italian man, with a rope casually hung over his shoulder, standing on the large rock outcrop—it was a perfect match, to the one that was clearly missing in the 1939 picture. "For once, Sam, you're right. Now what?"

"How do you feel about some high altitude diving, Tom?"

John Wolfgang was glad that his daughter had made the effort to see him before returning to Massachusetts. At first, he'd been concerned that she was there, but it had been nice to see her. Then, when he realized what had to be done, his concern turned to terror.

How could he use his own daughter like this?

But, as had been the case in previous times, in the end, the need outweighed his ethical reservations.

It took some convincing, but in the end, she understood what was required of her, and said she'd make the call.

The phone rang just once before Sam answered it.

"Sam?" The reception was poor, but he thought he recognized the eloquent soft voice; that distinctly American accent that contained a hint of European ancestry.

"Yes, who's this?" Sam asked.

"It's Aliana. Are you still in Europe?"

"Yes, I'm staying in Ötztal, how about you?"

"Ötztal! I spent some time in Ötztal when I was growing up. I'm in Berlin now, until the end of the week, but I was thinking about seeing you again before I leave for the States. If you're interested, maybe this weekend, I could show you more of the area, from a local's point of view?"

"I'd love to. Let me know when to expect you, and I'll change my schedule."

CHAPTER 13

Blake Simmonds felt every single one of his 68 years of life.

It had been a long time since he'd been so involved in field work, particularly one with such catastrophic consequences. It was certainly the most mentally demanding he'd done in years.

He felt like he was right in the midst of a second nuclear arms race. In truth, he still wasn't certain whether or not the involvement with his employer made him the good guy or the bad one.

At first, the thought of the work ahead had invigorated him, but now, after two weeks of putting in long hours, getting almost no sleep, and wondering about his floundering morality, Blake Simmonds was utterly exhausted.

He cursed himself for losing the upper hand. He was the only one who knew that Sam Reilly was still alive, and that he had flown to the Alps to join the rest of the damn treasure hunters. *Savages, every last one of them!*

At least he had the good fortune of knowing that Sam had hired one of their helicopters. The GPS locating device, mounted atop the Robinson 44, kept him updated on their every fruitless movement.

But what could they accomplish, which others had failed in the past 75 years?

It wasn't until he noticed their helicopter next to Lake Solitude, that he understood the severity of his mistake.

Blake had, at first noted their landing site, and assumed that it was just like every other place they'd landed and searched during the past two weeks. It wasn't until he focused his satellites towards the lake that he realized which side of the Alps they were on.

Then, it only took mere seconds before the mental image of Peter Greenstein somehow clearing the mountain pass, losing altitude, and landing in the middle of the frozen lake, entered his mind.

His mind then made the same connection that Sam Reilly's had—that an avalanche might have opened a rift in the frozen lake surface for the first time in probably a century. A quick internet search showed him that he was right.

But it wasn't until he brought up the centuries old map on his computer, that he suddenly knew with certainty, that Sam Reilly had been right about the final resting place of the Magdalena.

It was time to make his move—*but could he do it in time?*

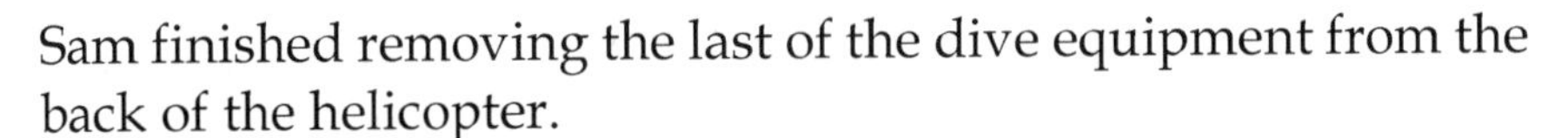

Sam finished removing the last of the dive equipment from the back of the helicopter.

He was glad that Tom had managed to put the 44 down on an enormous piece of solid granite, which formed a small island near the edge of the lake. Upon their first fly-over yesterday afternoon, he wasn't sure if this maneuver was even going to be possible. Considering the giant pine trees lining the lake's edge, there was a chance they might have to land miles away and hike in.

As it was, Tom had found this rock, as though it had been set in place just for them. Sam decided that the chunk of granite appeared to be slightly out of place in the turquoise-green lake, which was made up almost entirely of limestone. Sam could picture this rock forming part of the missing peak of the mountain above them.

The dive equipment was set up in front of the helicopter, ready for them to begin their safety checks and formalize a dive plan for their first descent.

They had spent the night camped on the edge of the lake. One of the hardest equations to predict with any certainty, is how much residual nitrogen a person may have from ground level to when they reached altitude. Although few scientific studies had been performed on diving at altitudes above 8,000 feet, it was generally considered sound diving advice to acclimatize to the altitude for a minimum of twelve hours before making a first descent.

At higher altitudes, atmospheric pressure is lower than it is at sea level, therefore surfacing at the end of an altitude dive leads to an even greater reduction in pressure and thus causes an increased risk of decompression illness. Such dives are also typically carried out in freshwater at high altitudes, and fresh water has a lower density than the seawater used in the calculation of decompression tables. The amount of time the diver has spent at altitude is also of concern, as divers with gas loadings near those of sea level may also be at an increased risk.

Sam sat and simply looked at the lake around him.

Despite the cold, Lake Solitude glistened in the sun's rays. They had picked one of the few weeks of the year in which the lake's surface had thawed, presenting the pristine waters below its surface.

In the distance, the enormous mountain peak of Mount Oztal could be seen, followed by a steep row of thousands of giant pine trees. At this distance, they looked like blades of grass until they reached the banks of the lake. There, the lake's shallow edge was a soft turquoise, and the crystal clear water of the recently thawed ice allowed Sam to see the limestone bottom as easily as if he were looking through a window, but impossible to hazard a guess as to its depth. He was able to follow the lake's bottom for some distance before the sunlight failed to penetrate the extreme depths at the center of the lake.

It was here that Sam hoped that the Magdalena had come to rest, thus remaining hidden, for all these years.

"Of all the places we've seen since we came here Sam, this must be the most magical of them all." Tom said, reverently.

"That's for sure. It's magical enough that I'm worried someone else must have surely dived it before now. Heck, if I had known about this place, I'd have made a trip to dive here years ago. Let's just hope that it releases its secret—the final resting place of our missing airship."

"Agreed. There's just one way to find out."

They each wore an inch-thick dry suit, under which they wore a thick layer of thermal clothing and a woolen beanie. The water was going to be icy cold, and having already checked and rechecked the math of their decompression requirements at this altitude, hypothermia would be their greatest risk.

On their heads, each wore a Neptune Space Diver Mask with a push-to-talk communications system (PTT), double LED lighting, and a camera to record the trip.

Loading their equipment first, Sam and Tom climbed down into the inflatable Zodiac, in which they were able to motor to the middle of the lake. Where the lake turned from light green to an almost black aquamarine signified that they'd reached the deepest section of the lake. There, they ran a dive line to the bottom.

"Let's see how deep this thing goes . . ." Sam said, as he started to feed the dive wire.

"100 feet, and still running freely," Tom said a few minutes later.

"Keep her going until she reaches the bottom."

"150 feet, and still going."

"If our airship is sitting at the bottom, I can see why she remained hidden so long," Sam said. "Diving near ten thousand feet is one thing, diving to depths below 150 feet while at such altitudes, is another thing entirely for the recreational diver."

"Forget the recreational diver. I'm a professional, and I'm still not keen on it." The wire stopped running at 180 feet, and the line went slack. They had reached the bottom. Tom looked at Sam, and asked, "Shall we see what's at her bottom?"

"Let's."

They would do their deepest dive first. Besides, they both were eager to know whether or not their hunch was right, and the most likely answer to that question was waiting for them at the deepest part of the lake.

Sam placed the regulator in his mouth, checked that his buoyancy control device (BCD) was inflated, placed his right hand on his facemask, and rolled backwards off the zodiac.

He broke the still of the morning's water with a giant splash, the icy water sending lightning signals up his spine.

I don't care how beautiful it is, I hate altitude diving.

A moment later, Sam was floating on the surface of the lake. He placed his hand on his head, forming a simple symbol for the letter "O" which meant that all was okay.

Above him, in the Zodiac, he watched Tom respond, using the same symbol, before following him into the water.

Once the bubbles settled, he heard Tom's voice through the PTT device in his facemask.

"You didn't mention how fucking cold the water is!"

"I didn't think you'd follow me in if I did."

"Come on, let's start the descent." Tom said. "Hypothermia's going to be a bitch the longer we wait."

The two of them started to descend.

The clear water made it all but impossible to determine distances. Sam was always baffled when people would talk to him about how scary it was diving in murky water. When the water was crystal clear like this, your depth perception became so warped that it was easy to make the kind of mistakes that get you killed, either during a descent or ascent. For that reason, both men kept their depth gauges out in front as they made their descent.

Sam's eyes feasted on the surreal environment they had entered.

The limestone gave a distinct green glow through the water, as the sun's rays penetrated the surface above. Near the rock where their helicopter rested, Sam could see a series of tunnels, all of which were much too small for the Magdalena to have entered, but which caused a myriad of reflective displays as the light traveled through. He made a mental note to come back and explore them later, if given the chance to do so before they left.

At a depth of ten feet, he opened his jaw, subconsciously equalizing for the change in pressure, as he continued his descent.

The rocks to his side appeared to be perhaps twenty feet away, in the exceptionally clear water. As an experienced diver though, Sam knew from the position of the zodiac, that they were more like 500 feet away.

At a depth of fifty feet they passed the two large air tanks which were tied to the dive line at the 50 foot marker. These were emergency air supplies, just in case something went wrong on their ascent.

One hundred and eighty feet was well beyond the realm of a no-decompression dive. It meant that what would be a quick drop to the bottom, would require a much longer and slower ascent.

"We're just under a third of the way down," Sam said. "How are you feeling, Tom?"

"Cold. How about you?"

"I'm all right. If I'd known what you were dragging me into, I would have brought along my ice diving gear."

"If I'd realized what we were in for, I would have done the same thing too," Tom remarked.

"Did you see the caves near our rock?" Sam asked, as he pointed toward them.

"Yeah, they were probably formed by the avalanche all those years ago."

"Seems a likely explanation. If we get a chance, let's make a shallow dive there later today."

"Sounds good," Tom agreed.

Descending into the deepest section at the center of the lake, Sam noticed that the shape of the lake, as seen from the air, varied greatly in the central section, which dropped to 180 feet, whereas the depth of the rest of the lake was somewhere in the vicinity of 30 to 40 feet, and had a silty bottom. The central section appeared to be more like the tunnel of a giant earthworm, burrowing its way down to the center of the earth.

Sam turned on his powerful hand torch for a few minutes as he continued his descent, and shined it along the rock walls.

My God, we're in ancient lava tunnel!

The walls were shaped as an ancient sinkhole, formed in the soft limestone over a period of millions of years. It was almost entirely cylindrical, as though something had intentionally created it. At its widest point, it was no more than 150 feet across.

"Hey buddy," Sam could hear Tom's voice, "I don't know about you, but something about this hole makes me feel like we're caught somewhere between reruns of 'The Abyss' and 'Journey to the Center of the Earth.'"

"Or, 'The Silence of the Lambs'?"

"Yeah, that's seems more like it. It's giving me the creeps," Tom murmured.

"I wouldn't worry about it too much. It's no different than the thousands of other naturally occurring limestone tunnels found throughout the Dolomites," Sam said, looking down at his depth gauge and at the darkness below. "Besides, what sort of monster could be bothered living in such an inhospitable environment?"

They were approaching a depth of 100 feet.

Below them there was only complete darkness.

"In a tunnel this narrow, at least we'll find our answer at the bottom," he heard Tom say. "If her remains are at the bottom of this tunnel, there's no way we could possibly miss seeing her."

"That's what I was thinking," Sam concurred.

The water temperature was becoming noticeably colder, too.

He was startled when a large fish swept past his leg.

It was the first sign of underwater life he'd seen, just as he was beginning to believe that the lake was utterly devoid of life.

At first, there was a total scarcity of underwater life, but as they descended deeper, the presence of large eels, crustaceans, and other fish became apparent.

"What do you think that thing is?" It was Tom who first spotted it approach.

It was a large fish, with a strange, bioluminescent organ hanging from a rod which protruded from its forehead and dangled in front of its face. The creature looked made up, or more like the type of creature you might have expected to have evolved at the bottom of the ocean, certainly not in a lake more than ten thousand feet above sea level.

"A night-light fish?" Sam guessed, flippantly.

"Yeah, I wouldn't have thought that a fish would need a light in this lake. Even at 180 feet, some light should be able to penetrate to its bottom. I wonder if things change in the winter when the lake freezes over."

"Maybe . . . or perhaps there is a more substantial system of caves and tunnels elsewhere around here, which has created a unique environment for such a species of fish," Tom said.

"Okay, we're at 150 feet. If the Magdalena's here, we should be able to see her on the lake bottom soon."

Sam flicked on his powerful LED and pointed it towards the floor of the lake.

What looked back at him scared him more than any creature of the sea ever could.

Below him lay the wrecked remains of a B26 bomber, in almost pristine condition. A single crack in its fuselage, just large enough for a man to swim through, could be seen at its rear, but otherwise, the cold environment had preserved her in the same condition as the day she crashed.

Sam angled his torch toward the front of the aircraft until its light reached the cockpit window. He paused just long enough to see the eyes of its long dead pilot staring back at him.

Only, it wasn't a corpse.

It was alive.

And a second later, a light in the cockpit came on, followed by a second one.

Whatever they'd found, Sam knew that someone else had just beaten them to it.

CHAPTER 14

John Wolfgang didn't believe it when he received the report that Sam Reilly was still alive, and that now he and Tom Bower, of all people, were preparing to dive Lake Solitude. He was bewildered that the man had survived, not that he knew much about him. On the other hand, he had known almost immediately when he'd first met Tom Bower that he would be a hard man to deceive.

What were they trying to achieve?

John had understood, simply enough, that Sam had made the connection between the threat on his life, and his friend, Kevin Reed's discovery of the gold, followed by the subsequent unexplained death of Kevin and his wife, Sally, and that he had then come searching for the Magdalena. What puzzled John was what could have possibly made Sam start searching on the southern side of the Alps? Surely, he knew as well as anyone else, that an airship could never have cleared such high mountains.

Whatever their purpose, he was certain that they were on the wrong track. But even so, what could he do about it?

The solution presented itself to him.

But, was he over playing his new friendship?

John decided that the risk was worth it, and made the phone

call.

"What do you have for us?" It was the same cold voice of the woman who had spoken to him previously.

"I know exactly where they will be by tomorrow morning," he said.

"Good." The woman's voice maintained its air of superiority and hostility.

"But you will need to hurry to get a team in place," he continued.

Serendipity, so it would seem, had provided him with the perfect trap.

Of course he'd checked out Lake Solitude years ago. It was one of perhaps a dozen early choices years ago, back when he'd first started looking for the Magdalena in earnest.

That was where he'd discovered the downed B26 Bomber.

And, at that depth, Sam Reilly would be an easy target.

At first, Sam thought he was simply seeing the remains of the pilot.

Then, he saw the light turn on behind the remains . . .

Followed by a number of others.

"Where the hell did they come from?" He wondered, aloud. Something instinctively told him to switch off his LED.

"Beats the hell out of me," Tom said, following suit.

One after the other, he saw the divers emerge from the crack in the bomber's fuselage, and swim towards them.

There was nothing obviously menacing about them, but he knew for certain that something wasn't right.

"I don't think they're recreational divers on a holiday," Sam noted.

"Neither do I—let's get the hell out of here!"

The dark figures started swimming rapidly towards them.

Sam didn't wait to count them, but at a glance, he could tell there were at least eight of them. And there was something familiar about them, too.

Sam couldn't quite put his hand on it to begin with. But there was something about the way they moved in such perfect unison.

Had he seen their dry suits before?

Then he realized that he had indeed.

They're Navy SEALs.

"They're Navy SEALs, Tom. We're in worse trouble than I thought. These guys mean business," Sam said.

"I think you're right, Sam, and I'm not sure if these guys are still on our side."

Sam and Tom both started to kick their fins, and ascend.

Below them, their assailants were gaining on them.

The first one fired his harpoon—much larger and more deadly than a spear gun, capable of traveling the thirty or more feet that separated them.

Sam watched as it shot past him. The clear water making it difficult for the shooter to accurately judge the distance, he missed by several feet.

Next time, the man wouldn't be quite so careless taking aim.

A second SEAL then took aim, and his harpoon sliced rapidly through the clear water. This time, it just barely clipped the neoprene of Sam's dry suit near his elbow.

Narrowly missing the flesh of his arm.

The freezing cold water poured into the small opening, and it stung him almost as painfully as if he had been shot.

"Shit," Sam swore.

"You okay, Sam?"

"Yeah, it's just a scratch, but we won't be so lucky a third time. We're going to have to make a rapid no-decompression ascent. What do you think?"

"I think at 150 feet, we're very likely to get ourselves killed. But, if we stay here, we're going to end up dead anyway, so why not?"

"Good luck, Tom," Sam said as he pulled the emergency release on his weight belt.

Instantly, they started to rise toward the surface.

Sam just hoped that the minimal amount of time that they had spent making their descent would allow them to resurface without too much of a nitrogen build-up in their blood.

They were about to lose 5 atmospheres worth of pressure in under a minute.

Sam exhaled one gigantic breath during the entire ascent, as the air in his lungs expanded as the atmospheric pressure lessened.

The Navy Seals below were unable to follow, having been down much longer than Sam and Tom. The nitrogen in their bloodstreams would have built up to a greater degree, the longer they remained submerged. Consequently, they would be unable to follow Sam and Tom to the surface, without almost certainly, dying.

Soon, the SEALs were little more than dark shapes moving at the dark bottom of the lake.

Sam and Tom stopped their ascent at about six feet from the surface, just below their Zodiac.

"How you doing, Tom?" Sam asked.

"Yeah, I think okay. How about you?"

"I'm all right. I think we've escaped."

"We've certainly beaten those at the bottom, but an advanced mercenary team like them, must surely have a surface team," Sam said, and then went on to say, "That is, assuming that we're not dealing with one of our own teams."

The consequence of his last words echoed in his ears.

What if they are one of ours?

That thought and the possibility it might be the truth, scared the hell out of him.

"You're right, Sam. Maybe the surface team won't yet know what's happened below. Let's stay underwater until we reach the rock, and then let's hope we can take off before they know what's happened."

"Good idea, Tom."

"Sam?"

"Yes?"

"What did you mean by 'one of our own Navy SEAL teams'?" Tom asked.

"Well, we already know that there was something more valuable than gold aboard the Magdalena when she disappeared," Sam said. "Whatever it was, it's attracted a large assembly of treasure hunters, and they're willing to stop at nothing to obtain their prize."

"And you think that assembly might include members of our own government?"

"Yep, and I just wish I knew what that treasure actually is."

Two minutes later, Tom surfaced at the edge of the granite rock where his helicopter was still resting. He turned slowly, his eyes scanning a full 360 degrees, trying to get a complete view of their environment.

There was nothing to alert him of their danger.

No shouts or shots fired.

"We're good so far, Sam."

"Okay then, let's go."

They both quickly scrambled up the edge of the rock and climbed into the helicopter. Before Tom had even began to remove his dive equipment, he flicked the switches to begin the slow process of warming up the engine.

On the other side of the lake, something moved.

Before Tom could see make out what it was, he had lifted the helicopter into the air, and disappeared into the narrow Tyrol Valley below.

CHAPTER 15

Disappointment still shrouded Sam when he arrived back at the cabin.

Instead of finding the Magdalena, and the answer to a mystery that had already remained hidden for three quarters of a century, he had nearly lost his life, and found a whole set of new, unanswered questions.

How did they know he was still alive?

Who were they exactly?

Why would U.S. Navy SEALs be involved in this mess?

And, finally and most significantly: *What is it about the Magdalena that I don't know that makes her so damn important?*

Once he entered the cabin, Sam checked his cell.

There was a message from her. It was the only good news he'd heard today.

The text message read,

> I'M FREE TOMORROW. WANT TO SEE THE ALPS FROM A DIFFERENT PERSPECTIVE?

The sudden increase in his heart rate told him that he did.

Sam immediately hit the call-back number.

"Hi, Aliana."

"Sam, is that you?" Aliana asked, in her distinctive voice.

"Yes. So, you decided to stick around a little longer?"

"I thought I might stay for the weekend."

"I'm glad," Sam said, and he meant it too.

"Are you going to be free?"

"Yeah, my work here seems to have reached a dead end."

"Then, do you want to see the Alps my way?" Aliana repeated.

"Okay, that could be just what I need. What did you have in mind?"

"I'll tell you when you get here. Can you meet me at the hotel where I've been staying? Say, at about eight o-clock tomorrow morning?"

"Sure, what should I bring with me?" Sam asked.

"Just wear some comfortable clothes. I've got everything else you'll need."

"Okay then, I'll see you at eight." Sam said, and ended the call.

The grin came over his face, like a child at Disneyland—relentless and uncontrollable.

He'd had a number of women interested him over the years. He was young, healthy, and had the physique of a man who spent his life outdoors—and, of course, he was rich, although he took great pains to ensure that few people realized the immensity of his fortune.

Tom was probably the only person who knew him well enough to understand that he'd only dated a few of those women and none of them had held his interest or lived up to his expectations.

Aliana was different.

She was both stunningly beautiful, and in possession of a mind sharper than that of any other woman he had known—and the people he often worked with were genuinely very bright. They were specialists in their own fields, but she was smarter than any one of them. She had a love of the outdoors which matched his own, and the tenacity to see it all, in its glorious wonder.

Aliana was a mischievous, playful, and captivating creature—and she had decided that she wanted to spend the weekend with him.

As far as Sam was concerned, the Magdalena could just as well stay lost forever. He had discovered something far more exquisite than a seventy-five year old mystery. He had found Aliana and she wanted to spend a few days with him.

His heart kicked up. Did that mean night's too? *It will if I have anything to say about it.*

Tom looked over at him, and asked, with a note of sarcasm, "So, I take it I can go to Paris for the weekend? And we'll both return to the task at hand on Monday, both feeling a little fresher?" Tom studied the besotted expression on Sam's face, and added, "Well, maybe not fresher, but at least your mind will have been cleared from our current predicament."

"That sounds like a good idea to me," Sam replied. "You sure you don't mind that I didn't invite you along?"

"Not at all. Besides, the last thing I want to do is stare at these damn mountains. Anyway, I'm keen on going snowboarding with some friends."

Sam watched from the ground as Tom pulled the collective on

his 44, and eased the helicopter back into the sky above, after dropping him off. As Tom rotated the helicopter so that he again faced Sam, he gave him one last smile, which said, *have a great weekend*, and then he flew off.

Sam looked at his watch.

It was only 0740, but he still had a five minute walk down the rickety stone road which led to the only accommodations at Tyrol. He walked into The Summit, the B&B where Aliana was staying.

He took a seat in the foyer, and casually picked up a magazine advertising an article bearing the headline, "Europe's Best Walks Above 4000 feet." He started to flick through its pages without paying much attention.

From where he sat, Sam could see a large, thick, glass window that allowed a stunning vista of the valley below, and the mountains towering high above. It was difficult to discern the height of those mountains; their distance was capable of tricking the mind into thinking they were higher than they actually were. Over the past few weeks, he had flown over all of them. He knew exactly just how high those mountains were.

A blonde-haired gentleman behind the reservations desk approached Sam, and asked, "Can I help you?"

The man, like so many Europeans, spoke perfect English, but his German accent was so thick that it was hard to distinguish whether or not what he was speaking English or German. Sam recognized his voice and realized that this was the same man he'd spoken to on the phone about his friend, Kevin Reed.

His name tag simply read, 'Carl.'

Sam wondered if this man knew anything about the deaths of his friend and his wife. More importantly, would he make the connection between him and his murdered friends? He dismissed the idea as unlikely, given how many tourists from around the world must visit here in a single year.

"Guten morgen," Sam said, using the only polite German phrase he knew. Then, in English, he added, "I am meeting a friend here, a Miss . . ." he paused, realizing that he still didn't know her surname, and then said, "Aliana."

"Ah, very good," Carl replied, now looking slightly uncomfortable, before quickly hiding his discomfort, and asked, "May I get you a drink while you wait, sir?"

Sam watched Carl's response carefully.

Did Carl's eyes just show a glimpse of understanding when I said Aliana's name?

It was not a look of understanding that one man might give another when he noted that you had an attractive girlfriend, or even a look of jealousy. No, instead, it was more a look that indicated the realization that Carl had also been waiting to meet this same person.

"Sure. A soda. Any kind, please."

Carl nodded his head and left.

Aliana then walked into the foyer, and Sam stood up to greet her.

Despite the cold air, she was wearing a white climbing tank top, and purple three-quarter length, Lycra climbing pants. European women, he'd discovered, never seemed to feel the cold. Her blonde hair was neatly arranged in an intricate braid, and she wore a mischievous smile that he would never tire of.

She was just as lovely as he remembered.

"Good morning, Sam. I see that you made it?"

She kissed him on both cheeks, a very European custom.

Her lips were full, soft and beautiful.

"Of course, did you doubt that I would?" Sam asked.

"I wasn't sure what I thought you would do."

"Do you want to grab a drink while we're still here?"

"No, but I know this great coffee place, built into the side of a cliff, it's down the road." Aliana said. "They have built a cantilever deck over the side of the mountain, so you can see all the way down—I don't know, perhaps 3000 feet."

"Sounds great," Sam replied.

Carl returned with Sam's drink, a pink soda, and asked if the lady would also like a drink. Sam paid him, and politely told him that they were a little pressed for time, and so they were leaving.

Aliana led the way outside.

The paths were narrow. While they might be large enough for a motorbike, they were not quite wide enough to accommodate a car. Sam was surprised to see a small Fiat parked out in front of The Summit with several inches of snow over its window. He would have liked to know how long it had been there, and how anyone had managed to get it there.

They walked down the winding path for about fifteen minutes, until they reached something resembling a small road.

A restored 1965 Cobra V12, American muscle car, was carelessly parked next to the vertical cliff, and on the narrow road, which lazily followed the Tyrol River along the valley floor. Anyone trying to get around it would have had to take the trouble of placing their side wheels on the uneven edge of the road and its lethal drop. Although not very high, the short fall from the cliff to the river below would leave the occupants submerged in its deep, fast-flowing, icy waters.

Sam hated alpine roads, and their European drivers.

"This is my ride," Aliana said.

"You rented this?"

"No, it's one of my Dad's. I borrowed it for the weekend."

Sam looked at her, impressed.

Sam had figured that her family wasn't short of cash. After all, no one goes to MIT, overseas student or not, unless they have a lot of money, or receive a scholarship because they're incredibly intelligent. In Aliana's case, he gathered that she was both.

How ironic, he thought, as he looked at the beautifully restored antique car, that he should find someone with a similarly endless bank account?

He removed the small back-pack he was wearing, opened the car door and sat down on the passenger's side of the two seat sports convertible.

Aliana inserted the key and turned on the ignition. It started immediately.

Sam could feel the powerful 6.4L engine enticing the driver to let go of the reins.

Aliana released the clutch, and started driving down the road. It hugged the winding road beautifully, as she carelessly made their way south, towards Italy.

"So, where are you taking me for the weekend?" he asked.

"It's a surprise." Again, her mischievous smile owned him. "You'll see soon enough."

"Okay, do I at least get a hint?"

"No."

"Okay then, so tell me what brought you to Europe?" Sam asked. "I thought you were heading back stateside to complete your PhD?"

"I was." She downshifted as they reached a sharp corner and

approached the start of a large hill. "But I was worried about my dad. He's been under a lot of pressure with work lately, and he sounded pretty stressed. Since my mother's no longer around, and I'm an only child, I kind of feel obligated to come and check up on him."

Once they'd cleared the sharp turn, Sam felt himself pushed back into his seat as she floored the accelerator on the straight, and the powerful 6.4 L engine kicked into the life it was built for.

Sam felt nervous at such speeds next to the cliffs, but Aliana appeared to be adeptly controlling the powerful machine, apparently ignorant of any danger that the narrow road and cliff sides presented.

"And, was he okay?" Sam forced himself to return to the conversation.

"Yeah, he's struggling, though. I know he's got problems, but he won't speak to me about them. I know that something is worrying him. He's a strong man, but I sometimes wish he wouldn't keep all his problems to himself."

Sam noticed that for some reason, her facial expression did not match her words.

"I know the type," Sam commiserated, and he did, thinking of his own father.

"Although my dad didn't say it . . ." Aliana began and paused, "I think he was glad that I made the effort to come here, even if only for a few days."

He nodded his head in agreement, certain that any father would be pleased to see his daughter, especially if that daughter was Aliana.

They came to the crest of a hill.

Sam could see miles of curves winding down the mountain

pass.

None of them with guardrails.

Aliana sped up as though she could sense his fear, "This is the famous Timmelsjoch Pass," she laughed at his obvious discomfiture. "Do you know it has been the background of a number of car ads over the years? We're now entering Italy."

He ignored the road, trusting in fate, and wondered just how much Aliana was enjoying scaring the daylights out of him, and wondering just how safe they actually were. She'd obviously driven these roads many times before.

Instead, he looked out at the Dolomite Mountains ahead, and said, "It's really beautiful here."

She smiled at him, in such a way that he began to wonder just where she was taking him, and then said, "Just you wait."

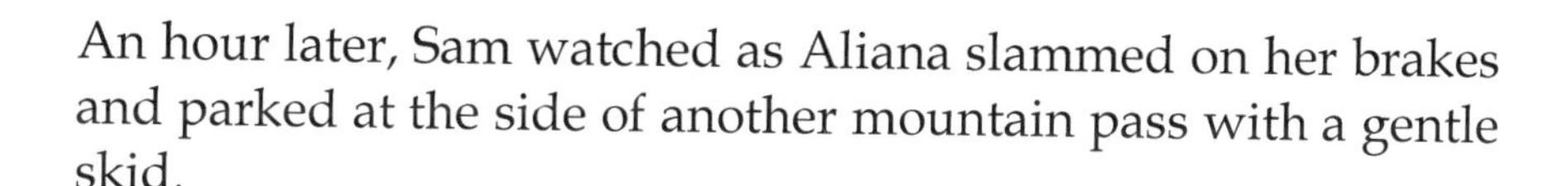

An hour later, Sam watched as Aliana slammed on her brakes and parked at the side of another mountain pass with a gentle skid.

It was halfway up a large mountain. A number of cars had parked in the small rocky outcropping at the side of the road, in the typical Italian fashion with no discernible method, yet their arrangement was a perfectly harmonized disorganization. It was as though they had been strewn there, like the toss of a several pairs of dice. Sam noticed three men who were organizing their climbing equipment on the hood of their red Fiat.

In the distance, the mountains seemed to stretch high up into the sky, with just a hint of white snow cover at their peaks.

"We're here," she said.

Sam looked at the mountain peaks around them and then turned his eyes back to her.

"That's great, where's here?" he asked.

She opened the small trunk and took out two large back packs. She handed him the first one, and took the second one for herself and then said, "The Dolomites, of course." With a grin, she carelessly added, "Somewhere . . ."

Sam drew the backpack over his shoulders, tightening its straps until the weight was comfortably distributed over his hips, chest and shoulders.

It was quite heavy.

He wondered how much heavier his backpack was compared to hers.

"Okay, I'm ready," Sam said. "Now where?"

"Follow me."

He watched as Aliana didn't quite skip down the dangerous path that hugged the side of the mountain precariously, but neither did she walk carefully either. Her stride was more of a halfhearted tramp than anything else.

She wore Merrel Perimeter, Gore-Tex hiking boots.

Watching as she casually placed her feet along the narrow path without any hesitation, Sam could tell that she was no novice, and had spent many hours in these mountains during her lifetime.

Ahead there was a little wooden arrow bearing the words, "Best Coffee above 5000 Feet."

They followed the signs until the path reached a sudden end. There were no more paths to follow, nor was there any notice posted that the path ended in a 5000-odd, foot drop.

He looked at Aliana and asked, "Now where?"

"Now, we go up."

Sam leaned carefully over the edge.

There was a sheer drop off that certainly appeared to be in the vicinity of the suggested 5000 feet, and apparently, it was a similar distance going uphill.

He noticed that alongside the cliff there was an old, metal ladder which had been bolted into the side of the mountain. It's slightly rusty, weathered appearance made it look as though the years of dilapidation was still trying to remove it from the rock wall.

"We're climbing up that?" Sam asked, incredulously.

"Yes, why, don't you like heights?"

Sam didn't fear heights, however he wasn't keen on taking needless risks with his life either.

"Ladies first."

Aliana opened her backpack and withdrew a climbing harness, a "Y" shaped lanyard with two carabiners, marked with the letter "K," indicating the German spelling.

"You have a climbing kit too," she told Sam, as she opened the top of his bag, if you care to use it.

She fitted her safety equipment, and then made sure that Sam was okay with his. He had gone through a small mountaineering phase in his younger days, trying to challenge himself, but he'd never developed any great love of heights. He possessed a good understanding of his equipment and how to use it, but he wasn't going to let her know that.

Besides, it was nice to watch her take care of him.

He could see her concern as she checked over him and his climbing gear.

"Now, we climb," she said.

"Okay."

"Don't take too long," she told him, as she reached the first rung of the ladder and started to make her way up.

Sam shook his head at her and then, just like all men when they are around a beautiful woman, he followed her up, despite his reservations.

The ladder appeared to be about forty feet long, and just before the top rung, he was relieved to see that Aliana climbed into a small opening in the side of the shale mountain.

Inside it, was a café.

They placed their orders and she took a seat on the counterweight iron ledge.

Sipping his perfectly prepared Italian macchiato, he stared in wonderment at the brilliant vista ahead. He'd flown over these mountains more than a dozen times over the past two weeks, but had never really taken the time to fully appreciate its magnificence.

It was beautiful.

Only in Europe, could you possibly find a professional barista willing to work inside a manmade cave located on the inside of a sheer cliff face!

He took a sip of the strong drink, looked at the face of the angel—or possibly devil, in front of him, and decided that he was in for a fantastic weekend.

Blake answered his cell.

He was still driving through the Alps, but like every other place on earth, he still couldn't escape from the ubiquitous phone coverage. "Yes?"

"Have you arrived?" The voice on the line was cold.

"Not yet, but one of my men has already made contact with them."

"Them? Who else is with him?" The voice became even colder and harder.

"He didn't say," Blake replied, as he drove around the corner and started up the enormous hill, pushing his right foot to the floor of his BMW M5. "Some girl. She's probably some European backpacker he picked up since he's been over here."

"You should have gone there sooner," the man remonstrated.

"Yes, well, we were waiting to see how far he got, weren't we?" It was a weak excuse, Blake realized, even as he gave it.

"And, now you know . . ." the voice remained cold.

"Yes, well, we really didn't have any reason to suspect that he knew any more than what he told me to begin with."

"Just make certain that he never gets there, all right?"

"Of course, I'll fix it. I said I would."

CHAPTER 16

Aliana watched as Sam looked out upon it all.

The steel cable ran from off the cafe's metal decking. The 220 foot cable spanned the distance from the café, to where it was attached to the wall of Mount Oztal, across the valley. The Tyrol River could be seen, lazily making its way along the valley floor.

About five thousand feet below.

The wire bridge allowed climbers easy access to the entrance of the Dolomite National Park. Like a giant game of snakes and ladders, it was the common starting point to a myriad of different climbs, all of which were part of the famous Via Ferrata.

Sam's blue eyes were full of wonder and Aliana sensed that there was something else there too, something which she couldn't quite make out—*was it fear and uncertainty, or was it something else entirely?*

"What do you think, Sam?" she asked.

"You're taking me along the Via Ferrata?"

"Yes, the Iron Road, but the Germans call it the Klettersteig." Again, her mischievous smile captivated him. "The guidebook says it takes two days, but we have three, just in case you're slow."

"It's an amazing piece of engineering, "Sam said, as his hand pulled on the steel cable for reassurance.

"It's a monument to the human initiative for adventure, but did you know that the first Via Ferrata was built in the early nineteenth century as a means of crossing these giant mountains?" She waited for Sam to acknowledge his wonderment that someone would have built such a marvel all those years ago, and then she continued, "At the start of the First World War, Austria secretly built a Via Ferrata in order to move 40,000 soldiers across the border in record-breaking time, to seize the initiative. It became the front line of the war."

"No, I didn't know that," Sam replied. "I can also gather too, that they didn't have the luxury of such safety equipment as this," he continued, pulling at his lanyard and harness.

"We'll be doing it in veritable luxury, as you say; it will be easy." She wasn't sure if Sam was just trying to reassure himself.

She then gave him a very basic run down of the process of climbing a Via Ferrata.

"The essence of a modern Via Ferrata is a steel cable which runs along the route and is periodically affixed to the rock at three- to five-foot intervals. Using a Via Ferrata kit, climbers can secure themselves to the cable, limiting their chance of falling. The cable can also be used as an aid to climbing, and additional climbing aids, like iron rungs, called stemples, pegs, carved steps, and even ladders and bridges are often provided. Thus, the Via Ferrata permits routes which would otherwise be hazardous to be undertaken without the need for heavy climbing equipment."

She watched as Sam nodded his head in understanding.

"I've read about them."

Aliana continued, "A Via Ferrata set is comprised of a

lanyard and two carabiners. The lanyard consists of an energy-absorbing system, such as this, and two arms which connect to the cable with the carabiners, and a means of connecting to the harness."

She then showed him how to clip onto the steel cable.

"You'll see that these carabiners are made specifically for use on Via Ferratas. Their design creates a larger-than-average opening, and they have a spring-locking mechanism that can be opened with one hand. They are also strong enough to withstand high fall factors. These carabiners are marked with a "K" in a circle, which stands for Klettersteig, the German term for Via Ferrata."

Aliana watched as Sam played with the mechanism.

Sam's intelligent mind took in the practical steps in using them, and the physics behind their simple mechanisms.

She could tell that, for someone like him, it was all easy to understand.

"So, it uses a spring-loaded sleeve on the carabiner gate?" He asked, pressing it with one hand. "While the gate is closed, the sleeve is held in place over the gate opening by its spring; to unlock and open the gate, the sleeve slides directly down the gate shaft away from the opening?"

"Yes."

"Anything else I need to know?"

"Probably, but we'll talk about it when you come across it."

Aliana watched as Sam confidently clipped himself in, tentatively looked down at the river which looked tiny from this height, then looked back at her, as if he were sizing up whether or not she was worth the effort.

He then gave her a defiant smile.

The small dimple that appeared on his left cheek when he

smiled, reminded her how often he looked just like that.

"So, I'll see you on the other side?" Sam said as he began to make his way across the traverse.

Sam carefully made his way across the 220 foot cable bridge.

It used three cables to form the bridge. One at the bottom to walk along, foot in front of foot, and two at his shoulder height which formed an imaginary triangle.

It was good, he decided, to allow him to settle in his own way. He had always been afraid of heights, and had taken great pains to attempt mountain climbing as a means of overcoming his fear. Somehow, it didn't matter what challenge he completed, he would always feel some degree of trepidation, above and beyond his basic survival instincts when it came to heights. All it had taught him, was how to push past his fears and complete the task at hand. It was all about learning how to fake it.

Although one might never completely allay an irrational fear, you could instill an ability to control it. Long before he ever joined the Corps, Sam discovered that skill. Life experience and its vicissitudes taught him to use his fear to heighten his awareness and narrow his focus on the task at hand, without permitting his fear to deter him from what he needed to accomplish.

After thirty one years of faking it, he'd learned to be very convincing, even to himself, at times.

He was waiting for Aliana on the far side of the bridge.

Sam glanced around at the walls of metamorphic rock, of which the Dolomites were predominantly composed. Fossils of ancient marine life could still be seen, embedded in the rock wall, the shells of long-extinct sea life formed the basis of the limestone, which, after many millennia of heat and pressure, had eventually metamorphosed into the shales, slates gneiss and schists comprising these mountains.

A horizontal set of iron steps ran along the mountain, as though someone had built a little pathway, high up in the mountain, but had neglected to complete it with railings. There were a multitude of ladders, iron chains, and rocky steps, which could be accessed along the way.

He wondered, which of these routes Aliana would take him on today.

Looking back at the bridge, he noticed that she walked along it as though she was on a simple footpath and nothing more.

"What direction are we going?" Sam asked, looking at the two paths which followed around the mountain.

"Now, we start going up." Aliana pointed ahead at the third set of ladders, and said, "That one, over there."

He followed her to the base of those ladders, where an iron sign, bolted into the rock face, read, "Via Capilano Con Grande.

"Are you ready for a workout?" she asked.

"You set the pace and I'll follow," he said, with a confidence that he was already starting to doubt. Sam calculated that he must be close to twice her weight. Although his physique was built of solid muscle, he knew that she was extremely athletic, and that her slim frame disguised the wiry muscles of a mountain climber.

They started to climb.

It was an almost entirely vertical climb for a while, followed later by a more diagonal approach across the mountain face. It took them all day to make their ascent.

By early afternoon, they finally reached the peak of the first mountain, which was the smallest of the four peaks they planned to traverse as part of this trip.

Each time Sam thought he was finally getting somewhere, he'd clip his carabiner into a new run, which extended further up the mountain. His thighs burned from the workout. As with rock climbing, his leg muscles bore the majority of the effort, rather than his arms.

Every time he saw Aliana slow down at a particularly difficult or technical section, he would begin to gain on her, but then she would pass it, and get ahead of him again, as if she was a mythical water nymph, acting like a mirage.

She was incredibly strong, he noticed, for someone with such a slim frame. Beneath which, he'd come to realize was an athletic, wiry machine, developed from a childhood spent climbing and exploring these very mountains.

By late that afternoon, the two of them reached the pinnacle of the smallest of the four mountains. At a height of 7,000 feet, its status as the smallest of the four mountains seemed irrelevant. Of the four, it was the only one which allowed a clear view of the entire Tyrol River, running between the mountains.

The panorama was stunningly beautiful.

"I was beginning to worry you would never make it!" Aliana said good naturedly.

"Yes, well . . . I was starting to doubt that you had any desire to allow me to make it to the top alive."

"Do you drink beer?"

"Yes. It would be a great place to have one now, if we had any with us." He then saw the expression on her face, and said, "There's no way that you bothered to carry beer along all this way, is there?"

"No," she laughed. "Of course not. I would never be so careless with the expenditure of my energy on a climb such as this."

"I'll buy you one when we get back," Sam offered.

"There's no need," she said, grinning, "You did!"

He laughed, as he opened his backpack and found a six pack of German beer.

"You've got to be kidding me! You mean I lugged this all the way up here?! You're terrible, Aliana.

"Am I? Really?" She looked so innocent, that it made him laugh again.

"No," he conceded, you're not," he told her as he came closer.

He took her small, but strong hands in his, and sheepishly looked into her pale blue eyes, which were the color of a clear sky in summer.

"Then what am I?" she teased.

"You're the most extraordinary and beautiful woman I've ever met."

He leaned closer to her, and to his delight, she kissed his lips.

There was nothing for it, he was in love. She was the girl he had wanted all his life. Of that he had no doubt. The only thing that he couldn't work out, was why someone as exceptional as her, would be interested in him too.

Back at his log cabin, where his satellite phone had been carelessly left with the rest of his equipment, glowed as it indicated that a new text message was received.

It read,

> SON, COULDN'T FIND MUCH ON WOLFGANG, BUT I DISCOVERED THAT JOHN WOLFGANG HAS A DAUGHTER WHO OFTEN TRAVELS WITH HIM, HER NAME IS, ALIANA. BE CAREFUL, THE MOST BEAUTIFUL WOMAN ARE OFTEN THE MOST DANGEROUS.

CHAPTER 17

The next morning, Sam woke up early. Much before the sun had risen.

Next to him, her carabiner still clipped into a bolt in the rock wall, slept Aliana. About five feet past her was a ledge, beyond which was a drop-off nearly 9,500 feet down to the river below.

His hand reached out instinctively to the wall for support. It was unwarranted, of course, since his own carabiner was still attached to the same bolt as was Aliana's.

She looked just as beautiful sleeping, as she did when awake, he decided, as the water started to boil. Sam then tossed a packet of dehydrated soup into the bowl, just in time for breakfast.

"Good morning," Sam murmured, as he softly nudged the nape of her neck with his lips.

Aliana's eyes opened slowly, and as they displayed recognition, her arms reached around his neck and pulled him towards her and kissed him.

"Good morning, you."

His lips responded eagerly to her kiss.

When it ended, Sam asked, "What's the plan for today?"

"Do you remember the four peaks we saw in the distance when we first started our climb, yesterday?"

"Yes, we've already climbed two of them. My thighs haven't let me forget it."

"Right," Aliana said, taking the small cup of warm soup into her hand. "So, we climbed the two peaks, progressively getting higher, yesterday. Now, we're going to climb the next two. That's, if you're up to it, of course?" Her tone of voice implied that all four peaks were of equal height, when in fact, they had climbed a total of 3,000 feet yesterday, but today they would be climbing more like 5,000 feet.

She's got to be kidding me.

"Sure, I'm game. I'll just follow you." Sam wasn't about to let her beat him.

"Good," She said, taking another sip of soup. It was basic, but provided a certain warmth that helped heal a person at 7,000 feet. "Thanks for breakfast."

Twenty minutes later, Sam and Aliana commenced climbing the next section of the Via Farrata.

Sam followed Aliana along the first Via Farrata of the day, which involved a number of stemples which followed the natural fault in the mountain in an upward spiral, like a giant circular staircase. It wasn't a very hard, by comparison to the previous day.

It took an hour before they reached the top, where Sam rested by leaning forward and supporting himself on one arm, like a tripod, for a few minutes, trying to catch his breath.

Clipping her carabiner into the start of the next Via Farrata, Aliana calmly asked, "Are you all right to go again?"

Her voice sounded natural, as though her lungs weren't at all strained by the climb. Naturally, she was fitter than him, despite his physically arduous lifestyle.

"Of course, lead on," Sam replied.

He read the sign attached to the wire into which he clipped his carabiner. It read, "Ladder De Grande," and above it was a steel ladder, bolted in the rock wall, for almost a 1,000 foot vertical climb.

I'm sure this will be fun.

Above him, Sam could see the finely defined muscles of Aliana's long legs, right up to her butt, as she all but danced her way up the never-ending, pernicious, ladder.

It was just enough motivation to keep him going.

Unfortunately, she was climbing faster than him and, as time went on, she outpaced him by an ever-increasing distance. He found himself struggling to keep up with her, which frustrated him, and caused him to take longer steps and to skip some of the rungs on the ladder.

And then his foot missed one.

Or, so he thought.

In actual fact, Sam had planted his foot squarely on the rung, but it had given way under his weight, causing him to fall.

The carabiner, which he'd attached to the V-rope, slid down along the wire as Sam fell, until it reached a bolt, on which it should have caught and held. The end of the wire, just like the ladder rung before it, also gave way, as though it had never been there to begin with and he continued to fall.

In that split second, Sam was certain he was going to die, as he fell from the wall from which he hung suspended over more than 6,500 feet of nothingness.

And then, his downward slide came to an abrupt halt.

Sam's V-rope had somehow snagged on an old, dilapidated

stemple, ending his downward movement with a harsh jolt. Then, before the rope had a chance to slide off the iron stemple, Sam reached up and grabbed hold of the steel ladder once more.

Quickly, he reached for his second V-rope, and this time he clipped his carabiner into one of the rungs on the ladder.

Above him, he could see that Aliana had only just noticed his absence.

"Holy shit, are you all right?"

"Yeah, I think I'll be fine," he said, starting to climb once again.

"Are you sure?" Aliana sounded concerned as she started to climb down toward him.

"I'll be fine. My pride might be just a little damaged, that's all," Sam admitted. Then, noticing that she was on her way back down to meet him, he said, "Just wait there, part of the ladder's broken. I don't want you to fall too."

"I'm coming down to meet you, Sam. It will take more than a dilapidated ladder to make me fall."

"Be careful," he warned.

Sam stopped when he reached the point at which the bolt should have stopped his carabiner from sliding through. Upon close examination, it appeared that a steel bolt had once been there, but now it had been cut clean off.

Although he had only a very limited experience in rock climbing, and none of that experience on the Via Farrata, it looked to him as though someone had sawed off the end of the bolt. And it appeared to have been done recently, too . . . there was no rust evident on the raw cut.

Am I just being paranoia?

Could the fast slide of my carabiner, as I fell have produced enough force to slice clean through the bolt?

Sam examined his carabiner, and it was completely unmarked and unharmed.

It might be nothing, or it might be something.

He then continued to climb until he reached the missing rung of the ladder, the spot at which his fall began.

On both sides of that particular rung, where it had once been welded to the steel sides of the ladder, Sam could see a clear marking of where someone had intentionally hacked away at the connection with a metal saw. At first, he thought he might have been imagining it, but then he noticed something else.

There were small specks of metal on the rung below—iron filings.

The sort you'd expect to find after someone deliberately sawed through the steel.

Who just tried to kill me?

Or was Aliana their intended victim?

Despite the warm summer air, the thought sent a cold chill down his spine.

Aliana carefully climbed backwards down the steel ladder.

Below her, she could see that Sam had stopped, and that he was examining the steel ladder rung. Something about his facial expression worried her.

Then, she watched him run his hand along the intact rung immediately below it, and then bring it up close to his face, studying it carefully.

Sam looked directly up at her.

It was the piercing look in his eyes, which removed all

doubt.

Shit! He knows the truth!

Aliana wasn't sure what her next course of action should be. Her father had been explicit when he told her what needed to be done, but had never explained how it was going to happen. And she certainly hadn't expected it so soon.

Aliana had agreed to help her father. She even knew that she would enjoy the task, but at no point, had she expected to fall for Sam.

Only just today, Aliana had found herself contemplating how she would find another way to solve the problem, without killing him. She'd even found herself grateful that her father hadn't known where she was going, but the instant Aliana witnessed Sam's fall, she knew with certainty that her father had caught up with her.

Now, what options were still available to her?

She gave serious consideration to continuing up the mountain, and leaving Sam behind and below her. Aliana even considered how much faster she could climb than him. Would it even be possible for her to outrun him?

It was Sam's next statement that made her realize that she could never do that to him.

"Aliana! Wait there." She could see him, frantically waving his hand at her. "Stop! I believe you're in danger. Someone has made an attempt on your life!"

She looked down at him, but said nothing.

After everything that's happened, he's most concerned about my life?

It filled her heart with guilt at her betrayal, and then she recalled what her father had told her, and she stilled her nerves to continue with her initial resolution—in all wars, good men, must pay the price of future generations.

Stepping an additional four rungs down the ladder, Aliana stopped her descent, and then said, "There's no way anyone could have known that we would be here today, Sam. That rung must have been damaged by the ice last winter."

Below her, Sam shook his head.

"There's no way that this damage occurred naturally."

"Really? How can you be so certain?"

"Look here. These are iron filings. The kind you would expect to see after someone intentionally cut through the rungs with a saw," Sam said. "But I haven't a clue how anyone could have known I was going to be here today."

They couldn't have. I'm the only person who knew you would be here today . . .

She was just about to change her direction and make her way back up the ladder.

Still undecided, she looked up at the ladder above.

There, a man could be seen, approaching with German efficiency. Aliana recognized him instantly as the solidly built blonde man from The Summit, the bed and breakfast where she'd been staying. His name was Carl.

She recalled thinking that he seemed out of place at the time. He'd told her that he was a rock climber. In her opinion, he had the more solid physique of a member of Germany's Military Elite GSG9 Unit, rather than the lithe muscles of a mountain climber.

Does he work for my father, or is he one of the others who were hunting for the Magdalena?

Aliana couldn't readily answer the question, and her life depended on getting it right.

Of the two men on the Via Farrata with her, there was only one whom she was certain she could place her trust. The man, despite never mentioning it, was after the Magdalena, of that Aliana was certain. But not for the reason that her father had told her.

Of that, she was certain.

For what reason would her father have lied to her? She didn't have an answer to that, her only chance now, was to trust her instincts. And they told her that Sam Reilly might be her only hope of survival.

Sam watched Aliana above him.

Her face looked torn, as though she had just witnessed a horrific accident, and knew that a decision needed to be made about what to do now, but remained motionless, and unable to make it happen.

She'd stopped again, and was looking up. He wondered what she could possibly have to do with the attempt on his life, and then dismissed the idea as impossible, soon after it crossed his mind.

In truth, he knew very little about her, but his years as a leader had taught him a lot about reading people. Sam was certain that whatever secret intentions Aliana had for bringing him up this mountain, murder was not one of them.

"We have to go right now!" Aliana said, as she started to move down the ladder toward him at a much faster pace than she'd used previously.

"Why, what's happened?"

"Look up there, Sam. It's the guy from The Summit," she told him. "I knew when we met him that there was something about him I didn't trust."

Above them both, the large man from the bed and breakfast was continuing to climb down. He was still a fair distance away, but Sam could see that in his urgency to reach them, the man hadn't bothered to clip his own carabiner into the running line.

It all seemed like too much of a coincidence.

The man had clearly just been starting his day at the bed and breakfast yesterday morning. Even the most expert of climbers couldn't possibly have caught up with them so quickly. Sam was positive that he'd noticed some sort of recognition dawning in the man's face when he'd mentioned Aliana's name.

How had he caught up with them?

Then, Sam realized that the man must have followed them when they left the B&B, and then made his way past them when they'd stopped to enjoy their macchiato yesterday.

Aliana then grabbed hold of Sam and kissed him.

"Thank God you're alive!" she said, with tears in her eyes. "We've got to go."

"You're absolutely right, but go where?"

"I have no idea yet. Let's just start making our way down the mountain, until we can find a place to traverse, and then get up above him."

"Agreed—I don't like the idea of someone looming above me who wants to see me dead," Sam said, as he started to climb downward.

Sam and Aliana had both climbed down the ladder a distance of about three hundred feet, until they reached a ledge. In that time, the man above them had significantly decreased the gap between himself and the two of them. He still hadn't said so much as a single word to them, but his machine-like approach could hardly be considered as anything but sinister.

Sam looked at the ledge in both directions.

"Do you have any plans or idea as to where we go from here?" He asked.

"No, I don't know this route very well. Let's see if we can follow this one until we find another Via Farrata that takes us upwards from here. We just need to get to a position above that man. I don't think he's got a weapon or anything," Aliana added.

"Why not?" Sam asked, moving as fast as he could along the ledge without falling. He was moving much faster than his nerves would ordinarily allow.

"Because otherwise he would have used it already, wouldn't he?"

Sam wasn't completely convinced by her logic, but he agreed that their priority was to get to a position above the man.

He cursed himself for his own stupidity in not bringing along a weapon, especially after the attempt on his life at the bottom of Lake Solitude. Sam had hoped that whoever had attempted to kill him down there, had done so in an attempt to protect whatever secrets the lake held, and not because they were specifically trying to kill him.

Like all fools, he had convinced himself that he would be safe, because whoever they were, they didn't know who he was or where he'd gone. He'd hoped that they were simply trying to protect their own interests, and hadn't yet discovered that it was him.

And he'd been wrong.

Taking a quick look behind himself, Sam could see that on

the flat ground of the ledge they'd neither lost nor gained ground on their opponent.

When he again turned his head, he was horrified to discover that the ledge had ceased to exist.

"Now what do we do?" Aliana asked.

"What about that?"

Above them was another set of stemples, old and rusty, leading upwards, and along in the other direction up the mountain. He could just make out where the top of it met up with a more recent, modern path.

Aliana's pupils dilated at the suggestion.

"That looks like it hasn't been used in a half a century!" Aliana exclaimed.

Sam grabbed one with his hand, and pulled on it with all his might. "I don't care how long it's been here. We're all out of options. I just hope it holds."

"I don't know how secure those stemples are."

"Neither do I, but would you rather wait and see what our friend wants with us?"

"No."

Acknowledging the danger they were in, Aliana started to climb. Without a running line to clip into, she was at the mercy of the bolts which she climbed. A single misstep here would mean certain death.

Fortunately, she was athletic, and had told him that she used to do this during her holidays as a child, and maintained a good pace up the mountainside.

Sam struggled, but managed to keep up with her.

Below, he could now see that the man who had gone by the name of Carl, had chosen to follow them.

Although Carl hadn't said a word, Sam was now certain that the man was there to kill them both. After all, no one risked their lives climbing a ruined set of iron rungs, unless they had something important to catch.

Sam took another brief look at Carl, down below.

There was something sinister about the mechanical way the man climbed the steps. He was much faster than either of them. At this rate, he would catch up to them well before they reached the top.

Looking around, Sam discovered that he had very few options when it came to looking for a weapon.

CHAPTER 18

Blake cursed his age, as he looked up at the mountain.

Years ago, he could have scaled these mountains as fast as the best of them. But those days were long gone now.

The Rockblitz was one of those ritzy climbing clubs, found all over Europe, where you could eat good food and drink good wine, while comfortably watching as your companions struggled to scale the distant mountains; and testaments of man's strength over nature.

There were a number of men around, carrying massive optical-zoom cameras, and taking pictures of the climbers today.

He noticed that one of them was standing at the end of the viewing platform, a Mediterranean man with long dark hair. The photographer had set up his camera on a tripod so that he could follow someone's ascent, and had now sat down to have a smoke.

"Excuse me, sir. May I borrow your camera for a few minutes to try to locate a friend of mine?"

"No, monsieur. I am using it to keep an eye on my own friend's ascent."

"Your friend will be there for a long time yet," Blake

reassured the man, and pulled out his wallet, extracting two purple 500 Euro notes, and said, "I only need to borrow your optical zoom lens for a few minutes while I locate my friends."

The man shrugged his shoulders, pocketed the proffered Euros, and sat back down to finish smoking his cigarette.

Blake sat down on the chair set up behind the high-powered lens. He followed the line of the Via Ferrata until he spotted the first climber. It was a woman, in her early twenties, her brown hair casually tied back in a ponytail, and nice legs, he noticed. At any other time, he would have enjoyed admiring her further, but having easily determined that she was not who he was after, he continued using the lens to zoom in further up the line.

There were literally hundreds of Via Ferratas in sight, and more than a dozen mountains ahead of them. It was one of the main reasons why this particular lookout, was the choice for avid climbing photographers and filmmakers. It could take him all day to find them, but his friend's message said that they had started their climb on the Via Ferrata Con Grande, and he was confident that he would spot them soon enough.

It ran for nearly a four hundred feet vertically, and once reaching the top of it, a climber could continue on another four pathways.

Blake continued following the line of the iron trail up the mountain, occasionally stopping when he spotted a climber, to see if he'd found them.

It was taking much longer than he thought it would.

He felt the tap on his shoulder, and turned to see that the owner of the telescopic lens was now extinguishing his smoke.

"I'll have my camera back now," the man told him.

"Please, monsieur. I have not yet found my friends, and I assure you that I will not be much longer."

"A couple more minutes, and then I don't care that you just gave me 1000 Euros, I have a job to do today, and it's worth a lot more to me than a 1000 Euros."

Without taking his seat again, Blake bent down until he could train his eye on the line. This time, he started at the top and quickly worked his way down.

Finally, he spotted them.

The woman was in the lead position, and Sam Reilly was close behind her on the wall.

His friend, he noticed, was pushing himself to his absolute limits, but was closing the gap between himself and the other two. The man was now about fifty feet below the next person up the ladder.

Training the lens just below the three of them, his eyes stopped scanning when he saw a fourth climber. This man was only a little further behind his friend, and he seemed strangely familiar. He focused in on the man's face—and even at that distance, he instantly recognized the man.

What the hell are you doing on the mountain?

There was no mistake about it.

There was no way the man was there purely by coincidence.

Blake thanked the photographer, and walked away from the camera, pulled out his phone, and made the call.

"Yes?" A surly man's voice answered.

"I have spotted him." He uttered each word slowly and deliberately.

"Good. Where are they now?"

"Halfway up a side track of the Grande Via Ferrata."

"Do you think they know about it, then?" The man's normally cold voice held a little more concern than usual.

"They must. The coincidence otherwise is surely too much," Blake Simmonds acknowledged.

"What are you going to do about it?"

"I'll have one of our own helicopters meet me here shortly and take me to the top, where I will meet them personally." Blake fidgeted with the cell phone, and then said, "I'll be prepared for any eventuality, of course."

"Excellent. I knew I could trust you," the stern voice on the line said.

"There is something else."

"Yes?"

"He's there also," Blake said.

"Really? But we were certain he was searching on the other side of the Alps. Are you sure it's him?"

"Yes, of course, I'm bloody certain."

"Now, that does change things, doesn't it?"

John Wolfgang's thighs burned with each step he took.

Above him, on the dilapidated Via Ferrata, he watched as the three figures struggle to reach the top. The one man trailing behind and therefore closest to him, John recognized as Carl, one of Blake Simmonds' goons. Maybe forty feet above Carl, was Sam Reilly. He still struggled to believe that Sam had somehow managed to escape off the Australian coast three weeks ago. After his men had reported back to him about it, he wasn't entirely convinced that they were talking about the same man, until now. Then, located above Sam, John spotted what could only be the silhouette of a woman.

At this distance, it was impossible to make out any defining features, but he noticed that she was getting closer to the next ledge.

At his age, it would be impossible for him to keep up with them any longer.

He hoped that Carl was there for the same purpose as he, but he trusted that possibility even less than he trusted that Blake Simmonds was still on his team.

No, the goon is Blake's man, and that certainly doesn't make him my friend. He's most likely here to kill them, but he could just as easily be there to help them.

John climbed up another eight rungs of the rusty ladder, and then stopped to catch his breath.

But what is Blake after?

John simply could not work with anyone with whom he was unable to manipulate with either money, women or the threat of painful death.

Looking up again, he realized that it was time for him to make a final decision about his next step in this most violent treasure hunt.

The first climber was just about to reach the top.

John pulled out his pistol and took aim.

Sam Reilly was close to the top.

If they could just get to the next ledge they could then circle the mountain, placing themselves out of the reach of the man who was trailing them like a machine.

That was when he heard the loud crack echo across the canyon.

At first, Sam thought that the sound might have been caused by a natural crack in the rock face ahead. The sound echoed throughout the entire Dolomite range.

It took a few seconds for its source to register with him.

Did someone just shoot at us?

He and Aliana both picked up their pace, and he watched as Aliana climbed over the mountain crest and disappeared.

As he climbed, his mind writhed to grasp how anyone could have known that he was still alive. He was certain that they had taken sufficient precautions while they were searching, so that the other treasure hunters wouldn't notice him.

But somehow, someone had taken notice.

He knew that he had been careful to tell no one where they were going. He'd intentionally neglected to even tell his own father, just in case someone else might have been listening. Carl, the man from the bed and breakfast, must have recognized him somehow, but Sam couldn't understand where they could have possibly encountered each other before.

Just before Sam reached the crest, he heard another loud report, quickly followed by two more.

The rock, about a foot to the right of his hand shattered into dust.

Sam had no way to protect himself from the gunfire. It was just enough encouragement to force him to take four more steps, and clamber onto the other side of the ledge.

"You made it!" Aliana sounded relieved.

"Yeah, but for how long?"

She ignored his question, and then, reaching for a boulder on the ground, said, "Quick, help me with this. It's the only chance we're going to get to beat this prick."

"I like your thinking," Sam told her, as he squatted down to help. Between the two of them, they managed to roll the boulder to the edge of the cliff.

One quick look over the side confirmed that the two men who were pursuing them, were still trailing close behind. The man nearest to the top was no more than fifteen feet away.

Sam didn't take the time to warn the man, or even ask him to stop, before rolling the boulder over the edge.

Sam could hear the man scream out from below, and he could only imagine the painful death he must have suffered when the boulder hit him.

Slowly and carefully, Sam ventured a peak over the edge.

The man's right leg had been crushed by the boulder, but he'd managed to clip the carabiner from his safety line onto a bolt, a split-second before the rock struck him.

A rapid succession of gunfire ricocheted off the limestone directly above Sam's head.

"Shit!" Sam swore.

"He's still alive?" Aliana asked.

"Yes, but I think it's the man below him who keeps shooting at us."

"Damn!"

Sam and Aliana both started looking around for anything that they could throw, but with the exception of the one boulder which they'd already put to good use, the entire ledge appeared to be otherwise devoid of loose rubble.

Sam continued to eyeball the ledge. A path followed the natural protection of the ledge, and alongside it were two more sets of ladders. Sam didn't have the strength to keep trying to out-climb the other two men, although he sincerely doubted that the younger of the two would be able to keep pursuing them for much longer, either.

"Any ideas?" Sam asked Aliana.

"There's a tunnel, just around there," she said, pointing to the end of the natural ledge.

Sam noticed that the tunnel's entrance was well hidden.

It was unlikely that their pursuer would not notice that they'd stopped climbing, but at least they could buy some time and remove themselves from the direct line of fire while he searched for where they'd gone.

He followed Aliana into the tunnel.

The mouth of the tunnel wasn't much bigger than Sam, as he fell crouched down on his knees to enter, but once he got inside, he found that the tunnel opened up, so that he could walk around freely without crouching.

"This way," Sam said, "there are a couple of different routes here, and we might be able to lose him. Stay close to me."

Aliana took his left hand in hers, and the two of them stepped further into the dark tunnel.

At the far end was another opening.

"There!" Sam directed.

They both made their way toward it as quick as they could manage in the darkness.

Reaching it, Sam looked down and was able to see that there was another long Via Ferrata ladder which dropped for a distance of more than a thousand feet on the other side. He then turned his head and looked up.

Absolutely nothing.

There was no way that he and Aliana would survive such a long, downward climb. Even if it took their attackers half an hour, they would eventually discover their location. Then it would only be a matter of time before they finished what they'd tried so hard to achieve.

In the vista below, rested an enormous lake. It was colored a stunning green and turquoise near its shoreline which turned an almost emerald darkness at its center. It was only then that Sam realized that this was the same lake that he and Tom had dived two days ago—Lake Solitude.

It appeared even more beautiful in the distance, viewed from this height.

On the other side of the tunnel, where they'd entered, he heard his pursuer speak in a thick German accent.

"Sam Reilly. Stop. I'm on your side. They're going to kill you!"

It was a ruse, and neither Sam nor Aliana responded.

"Blake Simmonds sent me here to tell you that if you get too close, they will never let you live!" The voice was clear, but the man's breathing sounded labored. Sam had seen his leg, and knew that he must be in agony.

So, it was Blake Simmonds who betrayed me.

Sam then heard the voice of another person, speaking in German, at the other end of the tunnel. It was relatively quiet, and despite the speaker's use of a foreign language, Sam could tell that the person was speaking calmly.

Aliana nudged his shoulder, and directed his attention to a spot that was located a few feet to the side of the tunnel's entrance. There, Sam could just make out the slightest outline of another opening—this one running deeper inside the bowels of the mountain.

He nodded his head in recognition of the fact that it might be their only chance to escape.

John Wolfgang was panting heavily by the time he made it to the ledge containing the entrance to the tunnel.

He walked up to the other man, and said in German, "Where are they, Carl?"

"Where are who?"

"Don't play dumb with me, Carl."

"Who's playing?" Carl asked.

"Okay, suit yourself," John said, as he pulled out his pistol, pointed it at Carl's face, and at close range, pulled the trigger.

A large hole instantly bloomed where Carl's head once was, and he fell to the ground on the narrow ledge. He tried in vain to breathe for a couple of seconds before his brain finally caught up to the reality that he had been shot at point blank range with a powerful pistol.

Well, at least one of those damned treasure hunters is now out of my way.

From the other side of the tunnel entrance, he watched, relieved, as his own elite team was now quickly making their way into the tunnel.

Sam followed Aliana down into the little hole, before he heard another crack of gunfire. It was dark inside, but a small draft reassured him that the crevasse extended even further.

They climbed down another fifteen to twenty feet, using their arms and legs to press against the rock walls and slow their descent.

The hole dropped down much further than either of them expected.

When they could no longer see the opening at the top of the crevasse, the two of them stopped their descent entirely.

Above them, Sam could hear the two men shouting at each other in German. It was the first time he realized that there were several people after them.

The yelling got even closer.

Sam would have loved to know what they were saying, but he didn't dare ask Aliana to translate for him, in fear of it giving away their hiding place.

The shouting quieted somewhat, and now sounded more like a series of distinct questions, as if his pursuers had drawn closer together.

Then he heard another sound, similar to that of a small rock falling, and it echoed down the same gap in the rock wall in which they were hiding.

Aliana, whose native German ears understood every word that had been spoken, yelled, "Grenade!"

They both released their pressure on the rock walls and slid downward in a complete free fall.

Above them, they heard a large explosion, followed by the sound of limestone crashing.

And still, they continued to fall.

CHAPTER 19

The entire tunnel that John had been standing inside shook after his grenade exploded. He instinctively raised his arms above his head to protect himself from any falling debris. For an instant he actually wondered if the entire tunnel was going to cave in on him.

He was wrong about that, but the thick dust that billowed out of the tunnel could easily be just as lethal. John ducked down and made his way to the tunnel's closest exit. Then, with the calm experience of someone who'd spent many years climbing these mountains, he carefully climbed down half a dozen rungs of the Via Ferrata below.

The air was fresh again—and it felt naturally crisp by comparison to the rock dust that he'd been breathing and from which he'd just escaped.

It was over. Sam Reilly was dead.

He'd just bought himself some more time.

In his pocket, John's cell phone began to vibrate silently. He slid his hand across its face to accept the call.

Its caller ID read, "Blake Simmonds."

"Speak."

"What are you doing, John?" Blake asked, in the coarse voice of a man who'd smoked too much for far too long.

"Never you mind, Blake. I'm trying to take care of something you were supposed to fix."

"And I will fix it. In fact, my guy is in the process of taking him out right now."

"I doubt that," John replied, chuckling. "I doubt that very much indeed."

"Why is that?"

"Well, for starters he's dead, and so is Sam Reilly."

"Carl's dead?" Blake's voice sounded irritated. "He was loyal. It takes a long time to make a man really loyal, doesn't it?"

"So it does," John agreed.

Both men subscribed to a world where loyalties could easily be exchanged for more money, better opportunities, and self-satisfaction.

"And Sam Reilly's really dead?" Blake asked, seeking reassurance.

"Yes."

"Well, that's something, at least."

"Now, what about the other thing? Are we close?"

"We're getting there, but it will still take some time," John replied.

"Don't take too long. The buyers are getting impatient, and you know what that means, don't you?"

"Yes, of course."

Blake Simmonds ended the call.

He noticed an unopened text message on it from Carl.

He opened it, and read, "For your information, boss, Sam Reilly is here with Aliana Wolfgang."

Blake Simmonds laughed aloud, in a way he hadn't laughed since this whole affair began, all those years ago.

The European backpacker that Sam Reilly had picked up was John's own daughter?

The implications of the statement were enormous.

Could it be possible that John didn't even realize that his daughter was with them?

Blake considered how this new piece of information might be useful to him, and then looked at the GPS on his cell phone. It displayed the location of his own team, and he wondered whether they would reach it in time.

Could it be that John doesn't even realize how close he is to stumbling upon it?

He tapped the helicopter pilot on the shoulder, and said, "Take us back—there's been a change of plans."

Sam slid deeper into the large crevasse with Aliana.

The crash of large rocks falling could be heard all around them. Sam had no idea where this drop would eventually take them, but the alternative was to be killed by the landslide that the explosion had caused above them.

At the bottom of the crevasse, they skidded along a flat section of the rocky fissure as it leveled out. A split second later, several tons of rock came crashing down, completely blocking their exit.

Sam flicked on the small headlamp, and then looked back at the mounds of rocky debris now strewn along the route they'd used when they had entered.

"Well, we can't go back the way we came," Aliana said, pointing out the obvious. Even if she and Sam could possibly move the rocks, their pursuers would be waiting for them on the other side.

"No, that's for certain."

"So, then, now what do we do?"

Sam turned his head to where the crevasse seemed to continue on into a natural tunnel.

A strange green luminescence could be seen emanating from the other side. He looked at Aliana, who seemed to be equally fascinated by it.

The strange glow so mesmerized Sam, that he nearly forgot the fact that someone had just tried, for the third time this month, to kill him.

The air in the tunnel was cool, yet it was warmer than the air outside.

"We may as well follow it," Sam suggested and they started to walk in the only direction that was left available to them.

The narrow tunnel led to a larger one, followed by a smaller one containing stagnant water. The number of glowworms scattered about on the limestone walls increased as they moved along, and formed the basis of a glow so strong that they were both able to turn off their headlamps.

They clambered over a large rock, perhaps twelve feet high, and lying on its side. Once they reached its other side, Sam saw an image that was as surreal as it was beautiful, and which appeared to be completely out of place.

Stagnant water filled the tunnel and a little wooden boat could be seen floating there; its leather painter still tied off on a rock, looking as though it was waiting for its owner, who'd only left it there a few hours ago. It might have been floating there for a hundred years or more. The glowworms provided just enough light to enable them to see that the subterranean lake stretched ahead for quite a distance.

"It looks pretty old," Sam said, as he tested the buoyancy of the wooden boat by pushing down on it, and was pleased to note that the old boat seemed to maintain his weight easily enough.

"I wonder how long it has been here?" Aliana said, as her beautiful blue eyes admired the enigmatic place, and then she added, "The limestone in this mountain has made it easy for many tunnels to form naturally. Armies, farmers and travelers alike have used such tunnels to cross the mountains fast, and in secret, as far back as the early 16th century, and perhaps, even earlier."

"This section of the tunnel must have collapsed many years ago near where we entered it, and this poor boat has remained stranded here, where this cold, dark environment, does not permit even time to pass."

"But where did it go?" Aliana asked.

"If someone took the trouble to leave a boat this high up and inside of this mountain, I can only guess that it goes somewhere, or at least, once did. I'd say, our chances of survival have just risen—at least a little."

Sam sat down in the middle of the boat and then gave Aliana a look which said, "Do you dare?"

She climbed aboard and sat down in front of him, and he started to push the boat forward along the underground creek. The waterway continued on much further than he had expected. There were a number of wider sections, followed by a couple of very narrow sections, barely wide enough to allow the boat to pass through.

A pair of ramshackle oars were lying inside the boat. A chain ran along the tunnel wall, and they were able to use it with relative ease to maneuver the small craft along the tunnel, leaving the oars untouched.

After what seemed a considerable period of time, Sam checked his watch and was surprised to discover that they had been aboard the little boat for more than an hour.

The air had changed.

It had warmed significantly, and the draft he felt had increased.

"This is really something, isn't it?" Sam said.

"It's beautiful. I've never seen anything like it," Aliana replied, the large dilated pupils of her blue eyes displaying a reflection of the tiny glowworms as though they were tiny stars.

It made Sam feel as if he were on the most magical date of his life, rather than fighting for a way to escape with his life intact, and from a woman whose loyalties were at best, uncertain.

In the back of his mind, he struggled with one thought, *How is she involved in all of this?*

As they continued to float their way through the tunnel, the ambient light seemed to intensify until the tunnel opened up into a gigantic underground cavern containing a lake. More than a million glowworms covered the walls and ceiling, illuminating the entire cavern, as though it were daylight inside.

In the middle of the stilled water of the underground lake, he saw an enormous, silver, structure.

Sam found himself holding his breath involuntarily, as though the mere sound of breathing, were enough to make the image disappear. In the middle of the shallow lake, rested the serene remains of the Magdalena, in all her glory.

As though she had floated inside the cavern, and then, the water had receded, leaving her stuck in the middle of the shallow underground lake. The passenger compartment of her gondola could still be seen, resting completely above the water.

"My God," Aliana said, staring wide-eyed at him in disbelief, "It's the Magdalena!"

CHAPTER 20

Aliana's words broke Sam's trance in an instant.

Turning to face her, his hands still holding hers, he said, "You know about the Magdalena?"

"Yes, of course, it was a story my father used to tell me as a child. He's spent a lot of time and millions of dollars searching for her over the years."

Sam desperately wanted to question her about how her father was involved, and more importantly, if she had been entangled in the attempt on his life. But his first priority was to find a way out of their current mess. He would have to focus on that first, and then return to the problem of her involvement.

"Well, if she somehow found her way in here, we should be able to find our way out."

"Yes, but out where? I don't see any other tunnels or crevasses," Aliana pointed out. "Besides, she's remained lost to the world for over 75 years! It's easy to imagine that the passage she took to enter here, may be long gone."

Sam had already considered that possibility, "The water level must have changed in the past 75 years. It's the only explanation as to how she made it here in the first place." Sam said, his gaze returning to the Magdalena once more. "Look at her, she's aged a bit, but otherwise she's completely intact. She must have crashed into the icy lake, and then somehow floated into here in the summer, when the ice had thawed. Since then, something must have changed to increase the water level, and block the passage that otherwise might have allowed her to float out of the cavern again."

"After all this time, she's been so close to all of us?"

"Yes, but it's really not all that surprising that she wasn't discovered. At this altitude, only a few people would go to all the trouble of diving, and even fewer would do so, knowing that they'd have to carry all their equipment up 10,000 feet of rock."

"If that's so, and the water level has increased since she crashed, why then is she resting high and dry on almost solid mud in here?" Aliana pointed to the sand-like silt upon which the Magdalena rested.

"That's a good question," Sam said, as he looked around the enormous cavern for an answer.

This is what I call real treasure hunting.

And then saw it.

A little subterranean creek, slowly feeding into the subterranean lake.

"That's why," he said, pointing to it. "See how the creek is moving the limestone sediment into the lake here? It's building up and, over time, is slowly making the lake shallower."

"Hey, I think you're right, Sam."

"Thanks for the vote of confidence." Sam checked his watch. "It's already nearly one a.m. How about we check out what's inside the gondola in the morning? As far as I'm concerned, we need to get some rest and call it a night. We can make a fresh start on finding our escape route tomorrow morning."

Aliana slept poorly, as did Sam.

"Are you awake?" she whispered.

"Yes, can't you sleep, either?"

"No, I just can't stop thinking about what we're going to find when we search her."

"What time is it?" Sam asked, rolling over.

"It's four o'clock. Shall we start our day?"

The time of day was irrelevant given their subterranean environment. They breakfasted on some dried fruit and nuts. It was a very basic meal, but it would provide them with enough nutrients to see them through.

"Okay, now what?" Aliana asked.

"You wait here while I see if it's safe. I'm dying to have a look inside that gondola," Sam replied. Then, looking sheepish, he said, "Actually, people have been trying to kill me to keep from looking inside that airship."

Sam hadn't gone as far as saying that he knew she was involved in the last attempt on his life, but the tone of his words suggested that he was intentionally letting her know that he was on his guard.

"Are you kidding me? No thanks!" Aliana hid her guilt with indignation. "If you're going to check it out, I'm coming with you! After years of hearing about her disappearance, do you honestly think I'm going to let you explore her by yourself?"

"Suit yourself," Sam replied.

They both climbed aboard the little boat and rowed out onto the lake toward the Magdalena.

Aliana watched as Sam fought to pull open the gondola's hatchway, which was pretty much stuck solid after all these years in this damp environment.

Just like all men, Aliana observed, Sam doggedly attacked the first hatchway he could find, while she, on the other hand, noticed that she could climb onto the open-air gangway and then try to open the door from there, into the gondola. The open-air gangway was above the water level, along with its hatchway. If they were going to have any luck, that would be the most likely hatchway to use.

She reached up to grasp the thin wire safety railing of the open-air gangway, and started to pull herself up, first by her arms, then by swinging her legs up to one side, before climbing over the railing.

She attempted to open the hatchway door with a strong push, but it didn't budge an inch. Then, she turned the door handle and pushed again.

It clicked as it opened.

"Are you coming?" She said, mockingly to Sam.

"I'm right behind you."

She waited as he quickly climbed up to stand beside her, before pushing the door open completely.

There was no odor.

After seventy five years, any and all flesh that might have been aboard at the time of the crash, had long since departed from the remains of the Magdalena's passengers.

Still, the ghastly sight in front of her took her breath away.

There were eight skeletons in total, who sat lifelessly, in the open gondola before her. Their clothing had almost completely disintegrated over time.

Aliana noted that one of them still wore a pendant around its neck. At its base, was the largest diamond she had ever seen.

She remembered reading about it in a book.

"It was called the Rosenberg Diamond," Sam told her.

"That's right. I remember reading about it one of my father's books which was about some of the greatest treasures ever lost without a trace."

Her eyes continued to scan the gondola.

Each skeleton was strapped into its seat, as though they were expecting a bumpy ride. The rest of the room looked as though it had been ransacked. The once majestic interior looked barren. She guessed that it wasn't the passage of time which had destroyed her, but something else entirely—it appeared to her as though someone had deliberately removed all of the fine things that once adorned the place.

As her eyes continued to glance around the room and take in the entire scene, she began to worry that they were not the first ones to discover the dirigible. It was obvious to her that fixtures had been ripped from the walls, and everything that hadn't been bolted to the floor had been removed.

"I wonder what went wrong," Sam said aloud. There was a sadness in his voice.

Sam had said the precise thing that she was thinking.

"They must have thought they'd made it. They were so close. Looking at them now, it seems as though none of them even realized they were about to die."

"Look at this," Sam said, pointing at the ugly, brown wooden box, which sat amidst the seated skeletons.

It was one of the very few items still remaining inside the gondola, which had not been bolted down.

"What do you think's inside it?"

"I don't know, but it's pretty heavy. Anything lighter would have washed away when the gondola was submerged." Aliana watched silently as Sam struggled to open the lid, until he asked her, "Can you help me with this?"

She came up alongside him and helped him pull the lid open. The box was made of some sort of solid hardwood, but the water had caused the wood to expand, locking it closed, permanently.

Together, they managed to pry it open, using one of the oars from the rowboat outside.

"Wow," Sam said, his eyes wide, "is that why your father wanted me dead?"

Inside, Sam saw that there were more than a hundred gold bars, each one bearing the letters G&O, artistically embossed in the center.

"Wow, that's a lot of gold!" Aliana said, pretending not to hear what he had just said.

"Enough to kill for?"

"What? Of course, any number of treasure hunters would kill to get their dirty hands on this," Aliana acknowledged. She appeared genuine, but the faintest of quivers to her bottom lip, reaffirmed her involvement.

Sam decided that now was not the time to corner her on it.

"Yes, well, I imagine that they were trying to get as much of their fortune out of the country as possible."

He'd seen a lot of wealth in his lifetime, but he'd never set his eyes upon so much solid gold in one place, at one time.

Their luster gave them a uniquely strong allure, which surprised him.

"There's another box over here," Aliana said.

It was smaller, and easier to break open, but no less filled with gold. Inside it were German gold coins and a small bag of precious gems, including diamonds, sapphires, rubies and emeralds.

"No wonder someone wants me dead," Sam murmured, as he ran his fingers through the cache of precious gemstones. He raised his eyes to Aliana, and said, "There's a fortune in treasure here—certainly enough to kill for."

"You still don't know what this is really about, do you?" Aliana asked.

"It's what everything is about—Money, Power and Greed."

"No, it's about something even worse than that," there was spite in her response.

It gave him pause.

Sam had expected her to be more contrite, instead, she was almost attacking him.

"Then what it is it?" Sam's voice was stern with her, for the first time since they'd started this journey. Aliana had obviously known much more about it than she'd ever expressed to him.

Aliana didn't speak a word.

The guilty expression on her face was, in itself, enough of an answer.

Sam ignored her. He had other priorities right now. He would deal with her later. He walked slightly further ahead and found a single small suitcase with a chain on one end. It terminated in a handcuff which was attached to what would have been the wrist of one of the skeletons. Unlike the others, this small case was entirely metallic.

He started to pull at it, but it was completely intact and strong as the day it had been built.

"Don't touch that suitcase!" At her strident tone of voice, Sam turned to look at Aliana's face. There was recognition in it.

"Why, what's in it?"

"That one must be destroyed. It is of paramount importance that we destroy it!" There was true panic in her voice.

"Okay, tell me why?"

"My father told me about a virus that my grandfather was commissioned to create for Adolf Hitler. It was supposedly more lethal than anything else ever created. If Germany had succeeded in harnessing its power, the allied forces would have never had a chance to win the war. Like the Japanese after the bombing of Hiroshima and Nagasaki, the Allied forces would have had no other option but to unconditionally surrender, and Nazis Fascism would have succeeded.

A sudden realization hit Sam like a thunderbolt.

He had just discovered the missing piece of the jigsaw puzzle.

"Are you telling me that the hunt for the last airship was never about the gold?"

John Wolfgang knew the second he'd ended the phone call with Blake Simmonds that the man had been keeping something from him. Simmonds was as ruthless as he was calm. His voice hadn't changed a bit when he mentioned that Carl was dead.

There was something else that Simmonds was withholding, John was certain of it. He knew people, especially some very deceitful people, and Blake was the worst amongst the lot of them. At least a thief could be relied upon to steal. Even terrorists believed in something with certainty, but Blake worked on an entirely different set of values, which Wolfgang couldn't even begin to understand.

And how can you trust a person you don't understand?

John replayed the conversation in his mind. There was something about the way that Blake seemed so overly focused about where he'd just been, almost as if he were worried about his location . . .

Did he know something about the Magdalena?

Then it hit him like a bomb.

Carl wasn't trying to kill Sam Reilly – he was trying to protect him – but from what?

The answer presented itself to him, simply.

From discovering the location of the Magdalena!

Holy shit! That snobby English bastard knows exactly where it is – and yet still he tries to chase me up for his boss! He's known all along where she is, and that means that he doesn't want his boss to find her either!

John picked up his phone, and punched in the phone number that he never wanted to call.

"Yes," said the man, in his dark, cold voice.

"I have it. I need you to send the team in," John paused for a moment, and then said, "I'll text you the GPS coordinates for the location where I'll meet them. You'll need to have them there within the hour to secure the location."

John gave serious consideration to telling the man that Blake Simmonds had been a traitor all along, but thought better of the idea.

Some hands are best played close to the vest.

After Sam had finished explaining to Aliana how he had come to hear of the existence of the Magdalena, and what really happened to cause him to sink, Aliana became even more confused and angry than she ever thought possible.

"I refuse to believe that my father had anything to do with this! I mean, he has spent his life trying to make up for what his grandfather did during the Holocaust."

"Then who else would have been trying to kill me from aboard a ship, with a helicopter bearing the name Wolfgang Corporation?"

That question, she was unable answer.

"I have no idea, Sam, but you have to believe me when I tell you that my father wasn't responsible for that. Can you believe me?"

"I do understand that you believe it to be the truth."

It was a diplomatic answer, but she could tell from the expression on his face, that he didn't believe it.

"How can you say that? Don't you trust me?"

"No. I don't," Sam told her, plainly. Even before he spoke, his eyes had given her his answer. And what made it worse, she knew that he had reason not to trust her.

Those words hurt her even more than acknowledging the fact that, deep down, she believed that her own father had been keeping dark secrets from her.

She started to speak, but couldn't get the words out.

Then, she made another attempt, "Why not?" She wanted to sound both strong and defiant, but her weak tone of voice betrayed her greatest misgivings.

How much could he possibly know?

"There was a moment . . . after I fell, when I saw something in your expression. It was only there for a second at most, but I've seen betrayal before, and I know how to spot it when it rears its ugly head. You wanted to leave me there. You considered whether or not you might be able to outrun me if you left me and continued up the Via Farrata alone."

"No, you don't understand . . ." Aliana tried to explain, but Sam cut her off short.

"I'm not done. It was only when you saw the other man, Carl, coming down the Via Farrata, that you changed your mind. Almost as if you were frightened, with a glimmer of uncertainty, about just who your enemies were on the mountain, and among them, who you could possibly trust. It was then that you grasped at your only hope, and sided with me."

"It was nothing like that, Sam . . . you don't understand at all." Aliana tried to offer him an explanation faster than her mind was capable of forming one. "Many years ago, when I was only a child, my father was so poor that we were on the cusp of starvation. The Berlin Wall had just come down, and my father was approached by a man who offered him financial backing to create his pharmaceutical company. That company was how he went on to become rich, and powerful. It eventually earned him a Nobel Prize. That man asked my father for only one thing in return for his backing—that my father find the final resting place of the Magdalena, and once she was found, to give him control of the deadly virus she carried on board."

"So, your father sold out the rest of humanity for gold?" Sam replied, in disgust.

"He was desperate, Sam. We all were desperate, and he truly believed that it never would be discovered. Then, when I saw him last week, he told me that the same man, who he hadn't heard from in twenty years, had contacted him with new information, which would help narrow the location of the Magdalena."

"Which was . . ." Sam asked.

"You."

Realization could be seen in Sam's eyes, as he came to grips with her role in it all.

"My father was obliged to repay his long-standing obligation to this man by offering him something that he never thought he could."

"The destruction of mankind?"

"Exactly. He wouldn't tell me what his plan was, but he did tell me that there were a number of treasure hunters after it, and that they were all closing in on it like a pack of hungry wolves. He said that he had a team of people searching, but had already learned that there were others who had come close to finding it. He told me that we needed to be the first to locate it, and that the cost of another person discovering it first would be catastrophic. He also told me that on that very same day, he had heard about a man from Australia who had come here armed with secret information, and that was who he perceived to be his greatest threat. I put two and two together and knew what I had to do. With your knowledge of underwater recovery, you would be the most well equipped to find her at the bottom of one of these lakes."

"And so you tried to kill me?" Sam's face looked more hurt than angry.

"No, of course not! I never could have done that. How can you say such a terrible thing? All I wanted was to discover what you knew."

"So, your father put you up to this. You only came to me for the knowledge. The kiss, the intimacy, all of that was just an act?"

She slapped him hard.

"No, the intimacy was real, Sam. My father had told me to discover what you knew, and that . . ." Aliana's eyes stared at the twinkle of the glowworms in the cavern's ceiling, but her mind was a thousand miles away, "he would take care of you, once I had the information. But, you're real, Sam. It may have been my intention to become close to you for the sake of gaining information, but since then, we've both become close. You are the most amazing man I've ever met, and for what it's worth, I love you."

"If you didn't try to kill me on the mountain before, and it wasn't your father, then who did?"

"The man's name was Carl."

"Yes, but why? I mean, what did he expect to achieve out of killing me?"

"That, I don't know. Can you believe me that I had nothing to do with it?"

She couldn't tell what he was thinking.

"I have no idea what to believe right now," Sam told her, and then smiled at her reassuringly. "How about we first destroy this damned virus, and then start over again with a clean slate?"

"Okay, so now I know why you're here, and you know a bit more about my family history. I hate to point this out, but all of it is going to be academic if we don't find a way out of here in the next few days."

She watched as Sam whistled to himself while staring at the Magdalena, as though, having now found what he'd been searching for, escaping to the surface was the last thing on his mind.

"Are you even listening to me?"

"What?" He feigned a small show of surprise. "I'm sorry, what did you want to know?"

"I said, 'we're going to die down here, if we don't figure out how to reach the surface in the next few days.'"

He didn't look worried at all, and just continued admiring the bulk of the airship's hull.

"You're as crazy as my father, Sam! You're completely obsessed and seem unable to focus on what's most important!" She stared at him and noticed that his countenance hadn't changed a bit. The entire time they'd been talking, he hadn't taken his eyes off the outer hull of the Magdalena. Irritated, she asked, "What the hell are you looking at?"

"The Magdalena, of course."

"And what are you thinking?"

"She's in remarkably good condition, don't you think?"

His insouciance was starting to really piss her off.

"Yes, and I'm sure she'd look lovely in a museum one day, our bones inside, if you don't stop staring at her and start to consider how we might escape!"

"I'm not trying to figure out how we can escape, Aliana."

"You're not? Then what are you trying to do?"

"I'm wondering if we were to re-gas her canopy, and repair her engines, if we could fly her out of here."

"You can't possibly be serious?"

"Oh, but I am, completely."

"But we don't even know how to get out of here, let alone the Magdalena," she protested.

"No, that I worked out before we went to sleep last night."

Sam waded into the deeper section of the lake, where the mouth of the cave was most likely situated. He knew that he didn't have much time.

The water was cold, lethally cold.

He'd just finished explaining to Aliana his theory on how the Magdalena came to be trapped inside the mountain, and it was now time to put that theory into practice. He was confident there was no other conceivable way that she might possibly have ended up stranded here.

When he and Tom had compared historical photos of Lake Solitude against current satellite photos, and current pictures taken from the western side of the lake, it was clear that the water level was now a good twenty feet deeper than it had been back in 1939, and how a distinct section of the rocky mountain above it seemed to be missing.

"If I'm right," he said, before entering the frigid water, "the Magdalena clipped the top of that mountain, and then, losing altitude, her pilot, Peter Greenstein, looked for a place to land. Seeing that he was surrounded by steep, rocky mountaintops and 100 foot tall pine trees, the frozen surface of the lake in winter would have appeared to be a snow-covered field. In his predicament, the view would have been a godsend. There he brought down his wounded airship, only to discover that the ice beneath the snow was pretty thin. Then, the gondola must have crashed through the ice, and with the water temperature at well below freezing, everyone aboard must have died within seconds."

Sam had waited for Aliana to grasp what he had imagined, before continuing with his theory, "The Second World War continued on, and during the next summer, the lake would most likely have thawed and the Magdalena could have drifted into the large grotto, where she became stuck in the build-up of silt and limestone. Sometime during the war, this section of the mountain must have been destroyed, sending millions of tons of rock into the lake, artificially raising the water level as much as twenty feet and forever concealing the wreck of the Magdalena—until now."

"That's a nice theory, but then, why didn't your search of Lake Solitude discover anything?"

"Because we weren't looking in the right spot."

"What do you mean? You said you dived the lake, didn't you?"

"Yes, but we were looking for signs of the lost airship on the lake bottom, we weren't looking for a tunnel close to the surface.

"What if you're wrong?"

"Then I'm about to go for a very cold swim for nothing," Sam said, his white teeth showing his comfort, despite the cold.

That said, he dived his head under the frigid water and disappeared.

The combination of the frigid water and Sam's lack of a diving mask combined to make for very poor visibility. In the distance, he could just make out a faint glow, which, he decided, must be the outside world, but he had no way to judge the distance.

Sam held his breath for just over a minute.

The glow didn't seem to change at all.

How far had he gone? Could he make it to the end?

The glow at the end of the tunnel could be as much as several hundred feet away. He might make it, but he probably wouldn't, and if he failed, what would happen to Aliana?

No, he decided, he'd better go back and rethink their escape.

Years of diving had taught him not to be careless.

His lungs burned as they fought the instinctive desire to take another deep breath, and his muscles ached both from the effects of the icy water and his lack of oxygen. .

It was a dangerous combination.

As he surfaced, he tried to plant his feet on the silt, but struggled to hold himself upright. He drew upon his remaining strength, and dragged his body to the shoreline.

Aliana ran to him instantly.

"Are you okay?"

He wanted to answer "Yes," but the effects of hypothermia made speaking too difficult.

"My god you're freezing!"

He felt her wrap her arms around him. It didn't feel warm; if anything, it stung him wherever she touched.

Still, he didn't have the strength to tell her to stop.

"Sam, you're going to freeze to death if I don't do something soon."

Freezing cold, soaking wet and with no means of warming himself, Sam watched, helplessly, as Aliana stripped naked in front of him. Her intention was obvious—to share her body heat with him. As near to death as he was, he couldn't help but find himself amazed by her beauty. Her body exceeded the many fantasies that he'd had of her.

All woman, Aliana's skin was so soft! She smelled feminine and divine. Sam reminded himself that she wasn't doing this for his pleasure, but in order to save his life.

Even in the cold and so near to death, his body still became mightily aroused. To his embarrassment, he felt himself stiffen.

He squirmed, trying to hide his erection from her.

She nevertheless wrapped herself tightly around him and clung to him even harder.

They lay there together, for what might have been minutes or hours—Sam didn't know. Half in a fevered dream state, he fluctuated in and out of consciousness, unsure of just how much was fantasy and how much was reality.

Then, he felt her press her lips hard against his. They were soft and wet, and her tongue met his with an eagerness that burned him with desire.

Was this a dream?

Sam returned her kiss with all the strength he had that remained.

Her arms were wrapped firmly around his neck as she kissed him again. Other sensations were starting to return to his body, and as they did, they were more powerful than he could ever remember.

The sweet sound of her moans, her delightful, feminine scent, and the soft touch of her skin, drove him to ecstasy.

Then came the soft sound of her gentle whisper in his ear, "I thought you were dead, you bastard."

He opened his eyes, and saw that hers were wet with tears.

"Not a chance, not when I've only just found you."

Before he realized it, she pushed her underwear down and off. She was wet, warm and welcoming as he drove himself inside of her. Her sigh of pleasure spiked his need.

"Oh, yes," she murmured.

A wave of intense desire rolled though him.

Sam groaned.

Their bodies molded together perfectly. He'd gone from utter Hell to the heights of Heaven in that once moment and wished that the entire experience could go on forever.

CHAPTER 21

John Wolfgang worked with his team of lethal mercenaries throughout the night.

They had been on standby in Tyrol—awaiting his orders, and were dropped off by helicopter half an hour after he made the call.

His grenade had destroyed most of the crevasse which made its way deep into the heart of the mountain. The drilling process itself was easy enough, since the limestone was relatively soft. What took up most of their time was carrying out the rubble, bucket by bucket. There was only room for one person at a time to enter the hole. That person was rotated every half hour in order to maintain maximum drilling speed.

If Simmonds knew about it, so would the others, and that meant that he didn't have much time. His team were heavily armed, but who knows what sort of men, the other God damn treasure hunters had employed.

He had suggested to the leader of the elite team that they just use dynamite and blow their way down to the lower level of the tunnel. The leader had replied that he would be happy to do so, just as long as everyone was also happy to be crushed by the mountain above them in the process.

By lunchtime the next day, they had progressed approximately forty feet.

"How deep are we going, boss?" It was Brent, the leader, who hadn't spoken to anyone since he'd given the initial orders for how he wanted the drilling to proceed.

"Until we reach the cavern below. She's in there, I know she is," John said, with an outward sound of certainty that he didn't quite feel inside. If he was wrong about this, it would be all over for him and Aliana.

"Understood."

Two hours later, the man returned once more.

"Have you broken through yet?" John asked eagerly.

"No, but there's a small gap, and we've been able to run a wire through it. We still have another 80 feet to go."

"How far have we gone in the past 24 hours?"

"We're approaching 50 feet."

"Okay, so another two days?" John asked.

"Yes."

"Is there any way that we can increase our progress?"

"No." Brent didn't have to say anything else. He was a highly experienced mercenary. His face said it all—"If I say 48 hours, then that is the fastest it can be done."

"Very good. Let me know the second you break through."

Sam wasn't sure how long he'd been asleep.

At the moment his mind was still groggy, but he was certain that he had something terribly important to do before time ran out—he just couldn't quite recall what it was. Despite the feeling of faintness, he discovered a sensation of comfort beyond anything he'd ever before experienced.

He opened his eyes and saw Aliana staring back at him.

"You're still here," she said, sounding relieved.

"Did you think that I was going to leave you while you slept?"

She kissed him, and said, "I wasn't certain that you were going to live. You were pretty cold when I pulled you out of the water."

So I didn't manage to drag my body up on to the shoreline, after all – she did.

"Thank you," he said quietly, and he meant it too.

"Did you make it to the outside?"

"No."

He watched her face as he said the last word, and as she tried to formulate her next question, without trying to rush his weary mind.

"Was that because there was no way out, or because it was too far?" Aliana asked.

"It was too far."

"So, that's it then?" She seemed to be taking it well for someone who had just received a death sentence. "I wonder how many more years it will take before someone sees the Magdalena again, and enlightens our long lost loved ones of what became of us?"

It was strange, Sam realized, he hadn't even considered the fact that if he couldn't swim that distance underwater, then they would be stuck in the cavern, most likely ending up just like the skeletons inside the Magdalena. It was quick thinking on Aliana's part, he decided, to have reached the conclusion that if he, an underwater dive expert, couldn't swim that far underwater, then it would be impossible for her to do so as well.

The morbid part of his mind began to wonder if it should

come to that, would he prefer to die on the shore or inside the Magdalena.

He took his time before answering, "You would be surprised at how ingenious the human mind can be when it's trying to save its own life. We have enough food to last us for another week, and an unlimited supply of water, so I wouldn't write us off, just yet."

Her face brightened a little, but her voice betrayed her loss of hope when she asked, "Do you have any other ideas?"

"Yes. All we have to do to cross the tunnel underwater is to simply figure out a way to carry more than a couple of lungs-full of air."

"Okay, and how do you propose we do that?"

"I haven't worked that part out yet, and we don't have much in the way of air-carrying devices in our backpacks to work with."

"Unless . . ." she began, her smile seeming to return.

"Unless what?"

"Unless we can use something from the Magdalena?"

"My God, you're right! Why didn't I think of that?" He grabbed her hand again, "Come on, we're getting out of here."

CHAPTER 22

Tom Bower flew the 44 over the Dolomite mountain ranges. It had been a quick trip. He had stopped on only three occasions along the way, twice to refuel, and once to use the bathroom.

He'd been drinking at an exclusive bar in Paris, and had just taken the most adorable Parisian woman back to his hotel room, when his cell rang. He was reluctant to answer it, but the person on the other end had been persistent, and after the ninth phone call, he thought it might have something to do with Sam Reilly.

Against his better judgment, he answered the call.

"Tom Bower?" A stranger's voice had asked.

"Yes, who is this?"

"My name is not important right now. Let's just say I'm a friend of Sam Reilly."

"Go on, I'm listening."

It took some convincing for Tom to trust the man on the other end. His coarse voice, alone, sounded sinister, as though he'd smoked enough cigarettes to have already died from lung cancer years ago.

"Sam and Aliana have gone down the rabbit hole and found

the Magdalena."

Tom's reflexes were now fully awake, *and he* said, "Those are a few names I haven't heard in a while. Tell me more . . ."

"Some people, let's say some unfriendly people, are currently making their way down that hole right behind them."

"Okay, that's not very nice."

"No, I thought you'd say that. Now, what I need you to do, is return to the only place from which they might escape."

"Might escape?" Tom asked.

"Let me tell you what I know . . ." the man coughed several times.

Maybe he does *already have lung cancer?*

"At this moment, Sam and Aliana are inside a tunnel and are most likely in possession of the highly sought-after contents of the lost Magdalena. An elite team of mercenaries is chasing them, cornering them like foxes; their only hope of escaping them is to exit from the other side of the tunnel."

"And you want me to help extract them from there?" Tom asked.

"Yes. Now, I'll give you the GPS coordinates of where I'm hoping they will meet you soon."

Tom wrote down the coordinates, and then read the latitude and longitude back to the man for verification.

He now knew exactly where he was supposed to go.

"Does this place mean anything to you?" The man asked him directly.

Tom had the good sense to answer, "No, I've never been there before."

The man laughed at Tom's denial, his coarse, dry laugh

indicated that he knew perfectly well that Tom and Sam had just spent the past week diving Lake Solitude.

But there was nothing in there . . . right?

"So, the tunnel comes out there?"

"Yes. But there's something else you should know, Tom."

"What's that?"

"No one's been able to find a way in for the past 75 years."

"And you're betting that Sam will find a way out?"

"No, I'm betting that Sam and Aliana will die when the fox catches up with the rabbits, but I thought you'd like to know nonetheless, just in case. Good luck."

The man ended the call before Tom even had a chance to thank him.

There was never any doubt in Tom's mind about whether or not he was going. He wasn't sure what he was going to do once he got there, or even what he *could* do. In all probability, Sam and his new girlfriend were probably already dead. In fact, if it hadn't been Sam, he wouldn't have even bothered going there to find out.

But Sam was different.

Sam's life of privilege had left him with the deep-seated belief that he could have it all, and as Tom had discovered early on in their friendship, that optimism seemed to have a carry-over effect. If there was anyone who could find a way to get out of this mess, it was Sam Reilly.

With a gentle kiss, Tom left the beautiful woman lying next to him. Her black, silken, negligée barely able to contain her ample breasts.

"You owe me for this one, Sam," he said quietly out loud as he left.

Then in the dead of night, Tom flew toward the given coordinates, where a crack team of mercenaries were swarming toward the mountain.

He still wondered what they knew, and more importantly, what they thought had been discovered. *Did they actually believe that Sam and Aliana had somehow managed to discoverer the lost Magdalena?* As he looked at the men swarming the mountain face far below, maybe another day's climb to Lake Solitude, he couldn't help but wonder what this really was all about.

The gold wouldn't even pay their fees, so what else were they after?

Looking at the altimeter, Tom noticed that he was approaching 6,000 feet. Lake Solitude was at 8,500 feet. The air was starting to thin out just a little, and he had to raise the collective to maintain elevation.

Some instinct told him exactly where to go, but what he would do once he got there was an entirely different matter.

And, it was a question for which he had no answer.

Sam located the engineer's compartment in the Magdalena's pilot house.

On a routine voyage, the Magdalena would have been carrying an engineer and enough equipment to repair any faults that might occur in flight, but from what he'd heard and learned about that fateful and final night, the Magdalena was flying with only a skeleton crew. Rifling through the equipment, Sam found what he needed in order to disconnect the 75 year-old, enormous air tank from the pilot gondola.

Aliana's eyebrow curled in surprise as he worked.

"After so much time, won't the air inside have gone stale?" Aliana asked.

"I'm sure it will have done just that," he said, as he managed to finally crack open its regulator with a hiss. "Yep, that's pretty dry, stale crap."

"So then, what are you going to use it for?"

"We're going to build a rudimentary diving bell." Sam released any pressure that still might be held within. He then began to work on cutting the air canister in half, as he continued to explain, "You see, I don't need a lot of air to get through this tunnel. There should be just enough air in here for me to take three or four breaths, which should be enough to get me through to the end of the tunnel."

"Me?" She looked concerned. "Do you mean we're not both going to go through?"

"No. You saw what the frigid water temperature did to me, and I've got a lot more body fat to help me keep warm than you do. Besides, the air isn't the best, as you know, so we shouldn't both risk going." He studied her face. She seemed to accept her fate with equanimity. "When I get to the other side, I'll contact my friend Tom. He's probably the only person that I know I can trust, and, once he gets here, with our dive gear, and some equipment, we'll come back to get you."

"And what will I do if you die along the way?"

It was a fair question, he realized.

"Wait a week. With my rations, you have more than two weeks' worth of supplies. If I haven't returned by then, take the second half of this air tank, and hope to hell that your luck is better than mine." Sam made sure that what he'd just told her, was getting through. "Then, you eat as much food as you can to increase your body's ability to resist hypothermia, and then swim as fast as you can toward the glow, in that direction. Once you make it through the tunnel, you should be able to ascend to the surface. You'll have to find some way to warm yourself up, and once you do, you walk out of this mountain range, following whatever trail or Via Ferrata you can find, and simply pretend that none of this ever happened."

He tried to meet Aliana's eyes, but she turned away.

"Okay, I understand," she acknowledged.

Sam watched as Aliana's eyes examined the now halved air canister. It resembled a giant steel bucket, and it was large enough that a man could fit his head and shoulders inside, and breathe the air.

"What I don't understand is how you plan to sink that thing?"

"Do you mean how will I make such a large air pocket neutrally buoyant?" Sam asked.

"Yes."

"Well, to do that is simple, really. All you need to do is to attach a heavy weight at the bottom using some of this wire cabling, until our new diving bell sinks."

"And what do we have that's heavy enough to sink something like that?" Aliana asked. "It must produce a couple hundred pounds worth of water displacement?"

"I estimate that it's around 300 pounds."

"So, what do we have here that weighs that much?"

"That part's easy, haven't you realized it yet?" Sam asked.

"No, I haven't. Please fill me in—what is it?"

"Gold."

"That's some pretty expensive ballast you're talking about!" Aliana laughed as she said it, and added, "Okay, you'd better get started then."

Sam gave her a big hug and then kissed her, saying, "I'll be as quick as I can."

"I know you will," she told him.

Their parting was easier than one might expect, both of them believing that even with the odds against them, they were going to be all right.

Sam swam along the surface of the water until he reached the rock wall which marked the beginning of the downward tunnel.

He then hyperventilated for about thirty seconds, blowing off whatever carbon dioxide as he could, in an attempt to increase the length of time that his cells could survive while he was submerged. The makeshift dive bell, he knew, wasn't going to get him very far. He needed to get as much distance under his first breath as possible.

He didn't even wave goodbye or notice the tears in Aliana's eyes, before he simply dived under the water, as he had done so many thousands of times before.

As he submerged his body in a little over a three feet of water, the little digital animation of a swimming frog appeared on his watch, and next to it, the number in seconds.

He didn't even bother to look at the watch, seeing no point in it. After all, he was either going to make it to the other side, or he was going to die in the attempt.

His strong legs dolphin kicked him forward as he used both of this arm to hold the diving bell. Once he reached the point at which the diving bell became neutrally buoyant, he was able to concentrate on swimming while nestling his head through the cable which descended to the gold ballast attached below.

This time, he'd covered himself with grease from the Magdalena's large articulating rudder, as a means of maintaining some of his body heat, while submerged beneath the bone-chilling water.

As he swam, he allowed his thoughts to return to the bliss of the previous night with Aliana, attempting to divert his attention from the pain of the lactic acid build up he was experiencing, and the overwhelming urge to take a deep breathe.

Next to the frog on his watch, read the time: 1 minute: 22 seconds.

He swam on.

Using long, breaststrokes, combined with slow, continuous, dolphin kicks.

The glow he saw before him was like a mirage seeming to draw continuously closer. Sam soon realized that the tunnel was not completely horizontal, as he had first assumed. It wasn't even diagonal. Instead, it was a giant vertical shaft. It might have once been an ancient lava tube, in which the Magdalena had somehow become entombed. As the flow of water became blocked at its base, the increasing depth of the water must have raised until it flooded the grand cavern.

Sam just hoped that he could get through whatever had caused the blockage in the first place.

As he sank down deeper within the tunnel, he popped his head up inside the dive bell and took a breath of air. Understanding just how little oxygen was contained in such a small container, he was careful not to become complacent, and would try to last as long as possible between breaths.

Next to the smiling frog, the time now read: 5 minutes: 48 seconds.

He continued this process more than a dozen times as he descended. Each time, he would expel the remaining air in his lungs prior to surfacing inside the dive bell. By so doing, he could avoid the risk of contaminating the bell with potentially lethal amounts of carbon dioxide.

However, he knew that each time he took another breath, the air inside the dive bell was decreasing.

By the time his took his fifteenth breath, he discovered there was no longer enough air for him to take another.

By now, without any air to maintain its buoyancy, the dive bell became a dive weight, and Sam hung onto it as it caused him to rapidly descend into the depths of the dark chasm.

And still, at the very bottom, Sam could only just make out a faint glow.

Sam continued to hold his breath. His lungs felt like they were burning. Only years of free diving, and conditioning had made him capable of holding his breath for so long.

He hoped that the cold water would help to reduce his metabolic requirement, but it did nothing to alleviate the pain.

When his mind started to swirl, he knew that his blood was reaching a lethal level of carbon dioxide content. In his head, where he'd been listening to the quick beating of his fatigued heart, he noticed that it was starting to slow.

A certain sense of calm settled over him.

Next to his frog, read the numbers: 14 minutes: 43 seconds.

He was ready to die.

But what about Aliana? I'm not ready to die. She's the only thing I've really wanted in a long time.

In front of him, his hand touched against a wall of limestone.

The glowing hole he'd been focused on in the distance had never been one giant hole at all. Instead, it consisted of hundreds of small chinks in the wall, formed by broken rocks.

Sam squirmed through the first one he could find, and a moment later, his head surfaced inside a small bubble of air.

Gasping, he pulled himself up and began to hyperventilate.

A minute later, the dizziness he'd been experiencing from the concentrated CO2, finally reduced, and he was able to start focusing on where he was and why.

Switching on his torch for the first time since they'd discovered the Magdalena, Sam looked around and discovered that he was in an underwater cave that was approximately 6 feet long by 4 feet wide, and that it was almost completely sealed by rock.

At one end, he could see a small passageway, no more than seven inches thick, leading to the surface. The source of the light would be of no use to him.

Sam continued looking around the small cave.

As far as he was concerned, the place looked more like a tomb than his salvation.

CHAPTER 23

Blake Simmonds contemplated where his loyalties rested. Such contemplation was rare for him. Not since he was a small child had he even considered what his priorities were. In the end, though, the answer was simple, as it always had been and would be: Blake looks after Blake.

Looking at the touch-screen in front of him, he selected his employer's phone number, and clicked "scatter." The "scatter" app on his satellite phone then ran through more than a hundred proxy servers before making the final connection.

It took a considerable amount of time, but if someone was listening, which was often the case, it would take them more time to find out where the call originated than they would get listening to what was being said.

He had only spoken with the man three times since this whole thing began. The man receiving the call, answered immediately.

"Speak."

"I have reason to believe that John Wolfgang is going to screw us."

"Really? That is unexpected." The man sounded calm, despite what was at stake. "Why would he do that? He knows we have Aliana, right?"

"He might just discover that she's already dead." Blake didn't hesitate before stating the embarrassing fact.

"Ah . . . shit! How could you have been so careless?"

"I could never have predicted that John would accidentally kill her himself!"

"That stupid prick," the man said, chuckling. "Are you confident that Sam will reach the Magdalena?"

"I'm almost certain of it, and if Aliana is still alive, I know exactly where she and Sam Reilly will emerge from the rabbit hole. But we're going to have to act quickly if we want to secure the place."

"Send me the coordinates and I'll dispatch the men."

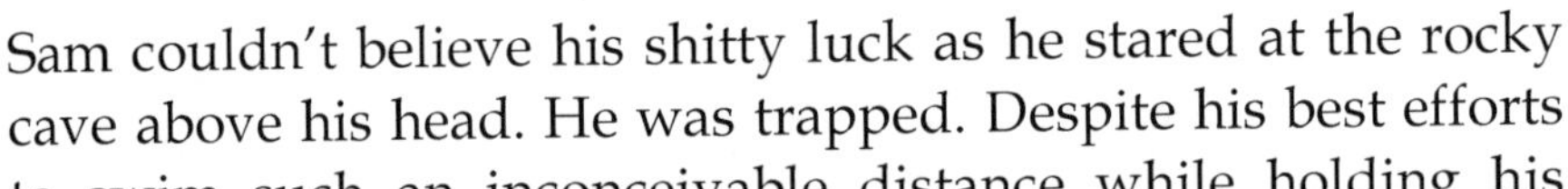

Sam couldn't believe his shitty luck as he stared at the rocky cave above his head. He was trapped. Despite his best efforts to swim such an inconceivable distance while holding his breath, he found himself no closer to the surface than before.

He allowed himself another two minutes to give his body time to allow its oxygen and CO2 levels to return to normal.

Hyperventilating once again, Sam again dived under the dark water below and tried to find another way out of his tomb. Despite having to hold his breath, he felt himself naturally relaxing after again submerging himself in the icy water. He had spent thousands of hours cave diving over the years, and it felt far from foreign to him.

Sam managed to explore three different tunnels.

Two tunnels were completely submerged and one contained a small pocket of air to support him, but neither tunnel offered a way to reach the outside surface.

At least he had a reasonable supply of breathable air on this side of the tunnel. If nothing else, that gave him enough air in which to exhaust the escape potential of each tunnel.

After four more attempts, Sam became concerned that the carbon dioxide levels inside his cave were probably starting to reach dangerous levels. He needed to find a way out and soon, if he was ever going to have a chance. If he couldn't make it out, Sam decided that he would rather return to the Magdalena and save Aliana the nightmare of swimming the submerged tunnel only to discover his corpse on the other side.

But could I even make that swim again?

Sam doubted it very much, regardless of his desire.

On his sixth attempt, he decided to try something different.

Sam knew that he needed to swim upwards in order to reach the surface of the lake, but thus far, all he'd discovered on his previous attempts was that each tunnel reaching upward towards the surface had ended in impenetrable rock barriers. Water was constantly flowing into the tunnel, but the surface marks around the perimeter of the underground lake appeared to remain relatively constant.

This meant that the water was obviously leaving the tunnel somewhere.

Instead of swimming upwards, Sam descended all the way to the bottom of the tunnel—guessing that he was at a depth of 30–40 feet. At the bottom, he could feel a gentle pull towards something beneath the largest rock that formed the barrier.

He allowed his body to drift for twenty to thirty seconds until he could be certain, and then swam underneath the rock.

The opening was narrow, and he scraped the skin of his wide shoulders attempting to get through.

The hole seemed to reach even farther down, he discovered.

It was far too narrow to permit him to turn around if it didn't lead to the lake's surface, and Sam found himself struggling to quell the terror that accompanied his fear of drowning.

For an instant, he saw his brother's face on the night that he died.

In a surreal moment, he felt as though his brother was encouraging him. As though, without words, he was telling him he was nearly there. Just keep going.

Sam had no idea how deep he had submerged, but even if he did have room to turn around, he realized that he'd already passed the point of no return. By now, even if he did have a way get back to where he'd begun, the lack of oxygen required to make such an effort would have rendered him unconscious before he made it.

With his lungs burning, he was very close to accepting his fate.

Ahead of him, he suddenly noticed a light on the rock below. It started to flicker, as sunlight would, through the tiny ripples of the lake's surface.

He began to rapidly kick with his legs, and pushed himself toward it.

Then, using his hands to reach through the opening, he pulled himself out of the hole and looked up. Above him he could see the crystal clear waters of a lake.

His watch indicated that he was under 30 feet of water.

Sam comfortably exhaled during his entire rise to the surface.

When his head finally broke free of the water, Sam took a deep breath of the most deliciously fresh air he'd ever breathed.

Above him, Sam heard the familiar vibrations of a helicopter coming up over the hill.

Oh shit, not now!

He quickly ducked back under the rocky ledge on the side of the lake. Having to hold his breath once more, his lungs burned instantly.

The sound of the helicopter overhead was amplified by the speed of the sound waves in the water.

Sam waited there for as long as he was able, until he was quite certain that the helicopter had passed, and then he resurfaced.

This time, he didn't wait to see if it was safe—he'd run out of time.

He felt dizzy and disorientated, exhibiting the first signs of cerebral hypoxia, and the muscles in his arms were beginning to cramp from the cold. His arms and legs had stopped shaking, another sure sign that his body was no longer attempting to compensate for the cold, and was now shutting down.

Sam knew that he had to get out of the water immediately, dry himself off and attempt to warm his body.

In the distance, he saw the back of a Robinson 44 helicopter as it hovered. At the back of its tail rotor Sam noticed a small yellow scratch.

Sam recognized that mark.

He'd made it with the yellow dive equipment four days ago, and then it hit him.

That must be Tom – and he was flying away.

Sam reached for a small piece of metal in his right zipper pocket, and used it to reflect the rays of sunlight toward the helicopter. He flicked it multiple times, so that the movement would cause an annoying flicker which the pilot would hopefully notice.

There was no immediate response, but Sam continued to try

to catch the pilot's attention.

Then, he watched as the helicopter turned and started to drop away over the cliff again, and off the mountain.

He was so close to being rescued, and now he'd lost it all.

CHAPTER 24

In the underwater lake, Aliana passed the time by taking stock of what worked, what didn't, and what could be repaired onboard the Magdalena. Sam had pointed out that if they ever wanted to get her off the mountain they would have to re-gas her.

It would be a prolonged process, taking many months, but if the Magdalena was ever to reach her rightful place in a historical museum, she would have to become lighter than air again. After that was achieved, a single helicopter would be capable of towing her.

In truth, Aliana realized that it was highly unlikely the Magdalena would ever escape from her watery confines. Sam probably knew it too, but it was better to try to keep her mind active with a purpose, rather than sitting around, waiting for death.

Starting with the pilot gondola, Aliana reached for the wooden steering wheel, much like that on a yacht, and found it still turned. She was even more surprised to discover, when she looked outside, that the huge rudder at the back of the airship still pivoted in response.

She could easily imagine the spectacular airship sailing through the sky.

It stirred something in her imagination, just as Peter Pan had done when she was just three years old, and she longed to see the old ship in the air again. But, just as with Peter Pan, she knew that it was little more than pure fantasy that it might someday fly again, but it made her happy.

Next, she turned the 14 valves which controlled the air input inside the canopy. To her surprise, they still had some air within them, but both compartments 13 and 14 leaked air out just as quickly as it entered them. She studied the diagram of the air valves, and noted that these represented the two forward compartments.

Aliana wondered if these were the result of the crash, or if they were what caused the crash. Had the Nazi's bullets damaged the Magdalena's bow compartments?

Next, she flicked on the helium tank valves.

As she expected, there was no sound of any gas moving.

She looked through the pressure markings, and tried to calculate exactly how much helium would be necessary to cause her to become airborne once again. She understood that the tanks that made up part of the hold in the pilot gondola were trivial in comparison to the amount of helium which would have been necessary to fill up the main airship canopy.

Aliana ran her hands along the rest of the controls inside the pilot gondola. There weren't many of them, and for the most part, they were merely monitoring devices: altimeters, pressure gauges, and engine pressure readers.

The Magdalena was a very simple machine compared to modern day standards of air travel.

Looking at the skeletons of the two pilots, she couldn't help but wonder, *what went wrong with your beautiful airship?*

Before leaving the gondola, however, she noticed a locker marked "maintenance tools." These airships were designed to be maintained by those onboard, come what may during their travels, in a time long before the existence of ground technicians and engineers, who nowadays could advise a pilot on his or her best choice of action with a simple radio message or computer signal.

Inside the locker, she found a number of tools, but only picked up a small metal box which contained a number of wrenches, and screwdrivers—just in case.

She then made her way along the airway, which linked the pilot gondola with the luxury passenger carrier, and then through that compartment to the one containing the engine. The engines were completely sealed in a protective casing. It appeared that the engine gondola had never been submerged into the water.

Much more basic than modern-day engines, the Magdalena's forward propulsion system consisted of four Daimler-Benz 32HP diesel engines. Unlike their modern counterparts, these engines relied on hand power to crank. They were primitive, but simple and reliable to operate and maintain.

I wonder if you could be coaxed into working again.

Sam had inspected them earlier, and had said that given enough time, he'd get them working again. She assumed, at that time, that he'd meant to repair them in a workshop or something similar. In reality, someone would probably just replace all four of them with brand new replicas, if the Magdalena ever made it out of here.

Her mind returned to the problem at hand—*that's if I ever make it out of here, for that matter.*

Aliana didn't allow herself to dwell on the thought. Instead, she decided to find the manhole, and climb into the giant canopy. From the outside, it looked entirely intact. But who knew what that meant in terms of the structural stability of its aluminum. Few things are designed to survive 75 years in a cold, wet environment.

She climbed up the aluminum ladder, unscrewed the manhole cover, and entered the canopy.

As far as she could tell, it seemed to be intact.

Exploring the canopy took longer than the rest of the airship, but again, as far as she could tell, the canopy, if filled with helium or another lighter-than-air gas, could, in theory, fly again.

She climbed back down and entered the main gondola, where the skeleton of Fritz Ribbentrop stared back at her. Its metal suitcase still securely chained to his wrist.

What were you doing here Fritz? And what are we going to do with your virus?

Something didn't seem to make sense to Tom as he banked the helicopter to the right in an attempt to get away from the strong reflection of the sun glistening off the waters of Lake Solitude.

He started to again descend off the mountain, but about two minutes later, he understood what was wrong. The powerful reflection he'd been trying to avoid, was moving in an up and downward direction! While that might mean very little to the casual observer, to a helicopter pilot, who had spent years flying over oceans and lakes, he knew that the up and downward flicker of the sun's reflection was only normally seen in the ocean or large lakes which had swells or ripples, whereas the waters of Lake Solitude lay perfectly still in the morning sunlight.

It must be a signal from Sam!

He knew it as intrinsically as his body knew how to maneuver the complex controls of the helicopter to return for a second fly-over. There, in front of him, sprawled over a rocky outcrop on the edge of the lake, like a lizard absorbing the sun's warmth, lay Sam.

At first glance, he looked as though he might be dead.

But, then he saw his friend sit up, smile at him, and raise the thumb of his left hand as if trying to hitch a ride from a passing motorist.

Tom carefully lowered the helicopter until he stopped its descent, hovering just above the rocky outcrop, mindful of the tall pines that lined the mountain to the east.

To his left, Tom watched as Sam opened the cockpit door, climbed inside and sat next to him in the front passenger seat.

"So, what took you so long?"

Tom immediately took off as soon as the door was closed.

"Okay, so what's our next step?" he asked.

"Can we get back to the Tyrol crow's nest?"

"No, not from what I hear. Your 'friends' know that you're here, and they're pretty pissed off about it. I'm sure they have some of their goons on hand, just waiting for your return."

"Okay, in that case, let's go to Lugano. There's a commercial dive shop there, and we're going to need to get some heavy supplies to rescue Aliana."

"Okay, you're the boss," Tom replied, as he started to input the details into his flight GPS.

Along the way, he waited patiently for Sam to tell him everything that had happened, including the discovery of the Magdalena, and about how Aliana was still trapped in the cavern below.

"We'll have to return with enough equipment to rescue Aliana," Sam said, through his chattering teeth. He looked dangerously cold. "We're going to need to get some dynamite too. At the moment, there's several hundred tons of rubble blocking our way."

"Gotcha."

When Sam stopped speaking, Tom said, "There's just one problem."

"Oh yeah, what's that?"

"There's an army on its way to Lake Solitude." Tom looked over at Sam's serious face as he continued, knowing that Sam wasn't going to like the next part, "They've discovered that it's the final resting place of the Magdalena."

"How the hell did they figure that out?"

Tom then told him about the man who had contacted him while he was in Paris, and also how the man had told him that he was unable to stop what was now proceeding in full motion—a race to retrieve the priceless cargo aboard the Magdalena.

Next to him, Sam Reilly's face displayed his incredulity at this piece of news.

"Well, that explains how they've managed to keep finding me."

"Now what are we going to do about it?" Tom asked him.

"Simple, we'll just have to make sure that she's no longer there by the time they arrive . . ."

CHAPTER 25

John Wolfgang heard the sound of falling rubble.

It might have been a massive cave-in, for all the sound that it made. A moment later, Brent came through the tunnel and reassured him that they'd finally broken through.

John checked his watch.

It was 0100. Just as Brent had advised him, it had taken 48 hours to accomplish. "Very good. Did you find their bodies?"

"No, but it's definitely where they went."

"How can you be so certain?"

Brent handed him a climbing bag, and said, "We found this at the bottom. Looks like one of them must have lost it when they came down the tunnel."

John looked at the bag. His eyes bulging with recognition, at the sight.

"Very good. Secure the location and I'll be down in a few minutes. I have to speak to the buyer before we kill them. No one goes any further without my orders."

Brent acknowledged him, and then added several additional orders in typical military fashion to his men.

John felt his head spin.

It was the first time since the Magdalena had first reared her wicked head that he'd actually felt physically unwell. He had seen that climbing bag before, and so he should remember it, since it was the same bag he'd bought for Aliana all those years ago.

Why hadn't she told me that she was climbing with him?

He had already considered the full extent of what might have happened. If Blake Simmonds knew that the tunnel reached the Magdalena, then perhaps they knew it too? If so, how would they try to escape with her?

Where would they come out? Then, as he looked out at the valley below, the answer finally became apparent to him . . .

Lake Solitude – of course!

John then considered how he could get there in time. If they had found the Magdalena, and then succeeded in finding a way out, it would mean that they already had more than a two-day head start on him.

It was time, John decided, to ensure that he had a second chance. He would never be able to flush them out from this end and secure Lake Solitude with his 5 men, even as efficient as they were. If he had more time, he could bring in additional help, but he hadn't expected these complications at all. The only chance he'd have was to bring in the Navy SEALs, who were already based near the lake, awaiting any additional information he could offer them.

If he reached Sam Reilly before he left the Magdalena, he could kill him, retrieve the virus, and save Aliana. She'd be mad as hell, of course, but he could deal with that later. After all, there were much bigger things at stake here than the life of just one man. If they did manage to find a way out before John reached them, the SEAL team could capture them, and he and Aliana could receive amnesty from the U.S. government.

John placed the call.

"We were right about something," he said, "Lake Solitude was indeed where the Magdalena disappeared. You'll need to secure the site within the next twelve hours if you want to catch them."

"We'll do that, and John . . ." the directness of the woman's voice sent a chill down his spine, "you'd better hope we get a return on our investment this time. We've already spent a lot of money toward this, and if we don't have something to show for it, we're taking you in."

"Don't worry. If I can't produce the goods this time, I'm counting on you taking me in."

Lugano was a little lake town in the north of Italy, shadowed by the dolomite mountains in the distance. Sam considered what he would need as Tom landed the helicopter in a small park at the town's southern tip.

"There's an adventure and climbing store here that meets the needs of tourists who are attracted to the lake and the Dolomite ranges. I'm not sure how much diving equipment they're likely to have on hand," Tom said.

"That's okay. For what I'm after, we won't need much dive gear."

After the short flight, during which the heating manifold was set to full, Sam's body temperature was beginning to return to normal, and with it, his usual level of confidence. The two men split up as Tom went to find out where he could get his hands on dynamite.

It was a clear sunny morning, but as cold as winter.

"Good morning," Sam said to the man standing behind the counter, as he entered the adventure store.

"Good morning, can I help you?" It was the welcoming voice of a Canadian, drawn to the town for the beginning of its peak climbing season.

"Yes, I have a list of the equipment I need," Sam said, as handed a slip of paper over the counter.

"An inflatable zodiac with a small two stroke engine, one large propane tank and burner, 200 feet of rope line, diving equipment for one person, a dry suit—2 inch thick, and dual air tanks." The sales assistant's left eyebrow raised in a tiny gesture, as though he couldn't imagine what Sam wanted with such a list of equipment, and then said, "Anything else?"

"Yeah, is there a marine mechanic here?" Sam asked.

"Just around the corner. Go out the door, and head up the street two blocks and you'll find a guy who's open."

"Thanks. I'll be back shortly to collect the gear, if you could please have it ready for me," Sam said, handing over Tom's Deep Sea Expeditions, company credit card.

"Not a problem."

Sam moved quickly to locate the mechanic.

He walked into the shop, knowing exactly what was needed.

Walking through the store, Sam discussed with the salesperson exactly what he needed, and after a short while, the mechanic returned with them.

He then purchased 20 gallons of fuel—it wasn't much, but it would have to do.

Sam thanked the mechanic who'd helped him and walked out with a cart filled with parts, which he then added to the other pile of dive gear, and waited for Tom to arrive with the now-refueled chopper.

He watched as Tom landed the helicopter, and then, leaving the rotors spinning, Tom carefully stepped out of it, lowered his head, and carefully walked up to greet him.

"I've got some bad news," Tom said.

"What now?"

"He called again."

Sam knew instantly who Tom was referring to, and he took great pains not to show his concern, as he asked, "What did he say?"

"They're not making an attempt at diving Lake Solitude as we expected they would." Despite the good news, Tom's face showed that his concern was justified. "Instead, they know about the ancient tunnel into which you and Aliana must have fallen, and they are tunneling down from above to reach it. Based on his predictions, they'll breakthrough in another eight hours."

"Okay, lets a get a move on, then."

They both boarded the helicopter, and as Tom flew over the southern tip of the Dolomite ranges, Sam spotted something.

At first glance, he assumed that it was just a climbing team on the Via Farrata. A closer examination revealed that they were all armed with military assault rifles.

"Oh shit, look at that," Sam said, pointing below.

"Who the hell are they?"

"There must be a hundred or more of them. Whoever it is they work for, they're not taking any chances, are they, now?"

"Yeah, but who do you think they work for?" Tom asked.

"What do you mean?"

"Well, we know that John Wolfgang and his team of mercenaries are trying to break into the tunnel you and Aliana fell through. So, if his team is in there, who the hell is responsible for these soldiers?"

"I have no idea, and I don't intend on sticking around long enough to find out."

"We just might be able to rescue Aliana, but we'll never have time to get the Magdalena's treasures out of there," Tom said. "There are just too many of these guys on the mountain."

"There still might just be a way."

"How?"

"What if we fly the Magdalena out of there?"

"Are you kidding me?" Tom's face displayed his incredulity. "You want to fly a 75 year-old dirigible, which crashed, mind you, when it was new, off the mountain?"

"Yes, I do."

"And, they called me crazy."

"So, are you going to help me?" Sam asked.

"Of course, I will. What are friends for?"

It was almost six o'clock in the evening. The last rays of the sun were edging their way to the side of the mountain behind Sam Reilly. As he quickly prepared his dive equipment, in the distance, he could hear the sound of Tom performing the tedious task drilling holes in which to place the sticks of dynamite.

"How much longer do you think you'll need, Tom?" Sam asked over his radio.

"It'll be ready to blow within the next three hours."

"Okay, let's sync our watches in five, four, three, two, one. Mark 15:05."

"Mark 15:05," Tom repeated.

"Let's blow this thing at 18:05."

"Copy that. Will do."

Just as Sam was about to make his dive, he asked, "How certain are you that this is going to work?"

"I've laid dynamite a number of times before. We've both done it, underwater. I know how to lay the stuff, but I just don't know for certain how big this thing is. I've added another 25 percent on top of what you estimated. You tell me? How confident you are about your estimation of the rock wall?"

Sam connected the last of his regulator fittings together and then said, "Okay, don't add any more than that. You don't want to blow apart the rest of the mountain. The Italian government's going to be pissed as hell as it is, when they find out we've blown up part of their mountain without approval."

Then, Sam dived under the water and started to make his descent to 30 feet, the depth at which he'd swum out of the underwater tunnel eight hours earlier. The tunnel was narrow, and he struggled with his underwater bag, which carried the equipment that was so essential for his plan to work.

When he eventually made it to the other side of the rock wall, he was amazed that he'd managed to get through there without using any dive equipment. The ordeal had really caused him to push himself to the edge of life and death.

"Can you still hear me, Tom?"

There was no answer.

As Sam expected, the solid rock wall precluded any form of electronic communication. Hopefully, the next time he made contact with Tom, the dynamite would have already worked and they would be on their way to freedom.

That is, if it did work.

If it didn't work, he couldn't imagine what their next move would be.

Sam kicked his fins slowly as he made his way through the enormous tunnel. It was a long way to go, but like most trips, this time it seemed to be a much shorter distance now that he had his dive equipment and could breathe.

In the distance, the green glow that he'd never forget could be seen illuminating the underground lake in which the Magdalena was trapped.

His heart raced as he thought about the prospect of seeing Aliana again.

As his head broke the surface of the lake, Sam could see her face. There were tears in her eyes.

"You made it!" Aliana said, as she raced to him and threw her arms around his wet body. "And you came back for me! Everything's really going to be okay?"

Sam kissed her. It was a passionate kiss, but it ended sooner than he would have liked.

"It sure is. But we're going to have to work quickly. We don't have much time," Sam said.

"Why, what's happened?"

"I'll explain on the way, but first . . ." Sam said, looking at his watch, which showed that it was already 17:10, "we have a few things that need to be done."

CHAPTER 26

John Wolfgang climbed up and over the rock inside the tunnel. On the other side were a number of glowworms, a smaller tunnel, and the shoreline of an underwater stream. At the end closest to himself, John noticed a steel bolt in the limestone wall. Its appearance suggested that something had been tied off on it at a previous time.

Had there been a boat tied there?

John waded into the water, followed by Brent and the other mercenaries.

It was cold, and the water deepened quickly. After taking his third or fourth step, he was unable to stand anymore, and started to swim. He was a slower swimmer than the mercenaries, but his need to get there first kept him focused.

John sensed that he was getting near.

He looked at his watch.

It read: 18:00.

Up ahead, he could hear a man and a woman speaking in fast, urgent words. His team was getting close. It drove him to swim faster through the tunnel.

Then he heard what sounded like a loud clap of thunder.

Brent looked at him and said, "That's either a cave in, or

someone's just used dynamite."

Sam watched as the large air bubbles underneath the Magdalena reached the surface. Aliana had looked at him as though he were mad when he told her that he needed to lay some dynamite. After 75 years, it was going to take a lot to release the Magdalena from the hold of the silty bottom, or at the very least, months of digging—and there was clearly no time for that.

He watched with satisfaction, looking down from the pilot house, as the limestone silt on the bottom, below the primary gondola, which had remained firmly locked, started bubbling like a boiling cauldron.

It continued for a couple minutes, and then a second dynamite blast exploded, sending another round of vibrations rippling up toward the surface.

"How confident are you that you're not going to blow us and the Magdalena to pieces?" Aliana asked.

Sam looked at her, a grin on his face displaying his self-confidence, as he recalled all the shipwrecks that he'd successfully resurfaced from the seafloor over the years, and then said, "I have a fairly good idea of what I'm doing."

"How many of those wrecks contained a virus so lethal that any damage to its container could literally threaten the existence of the human race on this planet?" Aliana asked.

"I was careful. Don't worry," Sam assured her.

The virus, inside its container, had been carefully moved to the pilot gondola, which sat higher up towards the front of the canopy, allowing it to remain dry once the Magdalena was once again floating freely in the water.

At just that instant, a large wave of water came barreling

towards them.

In the middle of the lake, Sam felt her break free from the silty bottom, and for the first time in 75 years, she was floating freely again, albeit, this time in water rather than in the air.

Sam pulled down on the two main propeller throttles.

The twin Daimler-Benz engines at the rear of the Magdalena roared into life, as fuel was allowed to increase its flow for the two engines at the rear of the Magdalena, which he'd managed to get started again.

Turning the wheel in his hands, Sam could feel her enormous rudder moving lethargically in the water. He increased the throttle, and the airship started to move forward, ever so slowly.

Tom would be blowing the tunnel entrance wide open any minute now, Sam thought.

And then the sound of gunpowder blasting echoed through the enormous cavern. His first thought was that the dynamite had exploded, but the sound of it didn't seem to be quite powerful enough.

Maybe it wasn't enough to blow the opening apart?

Then Sam realized where the sound had originated.

Behind him, he spotted men dressed in black military jumpsuits, rapidly approaching. Each man, in turn, took careful aim and fired at the Magdalena.

Outside the tunnel, Tom could hear the distant sound of a firefight.

It took him a second to realize that they weren't firing at him. On the opposite side of the lake, he could see the telltale sparks of gunfire; the tracers were lighting up the lake. He knew that they were on their way, but what he couldn't figure out, was how they had managed to get there so quickly.

Then he noticed that the gunfire was also being returned from the other side.

How many fucking people are *there searching for this damn ship?*

When Tom had originally heard the sound of gunfire, he'd assumed that it was Blake Simmonds' mercenaries attacking him. But, he could now see that they were firing at someone else, but who could it be?

The sound of gunfire was drawing closer.

If he wanted to get off the mountain in time to draw the attention away from the mountain, of any other helicopters that were patrolling, Tom was going to have to blow the dynamite soon.

Tom wouldn't permit himself to worry about or be distracted by potential problems that were out of his hands, and he continued to lay the last of the dynamite fuse lines.

Each of the lines ran to a central location where they attached to a central wireless router, allowing him to set off the charge from the air.

In the distance, he noticed that the first tracer bullets were approaching the edge of the area where his helicopter rested.

He was glad that Sam had suggested laying the extra charges and the line of aviation fuel, and he just hoped that the transmitter would work properly when he needed it.

Blake Simmonds continued to move along toward Lake Solitude with his team of mercenaries.

After coming to terms with the knowledge that John Wolfgang had betrayed his boss, Blake knew their only option was to help Sam Reilly escape, which would give him the chance to steal the virus once they were out of the mountain.

There was certainly no time left to make it to the top and then try to follow John's team in through the tunnels.

Blake's only hope was that by tipping off Tom Bower about the threat, he would come back and try to find a way to get Sam out of the bloody mountain. Once Sam Reilly was finally free, Blake could take out both Sam and Tom once and for all, and then steal the virus.

When Blake and his team had first arrived at Lake Solitude, he was at first worried that Tom might not have taken the bait. He was relieved when he spotted Tom's helicopter. Behind it, were the remains of thousands of tons of rocky rubble that appeared to have come from a landslide that must have occurred many decades ago.

That must be the spot where he's going to attempt to get Sam Reilly out.

His moment of relief was very short-lived, as Michael, the leader of his mercenary team, came to inform him that they'd spotted a team of Navy SEALs rapidly approaching the helicopter.

Where the fuck did they come from?

"Do you want us to remain concealed?" Michael asked, bringing his thoughts back to the matter at hand.

"No, I want you to engage, and make certain that they do not stop the man in that helicopter from blowing the mountain apart."

"Understood."

Tom flicked the connection switch on his wireless detonator.

The green light flickered briefly, and then changed to the blue symbol—indicating that the wireless connection wasn't reaching the helicopter.

He slid the power switch to maximum.

It would drain the power quickly, but provide a greater range for reaching for the wireless connection.

The connectivity light was still firmly locked on the color blue.

Behind him, he noted that there were so many tracer bullets flying through the air, that he could have sworn he was witnessing the Northern Lights. To make matters worse, this simulated aurora borealis was continuing to move steadily closer to him.

Tom's next decision was a simple one—he could either take off and escape now, or he could detonate the explosives on the mountain while he was still on the ground, and then take his chances by using the confusion to cover his take-off. In reality, either option left both he and his best friends in a deadly position.

He knew immediately that it was no choice at all.

Tom switched the master switch to "on," and started the rotation of the helicopter blades.

Sam Reilly couldn't believe their timing.

If Tom had blown the rock wall a minute earlier, they would have been too far into the tunnel, and out of the lake, to be attacked. Instead, John Wolfgang and his team were now stationed on the far banks taking aim at him.

He pulled each throttle to full.

Despite the fact that the tunnel at the end of the lake remained full of water, Sam motored towards its entrance. He knew that Tom wouldn't fail him.

The splendid red of the tracer bullets looked like shooting stars through the dark cavern.

Behind him, he could hear the sound of a dozen or more rounds spraying the back of the Magdalena's canopy.

He reduced the power of his port propeller, and then increased power to the starboard one, causing the airship to slowly turn on its axis to port. In so doing, he positioned the back of the Magdalena closer to the enemy gunfire.

Sam looked at Aliana, whose focus on her task hadn't wavered for a second, despite the gunfire, and said, "Hey, does this story seem somewhat familiar to you?"

"Sure does. Let's just hope that this time it has a different ending."

Sam felt the world shudder beneath him.

The water started to move towards the tunnel's opening.

Aliana pointed at the roof of the tunnel, still only a couple feet above the rapidly receding waterline and said, "We're never going to make it."

"Have faith, my darling. This tunnel is well above the height of Lake Solitude. If Tom has successfully blown the entrance to the tunnel, then this entire volume of water is going to quickly disappear."

"Sure, but if it doesn't make enough room for us soon, won't the suction drag us under anyway?"

"May do . . ." Sam replied. It was the best answer he could come up with under the circumstances.

Behind them, more bullets could be heard spraying the Magdalena's canopy.

Sam put both propellers in full reverse, but found that it had little effect over the strong suction of the current which continued to draw them forward, towards the receding water at the entrance of the tunnel.

Sam wrapped his arms tightly around Aliana.

He was quite certain that the nose of the Magdalena was going to collide with the tunnel's roof and smash it into a million pieces.

As the Magdalena was about to collide with the tunnel roof, the lake, now almost completely drained of its water, appeared to drop suddenly from underneath them.

It felt as though the Magdalena was sinking.

In reality, she was still floating on the water inside the tunnel, which was disappearing beneath them.

Sam waved goodbye to his attackers as he, Aliana, and the Magdalena disappeared below the surface of the now-empty lake.

CHAPTER 27

John Wolfgang watched in awe as the water level suddenly receded, and the Magdalena floated down and out through the tunnel with it, reminding him of the way a toy boat in a bathtub looked after the drain plug was pulled.

In the process, three of his men were swept away, and he presumed that they'd been drowned in the fast-flowing whitewater.

He didn't know whether to be happy with the knowledge that his daughter had survived, or terrified by the most likely outcome of this development.

Having failed to capture the Magdalena, John turned towards the remaining two men in his elite team—the men that his employer had sent.

"The buyer is going to be pretty pissed off that we lost them," John said, as he approached the two mercenaries.

"Who would have thought someone would pull the plug and the entire lake would disappear, taking them with it?" The first man responded.

"Yeah, that was pretty unexpected," John replied as he pulled his out Luger handgun, and shot each of them in the head . . . killing them in cold blood.

Circumstances made it imperative that John maintain his

allegiance with the other side. He felt no remorse in doing what he believed necessary.

Glad that he'd had the foresight to leave a number of radio transmitters along the way, John pulled out his radio and contacted the Navy SEAL commander.

"Ryan Walker?"

"Yes John, go ahead," replied the Navy SEAL commander in charge of the operation on Lake Solitude.

"They've escaped at this end. Expect them to surface somewhere on the lake any minute now."

"Understood," Ryan replied. "We have two targets here. One appears to be a group of fifty or more mercenaries, pretty heavily armed, and the other is a single helicopter—the same one our suspects used when they dived here a few days ago."

"Copy that. Hold your ground, but make sure that you don't let that chopper out of your sight. If you have to choose between the two, follow the helicopter."

"Copy that. Should we take it out now?"

"No, they have the virus. It needs to remain untouched. Do you understand how important it is that the virus not be damaged?"

"Yes, we've been ordered to protect it."

"I'm making my way back to the surface, but I'm going to need a ride from the mountain top."

"We'll send someone," there was a slight pause, and then the SEAL commander said, "The chopper's blades have just started to rotate."

"Don't you fucking dare lose it!" John shouted into his transmitter.

Tom had just enough time to close the helicopter door before raising the collective and lifting off. To his right, approximately three hundred feet away, out of the corner of his eye, he saw a number of tracer bullets flying towards him. Instinctively, he swung the tail of the helicopter around, providing a minimal amount of protection.

He then tilted the rotary blades, and made his approach toward the edge of the mountain. If he could manage to drop off it, he would be free.

Tom's eyes scanned the horizon and was relieved to see that there wasn't another bird in the sky. Even if there had been another helicopter on the ground, he knew that it would take them too long to start up and catch him.

He heard three bullets harmlessly rake the side of his tail, and then he dropped off the next cliff and down into the valley below.

He picked up speed as he lost altitude, and within thirty seconds, he felt that he'd safely escaped.

It's up to Sam now . . .

Behind him, Tom saw the two Blackhawks rapidly approaching.

Ah, shit! They're going to be a little harder to outrun!

He still had the altitude advantage over his enemies, but they had fighting ships, and all he had was an underpowered, unarmed sightseeing helicopter.

No, his only chance was to lose them and get rid of the helicopter before they shot him out of the sky.

Tom used the speed that he had picked up with his dive to maneuver around a mountain and search for a lake, or someplace where he could safely jump out of his copter. As he came around the narrow peak, he saw exactly what he imagined Peter Greenstein once saw—rugged mountains, lethal pine trees, and no flat surface anywhere.

He kept flying as fast as he could, but the Robinson 44 simply wasn't capable of keeping ahead of the more powerful Blackhawks.

Behind him, Tom could see that the two Blackhawks had slowed down and were following him carefully.

He continued watching as a number of tracer bullets flew past both his left and right windows.

It could have been less than a foot off his cockpit.

No pilot could miss that close a shot so many times, certainly not by accident.

"Robinson 44, this is the U.S. Blackhawk resting on your tail. You are hereby ordered to land immediately or we will take you out." Tom heard the voice of a typically relaxed American drawl, from somewhere in the southern states. For a second, he imagined that he could probably match the voice to a face.

"U.S. Blackhawk on my tail, do you mind telling me what jurisdiction you have over a privately owned tourist helicopter in Italy?"

"We're here with permission from the Italian government, on an anti-terrorism coordinated mission."

"Copy that. Can you then please explain your reason for firing upon a civilian aircraft?" Tom asked.

"We have reason to believe that you are in possession of some artifacts from the Magdalena. Please turn to 110 degrees and follow me in to a landing point."

"Acknowledged." Tom knew when the game was up. There was no way he could outmaneuver one, let alone two, Blackhawks, and to even attempt it would get him needlessly shot down. He'd survived one helicopter crash, but he doubted he would survive a second one.

Ten minutes later he landed his helicopter at an Italian military base.

He let the blades slow down naturally and then waited for members of the U.S. Marine Corps to arrive.

By the time the rotors had slowed down to the point where it would be impossible for him to take off instantly, several Navy SEALs came and ripped him out of the helicopter. He watched, bemused, as the highly-trained team took the helicopter apart in an attempt to find something.

A large man, with short red hair, and a grin that said, *"I'm gonna fuck you up,"* approached him and said, "Okay, where is it?"

"Where's what?"

The man looked at him, curiosity as much as pleasure, showing in his previously vacant eyes, and said, "Tom Bower, what the fuck are you doing caught up in all this?"

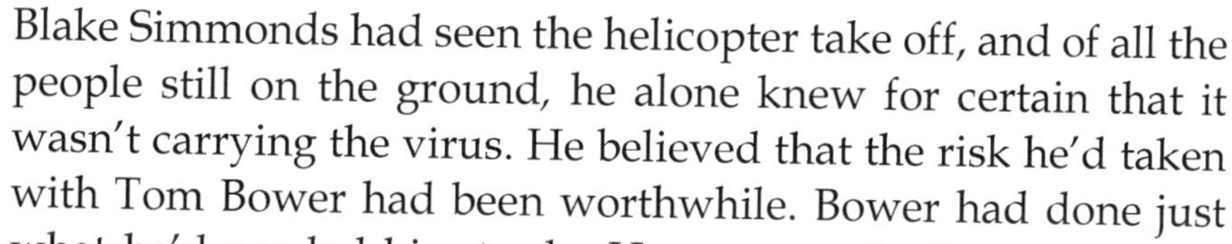

Blake Simmonds had seen the helicopter take off, and of all the people still on the ground, he alone knew for certain that it wasn't carrying the virus. He believed that the risk he'd taken with Tom Bower had been worthwhile. Bower had done just what he'd needed him to do. He was certain that Sam Reilly would soon appear from that tunnel on the side of the mountain.

"The helicopter's finally taken off, sir." It was the leader of his team, Mark Osborne, who then asked, "Do we have a secondary target?"

"Yes. The hole left by the explosion is the opening from which our target is going to exit. I am certain of it," Blake said.

"Will he be swimming, sir?"

"I have no idea. He definitely doesn't have any SCUBA equipment. He may have a raft, but nothing else. The priority here is to take control of that side of the mountain, so that we can secure the opening before he gets through it."

"Understood."

Blake watched as Mark issued a number of quick orders to the other men on his team.

Around Lake Solitude, the firefight between the Navy SEALs and Blake's team of mercenaries continued on into the night.

John Wolfgang climbed aboard the Blackhawk helicopter, as it hovered just a few feet above the mountain peak.

He wasted no time.

The outcome of the next hour would affect his entire life, and more importantly, Aliana's.

A muscled arm in military attire passed him a satellite phone.

"It's the commander on scene," the soldier said, "He wants to speak to you, sir."

John took the phone, and said, "Hello, John Wolfgang here."

"This is SEAL Commander Ryan Walker here," said the man's voice with military efficiency, "We have a problem."

"Go ahead."

"We've forced the chopper to land, but it wasn't on board."

"Shit! What about the Magdalena?" John asked, quickly.

"What about her? We were told that she was stuck somewhere inside the mountain."

"Yeah, well I have an idea that Sam Reilly has just made her unstuck."

"And you believe that he's going to bring her out of the hole in the mountainside?" Commander Walker asked.

"Sure do. I would make securing that your next priority."

"Copy that," Walker said, "there's just one problem . . ."

"What's that?"

"A second mercenary army is trying to secure Lake Solitude."

"Christ! Your team must have the upper hand. I was advised that you'd secured it earlier today," John told him.

"We did, and we will keep it secure, but we're outnumbered here, and the unknown army appears to be pretty keen on reaching the tunnel opening."

"I don't care what you do, or how you do it, just make sure that no one leaves the Magdalena."

"Copy that. No one's getting off this lake."

Blake Simmonds followed his team as they tried to gain further control of the region of the lake where the tunnel lay, toward the eastern end. He was long past the age in which he thought that he'd need to use his training as a military operative, but as it stood, what was at stake was far too valuable for him to entirely rely on someone else's training and expertise.

He'd already accepted that John Wolfgang had switched sides, but with whom, he had no idea. Whoever they were, they had considerable firepower and a professional team who knew what they were doing.

Blake had watched as the two Blackhawk helicopters chased the Robinson 44, and he hoped that they had taken the ruse, and consequently given him much more space and time in which to capture the Magdalena's most valuable treasure.

When his men approached the eastern side of the lake the incoming firepower increased dramatically.

Red tracer bullets now scoured the lake's bank.

So, they obviously know that Sam Reilly is going to come out from inside that tunnel, too.

As far as he could tell, all of the firepower was originating from a higher vantage point on the northern side of the tunnel. They would be able to reach the tunnel if they kept going, but to capture Sam Reilly, his men would first need to take out the enemy on the other side of the tunnel.

He pushed his men hard and offered an additional–half-million dollars to each of them if they were successful.

It was enough of an incentive to drive his men to push themselves literally to their deaths.

A tracer bullet suddenly flew past his head, missing him by no more than a couple of inches.

Shit, that was close. But where did it come from?

It wasn't from the north; instead it had been fired from the south.

Whoever the enemy team were, they had looped around the lake to approach him from behind. His men were now being outflanked by constant enemy fire from a stationary position in the north, as well as from a number of other attackers from the south, that were now moving in for the kill. To the west, Lake Solitude provided virtually no protection and to the east, the vertical limestone that formed the giant mountain range had them trapped.

It was a classic military strategy to outflank an enemy and thus divide their forces. Blake just hoped that he'd brought in enough men to overcome this maneuver.

Over the course of the next fifteen minutes, he was able to determine that his men outnumbered his enemies, but the enemy forces had superior firepower, and had bunkered-in earlier. He couldn't be certain, but to the north, there appeared to be three shooters with large, mounted machine guns.

His 72-man team greatly outnumbered the enemy, who, as far as he could tell, had somewhere in the vicinity of 12 men, but that wouldn't matter if he was unable to get control of those machine guns.

"Mr. Osborne, take your best men, and see if you can take out those gunners in the north," Blake Simmonds ordered.

"Understood."

He then watched as Osborne and 10 of his best soldiers climbed the debris field above the tunnel opening in an attempt to reach the machine gunners.

Below them, the fast-flowing, turbid water was surging through the tunnel opening and flowing into the lake. Its whitewater turbulence was tearing at the sides of the tunnel, and ripping out large chunks of limestone from its walls.

Any man who had the misfortune to fall into the raging maelstrom would be dead before he even knew what had happened.

Blake's eyes kept track of them for a couple of minutes until they disappeared from sight.

The myriad of tracer bullets continued to shoot through the air. It was hard to tell whether his team was winning or losing, and he had no idea whether or not the men he'd sent to destroy the gunners were even still alive.

Then, he heard the grenades explode.

The explosions emanated from north of the tunnel, and the entire area was lit up as if it were broad daylight. The surrounding pine trees caught fire. He heard loud screams of pain, but from whom, he had no idea.

The machine guns went silent.

Had his men destroyed them?

They were now in control of the lake. They would now be able to easily maintain the upper hand.

The fast-flowing water from the tunnel had settled as the water level inside the tunnel and that of the lake, had finally reached equilibrium.

Then, from out of the enormous tunnel opening came the unmistakable sound of large propellers spinning.

Blake Simmonds watched in awe as he bore witness to the nightmare of his father's past.

In front of him, in all its evil glory, he saw it—The Magdalena!

Her giant propellers spinning, they drove her inexorably towards the entrance of the lake.

"Get ready men, don't let her escape," Blake warned.

More than thirty of his men took aim at the propellers, ready to stop its forward momentum.

They never had a chance to pull their triggers.

The ground shook violently as another set of explosions detonated below their feet.

Blake watched, as the entire southern side of the lake burst into flames, as though someone had poured aviation fuel on the lake surface and tossed in a lit match.

The blast of heat that followed was so intense that those who weren't immediately incinerated dove deep into the lake trying to escape the conflagration.

Had the mystery military team set a trap for them?

Blake Simmonds couldn't answer his own question as he waded into the icy waters of the lake. All he knew, as he watched his professional team run for their lives, was that in the same instant in which he thought he had finally achieved the lifetime goal he once promised his father that he would fulfill, he had lost it all.

Without any other possible alternative or solutions, once he reached the western edge of the lake, he simply walked away from the disaster, finally free from the corruption.

In the background, the Magdalena sailed quietly into the night's water of Lake Solitude, unhindered.

Sam Reilly felt right at home as his hands ably steered the giant craft. It hadn't taken him very long to get used to its controls. It slipped out of the tunnel opening and sailed quietly into the lake.

Next to him, Aliana had the burner on full, expelling enormous volumes of heated air into the canopy of the Magdalena.

Sam could feel the pitch of the nose rising further and further out of the lake as the Magdalena slowly motored towards the lake's center. He wasn't completely certain that they'd made the correct calculations for the amount of heated air that was necessary inside the canopy, and he wondered, if it was even possible to now get the Magdalena airborne.

Then, like Peter Pan, the Magdalena started to lift out of the water and gently float upwards into the sky.

CHAPTER 28

The Magdalena flew through the night.

Sam Reilly was almost convinced that they had achieved the impossible. The enormous canopy slowly floated through the night sky like a dark rain cloud. He had flown many different aircraft in his life, but the Magdalena was one of the most magical. Like the child who dreamt of one day flying, the Magdalena seemed to belong in the sky. A part of him wished that he could have been around when airship flight was far more commonplace.

Sam watched as the beautiful girl, who was half asleep next to him, began to stir. He gently slid his hand forward and entangled hers. "Good morning," he murmured softly as she smiled at him.

"We're still alive?" Aliana asked, surprised.

"So far. I still haven't found a safe place to land. We haven't gone very far, perhaps 40 miles?"

"Now what?"

"I'm not sure about that, Aliana. You're the microbiologist. What are we going to do with this obscene virus?"

"You know that it must be destroyed, don't you?"

"I do. But when we land this ship, they'll never let it leave her."

"Then we must destroy it before we land."

"So many people have already been killed trying to acquire this weapon," Sam said. "How do we destroy it before they use it to destroy humanity?"

"The burner. That's what we'll use. We need to burn the entire container, so that as it melts, the virus won't have a chance to escape."

"Can't it escape as we open the container?"

"No, as long as it remains inside the burner, the virus will die instantly. The heat will most likely kill it before its container melts, anyway."

"Then let's do it."

Sam picked up the metallic suitcase, looked at it once more and asked, "Are you absolutely certain this will work?"

"Yes, I am."

Sam then tossed the suitcase directly into the blue blaze.

It took a few minutes for the shiny metal case to turn from a gloss to a blazing red, before suddenly combusting. The contents of the glass vials inside it bubbled as it was affected by the heat. Before long, the dreaded contents of the suitcase were finally destroyed.

"It's over, then?" Sam asked.

"Yes, it's finally over," Aliana replied.

He took her in his arms, and held her, as they both sighed with relief. Behind him, Sam heard the distinct sound of something he'd heard many times before. Sam didn't even have to turn his head to know that the Magdalena was being followed by two Blackhawks.

He only wished he knew who was piloting them.

Sam heard an American's voice, coming over a loudspeaker, and he gripped the Magdalena's steering wheel tightly, as he wished that it could help him find an escape route. Advanced as she was when first built, the Magdalena was more than 75 years behind the times when it came to her engineering and was certainly incapable of reproducing the speed and agility of modern day aircraft.

"Sam Reilly, this is Lieutenant Commander Ryan on board the U.S. Navy Blackhawk requesting that you land the Magdalena immediately."

Sam had no means of messaging the Lieutenant by radio, so he handed the steering wheel to Aliana, and then walked out onto the open-air gangway.

Next to him was the Blackhawk, which he presumed had ordered him to land.

He waved his arms, and then pointed to the mountains and pine trees below, as if to say, "Where the hell do you think I should land?"

"Sam Reilly, follow the Blackhawk in front of you. It will take you to the nearest landing site."

He waved his arms again to indicate that he would oblige.

It took more than six hours to reach the landing site. Sam concluded since they hadn't simply been shot down, that the U.S. government obviously wanted something that they had.

Finally, Sam saw a flat grassy area came into view below.

"Okay Aliana, I'll take over from here."

"She's all yours." Aliana said, looking relieved to turn the steering over to Sam.

Sam took the steering wheel in his hands again. It felt good. After making a couple of slight arm movements, he once again felt in control of the Magdalena.

Next to him, Aliana reduced the acetylene valve until the burner flame was almost entirely extinguished.

"Okay, pull the excess pressure lever," Sam said. "Remember, small bursts, we don't want to go crashing to the ground."

Following Sam's instructions, Aliana gently pulled on the excess pressure lever.

Above, they could hear the sound of heated air being released from the canopy.

There was no change in their flight.

"Okay, pull it a little more," Sam instructed.

After the fifth release, the Magdalena began to lose altitude, ever so slightly.

"Okay, let's increase the flame, just a bit. The ground is coming in a little too fast for my liking."

There was very little wind.

Sam would have appreciated a slight headwind to help steady the ship, but no wind was the next best thing.

Between the two of them, they continued adjusting the burner flame, the valve release and the speed of the motors, until the Magdalena eventually touched ground on the grassy field.

"Touchdown!" Sam exclaimed.

Aliana then pulled the excess gas release valve, so that the entire canopy released all of its heated air and the Magdalena's now empty three gondolas sank heavily onto the ground.

Immediately after landing, several Navy Seals stormed the

pilot gondola.

"Sam Reilly?" Asked the young man wearing military camos who greeted him. With the soldier's finger resting just above the trigger of his assault rifle, he gave Sam the immediate impression of a redneck hillbilly who wanted nothing more than an excuse to kill someone. The military needed people like that, he understood. They had their place, and for the most part, they could become excellent soldiers, but they were rarely bright enough to make it in, let alone to remain in one of the Navy's elite SEAL teams.

"That's me," Sam acknowledged.

"Stay where you are, and don't move. Who else is with you?"

"Just one other person. Her name is Aliana Wolfgang."

"Don't move or I will shoot to kill you both," the man said harshly.

"That's don't move, sir," Sam replied to his order.

"Who are you to tell me how to address you?" The soldier sounded irritated, and was just naïve enough not to show any concern.

"I can answer that one," stated the leader of the SEAL team. "Sam Reilly retains the rank of Major in the U.S. Marine Corps, as a nonoperational adviser, in his otherwise unspecified role—whatever the fuck that is."

The young soldier looked concerned, and started to justify his ignorance, but Sam ignored him completely and said, "Lieutenant Commander Ryan!" Sam looked genuinely pleased, "How are you, you old bastard?"

"Sam Reilly!" Ryan broke into a grin that matched the width of his enormous hand, as he reached out to take Sam's hand and shake it. "I never thought I'd see the day that I'd be the one breaking you out of a sticky situation."

"But how did you get involved here?" Sam asked. "And how did you know about me?"

"We had no idea that you were even involved until we captured Tom. It was just very good luck that the two of us once worked together in Afghanistan. He told me about your exploits. I was a little skeptical at first, and then when he told me that you were involved, I knew it had to be true."

"But why were we involved in any of this?" Sam asked, referring to the U.S. military.

"Surely you must know why, Sam."

"I can imagine, but I have no idea how your boss learned of its existence, especially since I first heard about it only two days ago?" Sam was genuinely surprised.

"I find that hard to believe, Sam. So, where is it then?" Ryan Walker inquired.

"The virus?" Sam didn't even bother to try to deceive his old friend. They had completed countless missions together over the years.

"Yes, what else do you think the President would be so concerned about?"

"What do you think I would do with a virus so lethal that it had the power to destroy the human race?"

Sam watched as Ryan's eyes slanted a look at the burner, its blue flames still a vibrant glow of amber.

"You silly rich bastard! You burned it?"

"Would you rather check the rest of the airship?"

"No, I can imagine there's no point." Ryan looked at him and said, "You know he's going to be pissed off about this, don't you?"

"Who?"

"The President."

"Publically, in his war room, I'm sure he'll appear to be mad as hell. But I'll wager a year's salary that he'll be relieved that this decision was taken out of his hands." Sam then looked at Ryan and said, "So, I guess that's it then. Shall we all go home now?"

"No, there's still the matter of the terrorist who has been after the virus."

"I thought we were the only ones after it?" Sam had decided early-on that the less information he betrayed about how he got involved in the matter, the better.

"No, there is someone even more dangerous than an altruistic fool like you, Sam. You're free to go, but we're going to have to borrow the Magdalena. Our one saving grace after losing the virus may just be to catch the man who wanted it so desperately."

He then explained to Sam exactly what they planned to do.

John Wolfgang stared at the Magdalena in the field ahead of him as the Blackhawk approached the landing site nearby. She had eluded him and his father for their entire lives. He wondered whether any of it was worth it, and wished that his father had never even discovered the damned virus.

The Magdalena was much smaller than he'd imagined she would be. The sharp lines of her aerodynamic canopy appeared more like sinister blades that took life than the beautiful airship that he'd imagined.

He wished the airship had never been built.

"Is my daughter onboard?" He asked of the soldier who had greeted him kindly in the Blackhawk, but who now acted as his guard. John had a slight quiver in his upper lip, the only visible sign that he was no longer in control.

Aliana was all that mattered to him now.

"Yes, she is," the soldier answered.

"And is she okay?"

"I'm told that she's fine."

"Thank goodness," John said.

"You'll be able to see her soon."

The pilot then landed the Blackhawk.

"So, it's over then?" John asked.

"What is?"

"Everything. The deal, the virus . . . it's all now under your control, and I hope your government uses it wisely for the prevention of war instead of as a biological weapon."

"It's not over yet. Lieutenant Commander Walker will explain it to you in more detail. He's waiting for you on board, and will explain everything."

The soldier then escorted John to the Magdalena.

A Navy SEAL with fire red hair and a confident smile shook his hand when he came aboard.

"John Wolfgang?" He asked.

"Yes."

"My name is Ryan Walker," he said, shaking John's hand. "I'm charge of this entire operation, and I'm here to tell you that we have a problem."

"We had a deal, Mr. Walker. It was quite clear. I get you the virus and the terrorist, and you get me my life back. Am I to understand that the United States government does not keep its promises?" John asked.

"We're more than happy to keep up our end of the bargain."

"Then, I want my life back."

"But the virus has been destroyed," Ryan told him.

The new information made John stop suddenly.

"After all these years, the countless lives that the search for the virus has taken, without ever even infecting any one of them, and you're now telling me that it had been destroyed back in 1939?" John asked, incredulously.

"No, you can blame Sam Reilly for that," Walker said.

"Sam Reilly destroyed it?"

"Yes."

John laughed out loud at the stupidity of it all.

"Well, at least he finally did something right."

"I won't lie to you, Mr. Wolfgang. My superiors are pretty upset about the loss of the virus. They have agreed to uphold the original deal if you help us capture the terrorist, Abdulla Azzama," Walker told him.

"And just how do you expect me to do that?" John asked. "You already know exactly where he lives. Why don't you just send in an unmanned drone to take him out?"

Ryan Walker laughed, and then said, "It's not as simple as you would imagine. Abdulla Azzama moves around a lot. Using an unmanned drone, we'd never be quite certain that we got the right man."

"So, tell me, exactly what do you want me to do?"

Walker then told him the entire plan, and then asked, "Will you do it?"

Sam Reilly watched as the older man came through the open-air gangway into the gondola. He recognized the man as John Wolfgang, but noted that his blonde hair was now more white than blonde in color.

Aliana ran towards her father and threw her arms around him.

"Dad!"

"Aliana!" John held her tightly to him. "Are you okay?"

"Yes. Tell me, is it true?" She asked, with tears in her eyes.

John didn't say anything at first. He looked almost too ashamed to speak, but he finally said, "You don't understand. There was nothing I could do about it. They threatened your safety. You must believe me, it was never about the money, I did it all for you, I promise. I'm so sorry."

She kissed him and said, "I believe you Dad," pausing briefly and then said, "Dad, I want you to meet a friend of mine. His name is Sam Reilly."

Sam shook his hand and said, "It's nice to meet you, sir. Aliana has told me of many of your extraordinary accomplishments."

"Thank you, and it's good to meet you, too." John smiled, but his intensely intelligent blue eyes refused to meet Sam's, and he quickly added, "I've also heard about a few of your accomplishments over the years, as well. Your father, of course, is a great man."

"That he is." Sam studied the man more closely, and couldn't help but recall the face of the man who tried to kill him while he was onboard *Second Chance.*

There was not a doubt in his mind.

Aliana's father tried to kill me.

"I'm sorry to interrupt you all here," Ryan said, "but we're going to have to get a move on if we're to reach the rendezvous point within four days. Time is everything here—we're going to get one chance only at this."

"Yes, of course," John agreed.

Sam spent the next few hours explaining all that that he could to help the man who had tried to kill him. In the end he said: "That's it. You'll find it's pretty simple. You'll get the handle of it by the time you get there."

John shook his hand.

This time, his eyes met Sam's.

"Thank you. I know how difficult this must have been for you." It was as much of an admission of guilt, as John would make. "If I don't make it, please look after my little girl. There are few men out there who I believe could be worthy of her affection. I believe you just might be one of them."

"I will, Mr. Wolfgang. You have my word," Sam said, and his word was just about as solid as you get, "Good luck. I mean it—I hope you nail this bastard."

Just before he and Aliana got off the Magdalena Sam watched as Aliana hugged her father and told him that she forgave him, for everything.

CHAPTER 29

Middle East, October 22nd

John Wolfgang had acquired some degree of confidence with the controls of the Magdalena by the time he reached his destination. His view of the desert oasis seemed so different from the air than it had a month earlier, now that he was at the controls.

That seemed like such a long time ago.

He lined up the airship with the runway. And it struck him as strange that the airship should even require a runway to land. Sam had explained the basic aeronautics of the airship before leaving Italy. In general, it was simple enough that even a child could keep it in the air, but it required some serious thinking to ensure that it landed safely without self-destructing.

John started to sweat as he began to make his descent.

It was the Middle East after all, and he couldn't deny he'd been sweltering in the heat for the past two days, but somehow, it seemed that he was sweating even more so now. He wasn't sure what he was more frightened of, landing the Magdalena, or meeting Abdulla in person, under the terrorist's terms. The man was powerful and used to getting his way in life. It would be a rare day indeed when someone bested him.

John just hoped today would be that day.

He followed the instructions, and slowly guided the airship to the ground.

Next to him stood a man wearing civilian clothes. The man was clean shaven, and had short red hair. He wore loose clothing and helped manage the buoyancy system on board.

The man looked at him confidently, and said, "You can do this, Mr. Wolfgang."

"I'm not worried about landing," Wolfgang told him, "I'll do my part, you just make sure that you do yours."

"It's a deal," Lieutenant Commander Ryan Walker replied.

John gripped the mahogany steering wheel so hard that the whites of his knuckles had become clearly visible.

They had dropped to an altitude of two hundred feet.

He would soon be on the ground, and then it would finally all be over—one way or the other. It was the not knowing that frightened him the most.

"How will you do it?" Wolfgang asked.

"It's better that you don't know until it's already been done."

"You mean—you'd rather I didn't give you away?"

"Yes. Look, Mr. Wolfgang. We train for this every day. During the few minutes when the action takes place, we're not conscious of what we're doing. It's only muscle memory we've built up over years of repetitive scenario training that guides us. We have no idea how you will respond, but I guarantee my men will successfully complete this mission," Walker said.

"I understand."

"Good. Now, let's land this relic and get this over and done with."

John Wolfgang noted the three armored Bentleys parked along one side of the runway.

"That'll be Abdulla there, I suppose," he said.

"Let's hope so," Walker replied.

"It's him. I'm sure he'll come today. This is too important for him to ignore."

"We've been closely following this man's movements for more than ten years. He's had a price tag of more than 10 million U.S. dollars on his head for most of that time. It takes a very cautious man to stay alive despite that kind of surveillance. His own men are extremely protective of him, with a religious fanaticism. I would be very surprised if he simply came in on his own."

"What should I do if his men want me to leave with him?"

"Then I suggest you do so," Walker said.

"Then what?"

"Then, you'll have to convince him to return to the Magdalena. I don't care how you do it, but it's the only chance we have."

"And if I can't?" John asked.

"We both know the answer to that question, don't we?"

John nodded his head, and said, "I suppose we do."

"Okay, we're now at fifty feet. I've slowed our rate of descent to ten feet per minute. I'll count you in for the last ten feet. Brett is ready at the rear of the gondola with the anchor ropes. I'm sure Abdulla's men will want to secure us to the ground as soon as possible."

"Copy that."

The Magdalena sank slowly toward the tarmac.

"Ten feet."

"Five feet."

Next to him, Ryan Walker gave three small bursts of flame to terminate their descent.

John flicked the directional switch, and the propellers swung into reverse.

The Magdalena slowed its forward and downward momentum until it rested just two feet off the ground, directly across from the armored Bentleys.

Several men ran up to the Magdalena, and took all four of the anchor ropes, tying two of them to the cars and the other two around large wooden stakes, which were rapidly being hammered into the sandy ground by two other men.

Then, between the twenty or more men, the Magdalena was pulled out of the sky until it was held firmly on the ground.

"Well, here goes . . ." John said, walking to the door of the pilot house.

"Good luck," Walker said. "You'll be fine."

John opened the pilot house door and stepped out onto the open-air gangway. He held his hands up and apart to show that he wasn't carrying a weapon.

He noted that there were now more than a hundred men on the ground surrounding the Magdalena.

All of them were armed with rifles.

Several men then quickly came to meet him, one of whom told him, "We would like to come on board and make certain that the ship is safe before our master enters." The man spoke in broken English, but with a confidence that more than made up for it.

"Understood. Help yourself. I have two of my men on board, and they will show you around."

"Very good, please tell them to come out here, too."

"Okay," John agreed. "Ryan, Brett. Come on out here so that they can see you."

I really hope this isn't the part where they machine gun us all to death.

John fervently hoped that Lieutenant Commander Walker was correct when he told him that the virus was too valuable for them to risk hurting him.

After several minutes each of the men returned after searching the ship.

"My apologies, but it was a necessary task. As you know, my master has been threatened from time to time."

"That's okay. I understand," John said. "Would you like to invite your master into the passenger gondola where we can discuss the final arrangements for the transfer of the virus?"

"Yes, of course. He will come with his guards."

"Of course."

The man then signaled someone near the car, and a confident Abdulla Ashama exited the vehicle and walked out to greet him.

Abdulla entered the Magdalena, escorted by five heavily armed men wearing balaclavas.

"My apologies, Mr. Wolfgang. These are members of my elite personal guard. I hope you do not take offense to them being present."

"No, I understand," John replied. "This is my co-pilot, Ryan and his assistant, Brett."

The man nodded his acceptance, but otherwise took no notice of John's two crewmen.

"How is your daughter, Aliana?" Abdulla asked.

"She is well. And your family, how are they?"

"Good," Abdulla commented. "Last time we spoke of the other contents on board . . . please, humor me, what were they?"

John thought seriously about where this question was going. Abdulla had previously stated that he cared little about the artifacts aboard the Magdalena, and then said, "There was more than ten million dollars in gold bullion on board, a diamond which has yet to be appraised, but which must be worth several million dollars, and there was a multitude of other precious gems as well. Their value is entirely irrelevant when compared to the agreed-upon price for the virus and its vaccine. Like the A-bomb dropped on Hiroshima, this virus will alter the position of the world's superpowers so greatly that they will have no choice but to cower and comply with your demands."

Abdulla stopped suddenly.

"Please forgive me, but I am not the man you should be talking to," Abdulla said.

Oh shit – they know!

John had no idea what his next move should be or how he could even warn the Navy SEALs who were there.

One of the armed men, standing behind the rich oil Sheik began to remove his balaclava and stepped forward.

"Alkmaar, you have served me well. You may now take your normal place." After removing his balaclava, he revealed himself as the true Abdulla Ashama. "Now, I wish to talk to my friend Mr. Wolfgang," he said.

The entire thing had been a ruse on their part to ensure the safety of Abdulla.

"I'm hurt that you didn't trust me," John said.

"I didn't, but now I see that you are a man of your word," the real Abdulla said, and then continued, "Mr. Wolfgang, I had my doubts that you would be able to locate it, but I never thought in a million years that you would show up with the Magdalena herself, right at my doorstep."

"It gladdens me to see that I have pleased you, my friend," John said obsequiously.

"So, it has survived all this time?"

"Yes."

"May I see it?" Abdulla asked.

"Of course."

John reached into the compartment beneath the seat and withdrew a metallic suitcase.

An electronic keypad was located at its base, and John tapped more than twenty keys in quick succession. A green light flashed, indicating that the correct sequence had been entered, and then the suitcase snapped open automatically.

In the middle of the suitcase lay three vials of an almost entirely clear substance.

"For a substance so powerful this appears to be rather small," Abdulla said, making no attempt to hide his disappointment.

"They are small, but don't forget that a nuclear bomb works by only minute, subatomic particles and yet still it has the ability to level entire cities."

"Of course, of course," Abdulla said, nodding his head. "And the vaccine?"

John didn't reply immediately.

Instead, his hands reached below the same hidden space, below the seat, and withdrew a second metallic case. After repeating the same process as the first, he opened it for Abdulla to see.

This one housed a laptop computer and a satellite phone. He switched it on and the image of a bank in Zurich appeared on the monitor.

"I would like you to transfer the money into this account. Once I have confirmed that the final 10 billion dollars has been deposited, I will provide you with the antidote to the virus," John said.

"You seem like a fair man to me. But how can I trust you to complete the transaction after I have transferred the entire amount to your bank?"

"Well," John said, looking out of the large glass windows at the men who now surrounded the Magdalena, "I should think that if I fail to provide you with the antidote after I've received payment, you will kill me, probably after first torturing me. No, I think you can trust me to make good on our deal."

Abdulla laughed again. It was a big hearty laugh from a man who was unaccustomed to men speaking to him so frankly.

Abdulla then picked up his own phone and began to speak rapidly into it in Arabic.

Afterwards, he looked back at John, and said, "Okay John, it will be done."

"Very good."

About three minutes later John watched as his computer registered the 10 billion dollar funds transfer. A quick phone call to his personal bank manager assured him that the money had been successfully deposited.

"Are you satisfied?" Abdulla asked.

"Yes, very."

John opened a trapdoor located beneath his seat and extracted a third suitcase. Upon opening it, Abdulla could see that the suitcase held 100 hypodermic syringes of the vaccine, with the needles attached.

"As you can see," John said, "I was more cautious with the vaccine than I was with the virus."

"So, this is goodbye then," Abdulla said. "It's been a pleasure doing business with you, Mr. Wolfgang."

Then, he stood up as he and his men turned to leave.

Abdulla clutched at his chest.

Shock and dismay could be seen, planted firmly in his eyes, as Abdulla came to the abhorrent realization that he had been betrayed.

Abdulla looked down at the hundred or more tranquilizer darts now piercing his body.

He never spoke, but his eyes told John that Abdulla wanted to kill him.

John, as well as everyone else in the room, had also been pierced by hundreds of the same tiny tranquilizer darts, and he was also starting to feel their paralyzing effects.

John felt sorry for his enemy, who could never have guessed that all of the three men in that room would willingly sacrifice their own lives so that he could be captured.

John never saw Abdulla suddenly lunge at him with a deadly knife.

It sliced directly across his throat.

John was surprised to feel no pain.

The injected sedative had a calming effect, and John felt a sense of peace come over him as he quickly bled to death, a feeling of peace which he'd not felt for the past twenty years.

He wanted to raise his hand to his throat to put pressure on the wound and slow the bleeding, but the toxin had already taken effect and despite his desire to live, he was unable to save himself.

Completely paralyzed, John Wolfgang had no way to stop the rapid flow of blood from his severed carotid artery.

Now it's really over, and at least my girl is safe – were his final thoughts as he was claimed by death.

Sam Reilly slid open the secret safe beneath the gondola's carriage, which he'd discovered on the night that he and Aliana had first found the Magdalena, and he stepped into the room where all eight people lay quietly, no longer breathing.

The weapon that Ryan Walker had installed on the airship had served the purpose for which it had been designed—to disarm every single person within the room quietly and without a fight.

He looked at the 100 loaded antidote syringes in the suitcase in front of him.

John Wolfgang had done his job – the antidotes were right where he needed them to be.

He injected Ryan first, and then Brett.

"Quick, John's been hit," he told them.

Lastly, he went over to do the same to John, but a cursory glance told him that the man had already lost far too much blood.

Without hesitating, he stuck the needle into John's deltoid muscle, and expressed the full contents of the syringe.

The antidote began to work within seconds.

Sam could hear the sound of gurgling blood coming from John Wolfgang's mouth. He'd started to breathe again, but Sam guessed that it would not be for long.

"Help me sit him up, Brett."

It only took a second, and the gurgling sound cleared for a moment as the blood slid down John's throat.

"I'm sorry John . . . I never meant for you to get hurt," Sam apologized.

His pale white face stared blankly back at him.

John was already dead.

Aliana was going to be devastated by the news.

"I'll get the Magdalena ready to launch," Sam said.

"Good," Ryan commented, as he then picked up the satellite phone, scrolled down to the second number and pressed enter.

When the call was picked up, he said, "I need you to eliminate the three targets on the map."

On the other side of the planet, the President of the United States and several military aides, stood in a secure room as the order was given for three computer guided missiles to be discharged from a drone now in place 90,000 feet above an almost deserted runway in the Middle East.

Sam watched as all three cars exploded simultaneously.

The shockwave produced was almost enough to destroy the Magdalena and definitely enough to injure every single person who surrounded her on the ground.

No more than a few seconds later, he felt the Magdalena lurch forward as Ryan and Brett cut the anchor ropes.

He pushed the throttles forward to full, and the airship began to pick up speed.

Behind him, Sam heard the scattered sounds of gunfire.

"They're waking up!" Sam yelled.

"We're on it," Brett replied, as he ran out onto the open-air gangway.

Sam adjusted the settings so that the Magdalena was ready to fly at maximum speed.

Then he heard the sound of the grenades exploding below.

Once the explosions settled, the sound of gunfire ceased.

Sam set a course, and sailed the Magdalena toward home.

CHAPTER 30

Sam knocked on the door of his father's Boston penthouse. It always irritated him that he should still have to do this. The place was guarded more heavily than the Pentagon, his father would have already known that he was on his way up, or else Sam would never have been able to reach his floor. It was that simple.

Standing next to him, Aliana was wearing a flowery dress, which he thought made her appear even more beautiful, if that was even possible. Despite receiving the sad news of her father's death, she was determined to see the good in the world, and vowed to make the Wolfgang Corporation the leader in medical research using the additional 10 billion dollars now in her father's bank account.

Aliana, Sam decided, would make his father happy, if nothing else.

"Enter." His father's voice sounded as though he really did believe that he was right up there with God.

Sam walked in, holding Aliana's hand in his.

"Afternoon, dad." He said, as he found his father sitting next to another, older gentleman wearing an Armani suit. He might have been any one of his father's many employees, advisers, politicians, or anyone whose name appeared on the Forbes Top

Ten Rich List. "This is Aliana, the girl I told you about."

His father stood up and kissed her on both cheeks, "I'm James Reilly, and it's an absolute pleasure to meet you."

Sam noted that his dad didn't bother to introduce the old man with whom, he'd been sitting, and Sam didn't bother to inquire. If his dad didn't choose to make the introduction, it was because he didn't want to. His father might be an arrogant, certified megalomaniac, but no one ever said that he was anything less than exceptionally intelligent, precise and deliberate in everything he did.

A butler entered, and handed Sam a glass of red wine. Grange. 1994 vintage. Then he gave Aliana a glass of white Muscato. She looked at Sam as if to say, *how did he know exactly what I like?* "Don't feel too excited, Aliana," he said, "It would have been Martin, my dad's butler, who took it upon himself to find out what you like to drink. My old man wouldn't have thought about offering us any refreshments at all."

"That's not true, Sam. I don't like to be the only one drinking, when I'm not alone." His father continued to completely ignore the older man, who still sat quietly at his side, sipping his drink. "And where's Tom?"

"He's back on the Maria Helena."

"Ah, at least that makes one of you who actually does some work for what I pay you," James Reilly said. "And, Aliana, what type of work do you do?"

"I'm a microbiologist. I'm soon to complete a PhD in microbiology at MIT."

"Excellent. And when do you start working for me?" His father said, assuming that all intelligent people should be under his employ.

"Thank you, but I plan to lead the research department of my late father's company." She then smiled politely at him, and said, "I'll let you know if I'm ever in need of a job."

"You do that, won't you?" He then turned to Sam: "So. What's your plan now? When do you return to the Maria Helena?"

"End of the week. First, Aliana and I are going on a holiday. A real one this time and then we're both returning to work. The Maria Helena is off to the Gulf of Mexico, where a large amount of dead sea life has recently washed up ashore. My money is on one of the big mining companies doing something they shouldn't be doing."

"Mexico? Well, they can't pay very much, surely?" His father said, sounding disgusted.

"They don't pay at all," Sam corrected.

"You're doing pro bono work now, son?"

"No, technically, I'm still being paid by you," Sam quipped and then laughed. It was a rare day when he got the best of his father.

"Hurry back, and do some real work—something that at least brings money into the company, will you?"

"You do know that dead fish in Mexico will lead to dead fish in the U.S., don't you?" Sam asked.

"Ah, that's not my problem," His father said, arrogantly.

The older gentleman sitting next to James Reilly turned to look at him, and said in his upper-class British accent, the precise class of aristocratic British snobbery to which his father could relate, "Thanks for the drink James, but I must be on my way home. I have a flight to catch. They won't hold my Lear Jet indefinitely. Glad to hear it all turned out well for you."

"Thanks Blake, I do appreciate your help," Sam's father replied, shaking the man's hand.

"Of course," the man nodded his head solemnly, "when its

family." The man then turned to leave, but hesitated briefly. "Oh, and I almost forgot to mention, here's that painting that was stolen from you."

"Ah, much appreciated," James said.

Then as the others were admiring the original Monet, James Reilly tore the back off of it and removed a small sealed vial labeled, Hitler's Virus: Antidote.

"I do appreciate your efforts, Blake, but this thing is virtually useless now."

Mr. Simmonds gave it his most basic perusal, as only a fine European antiquities collector could, and then said, "Excluding of course, the almost priceless value of Claude Monet's first attempt at painting water lilies."

"Well, I suppose that's of some consolation. I'll have it put up somewhere around here, I'm sure. If Sam's mother was around I'm sure she'd insist it be hung in the kitchen, or some other silly notion. Perhaps I'll have it hung in the study, as a reminder not to be so frivolous with my money again."

"Yes, I imagine that's probably the only real value of it," Blake agreed, before closing the door behind himself as he left.

Sam looked at his father.

"Well, you do look pissed, don't you?" James Reilly said.

"That man tried to kill me and steal the virus whose only purpose was to destroy humanity. I thought you said I could trust him?" Sam said, belligerently.

"Me? No, I never said you could trust him. I merely said that he could provide you with answers. As it was, I didn't realize that he worked for someone who wanted more than answers to your mystery, and who was willing to stop at nothing, including murder, to achieve his goal."

"What now, then?"

"What do you mean?" His father looked genuinely surprised at the question. "Now we carry on with our lives. What you choose to do with yours is entirely up to you."

"No, I mean, what about Blake Simmonds?

"I still don't know what you're referring to, son. I suppose he will go on with whatever it is that strikes his fancy, just as both you and I will do." He then looked at Aliana, and glanced back at Sam, adding, "Although, I think that among the three of us, you have the better deal."

"So, that's it? He tries to kill me and you write it off as nothing?"

"My goodness, no." His father mocked his son's genuine concern. "He's a rich and powerful man, and like all rich and powerful men, he is completely devoid of morals." There was an inherent implication of his disapproval of Aliana's father in his statement. "I should think, now that the virus has been destroyed, that he would cease to have any further dealings with you, alive or dead."

"So, it doesn't bother you that he's made several attempts to kill me in the past month?"

"No, not really. Should it?" His father said, looking at him curiously.

"Yes, of course it should!" Sam answered, adamantly.

"Why? I thought that it was more revealing of your carelessness to involve a man like Blake Simmonds in a treasure hunt for something that was so valuable."

"You gave me his details!"

"Yes, but I had no idea at that time just how valuable your treasure was." It was as much contrition as he'd ever heard his father offer.

Blake Simmonds rested his head into the soft leather of his Lear Jet.

He sat alone, and had told his pilot and crew to leave him that way for the duration of his flight, home across the Atlantic.

After so many years, it was finally over.

He then opened a $50,000 bottle of whiskey dated 1939.

It had taken some serious effort to track the stuff down, and once he'd acquired it, Blake had stored it in anticipation of this very day. He poured himself a glass and then added ice cold whiskey rocks.

From inside the secret safe at the end of the room, he withdrew his father's military badge.

It was a brass double rune emblem of the German Schutzstaffel, followed by the number 3, denoting the wearer as SS party member number 3.

In terms of seniority, this placed his father only just below Emil Maurice, the founder of the SS, who was member number 2, and Adolf Hitler, who was, of course, SS member number 1.

Blake Simmonds examined the precious historical artifact as his mind considered the life of its original owner.

As a senior SS officer, placed in charge of the capture of Fritz Robentrop by the Fuhrer himself, August Frank had mistakenly allowed Fritz to escape, in the expectation of catching his partners in crime, and consequently then having more to show for his efforts. In retrospect, he soon came to realize that he lost something far more valuable—the virus.

Frank placed all of the blame for that fiasco on Walter Wolfgang. Then, when it became apparent that no matter how ruthless the SS had become, Germany's people would not rise up strongly enough to beat back the Allied invaders and Hitler was going to lose, he decided to take matters into his own hands.

By the end of the war, Frank had reached the highest echelons of Nazi seniority. He used his power and position to take charge of a large stockpile of German gold, before escaping Germany as a refugee and moving to London. As an old graduate of Eton, he had many rich friends in the British aristocracy. He purchased a large estate and set himself up as a rich gentleman, always with the intention of one day returning to Germany and finding the lost Magdalena and the virus she carried. He was determined to one day rectify his mistake by acquiring the virus, and making Germany the supreme leader of the world, just as Hitler had tried and failed to do.

His need to make amends to his beloved Fuhrer became an obsession, one that only he could accomplish with the enormous wealth that he had taken with him as he fled.

As the years passed, and he realized that all the money in the world could not help him. He married and had a son, who Frank raised as a British gentleman. By the time the Berlin wall came down, Frank was an old man in his nineties, but he nevertheless believed that his son could one day achieve his dream. He was disappointed to discover that Walter Wolfgang was now dead, but motivated by the knowledge that Walter's son, John Wolfgang, had become a world leader in the field of microbiology, and desperate for the money required to set up his pharmaceutical business.

It was an easy deal to make. He would have to help John Wolfgang find the Magdalena, and then figure out what to do with the virus.

The hardest part, was to convince his only son that it was the right thing to do.

Blake Simmonds then took a long drink of the whiskey,

"Here's to you dad—the man who inadvertently lost the war for Germany, but saved mankind."

CHAPTER 31

Sam Reilly opened the doors to the elevator.

Aliana had left earlier, while Sam remained behind to have his annual twenty-minute catch up chat with his dad.

His father owned the top ten floors of the building. The highest two and the roof were part of his grand residence, while the other eight floors were places Sam had never seen, nor had he ever bothered to wonder for what purpose his father used them.

Today, the elevator stopped at the 76th floor.

Four levels below his father's residence.

The doors opened, and a tall woman with tidy, short cropped, dark red hair walked in. She was slim, and the hardened bony features of her face betrayed the arrogant confidence of someone accustomed to power, and none of the signs of age which often afflicted other women in their early forties.

Sam watched her enter and felt his heart beat just slightly faster, as his hands turned clammy.

The doors closed but the elevator did not resume its downward movement.

"Madam Secretary," Sam Reilly smiled, unsure of how genuinely happy he was to see the U.S. Secretary of Defense again. "You could have saved me a lot of trouble if you'd shared your interest in the Magdalena with me from the start."

It was as much of a reproof as even he was willing to give the leader of the world's most powerful Armed Forces, her position second only to that of the U.S. President, America's Commander in Chief.

"Sam Reilly," she said, her voice was quiet but nonetheless scolding in its tone. "You have cost your own government a fortune, not to mention the loss of the single most dangerous bioweapon in history. Do you realize how long we have been manipulating John Wolfgang to both find the Magdalena and catch Abdulla?"

Sam opened his mouth and started to answer . . .

"I'm not finished yet, Reilly," she continued, "It wasn't until the very end that we were even convinced that we had any control over the man, and we never did learn the identity of his original financial backer, and, we could only imagine what that person's interest in all this was. So, what do you have to say for yourself, Reilly?"

"You should have let me in on the game from the beginning, "ma'am."

"Reilly, you impudent fool! We weren't convinced you hadn't gone rogue, especially when our surveillance showed you fraternizing with Wolfgang's daughter. How could you have been so stupid? Haven't you ever seen a pretty girl before?"

Sam kept his mouth shut this time.

"I want you to know, I expressed an interest in having you taken out from the onset, Reilly . . ." Her voice betrayed not one iota of an apology, and she continued to say, "but the

Commander in Chief vetoed the idea, advising that your unique attributes made you useful and although it appeared that your loyalties may have been misplaced, perhaps through your bungled efforts, our surveillance might be successful in finally obtaining the identity of the person who was really controlling our puppet, John Wolfgang, from the beginning. I'm not sure whether or not the President really believed any of that, but if we inadvertently managed to kill James Reilly's only son . . . well, we can only imagine how that might affect your father's future presidential contributions, I'm sure."

Sam had never even considered the President's relationship with his father, but he had no doubt that she was telling him the absolute truth.

"After all, with your finances and your standing around the globe, who could possibly be entirely convinced as to where your true loyalties lay?" the Secretary of Defense said.

Sam knew that it was a hollow threat.

She, of all people, knew exactly how much honor meant to him. His word was like an ironclad bond, and when he gave it in service to his country, there was nothing and no one who could force him to break it.

"That's rubbish, ma'am, and with all due respect, your naiveté nearly got me killed this month."

"Should I take that as your formal request for resignation?" She asked, a seductive smile just forming.

"No, would you like to ask me for it?" It was Sam's turn to be provocative.

She paused, her head tilted just slightly to the left, as she mulled it over.

"I would like that, you know I would, but I am duty-bound to the defense of this country, and in that regard, I'm obliged to retain the services of the most competent person for any position." She eyed him up and down and then said, "And you, Reilly, have the most extraordinary credentials, which make you particularly useful. You've been an exemplary Navy SEAL, with the highest marks on record of any recruit, a highly-respected leader in marine biology and in the maritime world, and since you're wealthier than any playboy pup, the world opens its arms wide for you, whereas any other official investigator would have their arms tied. No, we need you, Reilly. Just try not to fuck up our mission the next time out of your own good will."

The elevator door then opened, and she stepped out.

"Yes, Madam Secretary."

The elevator continued its descent, and Sam couldn't help wondering, *just who was blackmailing John Wolfgang?*

Sam Reilly took the helm of his newly built ship, *Second Chance II,* as it sliced through the crystal clear waters of the Caribbean. Aliana was at his side, as beautiful as ever, and they were sailing alone through some of the most pristine islands on earth.

"Where did the name *Second Chance* come from?" Aliana asked him.

"It's exactly what the name says—it's my second chance."

It was an answer, but Sam knew that it wasn't what she wanted to know.

"But, there's more to it, isn't there?" she persisted.

Sam considered evading her question, or even making up a simple answer, as he'd done so many times before, but today was different. Aliana was different, and he had no desire to lie to her about it as had been his usual reaction to that question.

"Did you know that my mother was a very good sailor?"

"No, you haven't mentioned it before, or even said much about her for that matter."

"She was Australian, and in her youth had won a number of the Sydney to Hobart races."

Aliana's gaze widened as he spoke.

"She and my father used to be very well matched. They loved each other almost as much as they loved the sea. As you can imagine, my brother and I spent more time on the ocean than we did on land."

"I didn't know you had a brother."

"I don't anymore, he died many years ago."

"Oh, I'm so sorry," Aliana said, throwing her arms around him.

"It's okay," Sam said quietly, but there were tears in his eyes. "My brother and I were both good sailors, but we were driven to prove ourselves to our father who was the skipper of the racing yacht. So, one year, when the Sydney to Hobart race advisers considered whether or not to cancel the race based on the tremendously violent and unpredictable weather patterns, my brother and I decided that's how we would prove ourselves."

A part of him hoped that Aliana would accept his answer and not push to hear more about how it happened, but another part of him wanted her to make him continue.

She persisted.

"What happened?"

"It was a particularly bad storm. More often than not the sea can be as kind as it can be unforgiving, but on that night it was entirely unforgiving. My brother and I had received numerous reports of other ships dropping out of the race, or being dismasted. Worse, we learned that one ship had already sunk.

But, like all young fools, we thought we were invincible. At about three a.m., while desperately needing to furl our headsail before the wind literally knocked our ship over, a small loop caught hold of a cleat at the front of our yacht. I noticed it, and should have gone forward. It would have been easy to unclip it, or at worst cut, but I hesitated. I was frightened. I knew that the sea was more interested in being unforgiving that night than it was in being kind. As it was, my older brother noticed my hesitation, and he told me that he would go and do it instead, and that we would then try to ride the enormous wave at a thirty degree angle, so as to avoid broaching." His tears were falling more frequently now.

"It's okay, it wasn't your fault."

"My brother was an exceptional sailor. He alone could have beaten my father, and on that night, he saved my life. He unclipped the catch on the headsail, but while making his way back to the cockpit, he was caught by a secondary wave that crashed down from the other side of the one we were riding. There was no way he could have known it would happen, and by the time the water that crashed over the deck had dissipated, I could no longer see my brother. I sent out the alarm, and I tried my best to remain at the same location, but I never did see my brother again."

"My god, that's awful," Aliana said, holding onto him as she spoke.

"I promised myself that night that if I survived, I would never return to the sea again. I meant to keep that promise too. I had completed a master's degree in marine biology, but the next day I joined the U.S. military and became a helicopter pilot. My mom blamed my father, and try as they might to repair their relationship, she never forgave him for it. When I got out of the Corps, something just told me that it was time to come back to the ocean, to give myself a second chance at the life that I was meant to have. I've been trying to recreate that night for years so that I can finally say goodbye to my brother properly, but I have never found just the right conditions."

"So, tonight, you sail on towards your second chance and this time, with me."

"And I am so very much the happier for it," he said as he kissed her. "Come back with me."

"Where?"

"Wherever the perils of the world take us. Anywhere you want to go. Just come and do it with me."

"I would love to, but I still have my PhD to complete," she said. "And, I intend to keep my promise to head up the research department for the Wolfgang Corporation."

"When you're finished with your studies, give me a call. Work for me, we could certainly use someone with your background aboard the Maria Helena. Your corporation will still continue to produce brilliant medical research where it can help people in ten, perhaps fifteen years' time, once it's beaten the various ethics committees. Work with me, and I promise that you will get to see firsthand what a mind like yours can do for the good of the world in the present, rather than the future."

"If I work with you," she said, grinning lasciviously, "am I still able to sleep with the boss?"

"Not usually, but for you, I'll make an exception," he said, as she wrapped her arms around his neck and kissed him.

The End

Want more?

Join my email list and get a FREE and EXCLUSIVE Sam Reilly story that's not available anywhere else!

Join here ~ http://bit.ly/ChristopherCartwright